the
never never
sisters

L. ALISON HELLER

NEW AMERICAN LIBRARY

New American Library
Published by the Penguin Group
Penguin Group (USA) LLC, 375 Hudson Street,
New York, New York 10014

USA | Canada | UK | Ireland | Australia | New Zealand | India | South Africa | China
penguin.com
A Penguin Random House Company

First published by New American Library,
a division of Penguin Group (USA) LLC

First Printing, June 2014

 REGISTERED TRADEMARK—MARCA REGISTRADA

LIBRARY OF CONGRESS CATALOGING-IN-PUBLICATION DATA:

Heller, L. Alison.
    The never never sisters/L. Alison Heller.
        pages cm
    ISBN 978-0-451-41624-7 (pbk.)
    1. Marriage counselors—Fiction.   2. Sisters—Fiction.   3. Family secrets—Fiction.
4. Domestic fiction.   I. Title.
    PS3608.E453N48 2014
    813'.6—dc23 2013050247

Printed in the United States of America
10 9 8 7 6 5 4 3 2 1

Set in Walbaum MT
Designed by Alissa Rose Theodor

To my mom and sister—whose love and goodness I know as well as anything—and also to my dad, whose love and goodness we remember

acknowledgments

Ms. Kerry Donovan, you are a writer's dream come true: smart, talented, passionate, crazily efficient, a highly entertaining lunch date and a supportive friend to boot. Thank you, K, for all of that and specifically for kicking the stuffing out of the Reinhardt Sisters (editorially, of course). I'm beyond grateful!

Big thanks, of course, to Elisabeth Weed, as well as to the wonderful team at NAL: Kara Welsh, Isabel Farhi, Daniel Walsh, Jane Steele, Katie Anderson, Alissa Theodor and everyone else who helped this book evolve from manuscript to novel.

I'm blown away by the thoughtfulness of the following dear friends, who, in the midst of their own busy lives, have provided support and/or an ear and/or a boost at a crucial moment: Diane Simon, Joanna Costantino, Kevin "Easter Egg" Costantino, Donna Karlin, Matt Karlin, Konrad "No C" Tree, Toni Guss, Jenny Guss, Lois Ravich, Carroll Saks, Anne Joyce, Jacqueline Newman, Lori Dyan, Jen Hsu, Justin Hsu, Bethany "Emoji" Chase, Meg Donohue, Solana Nolfo, Patty Lifter, Michele Brown, Carolyn LaMargo, Ginny Markovich, Amy Montoya (for beans and more!) and Neil Bagchi. Hugs and kisses to all whether you want them or not!

For their time and valuable wisdom along the way, thanks to Alice Peck, Alicia Cowan and Tanya Farrell.

To my wonderfully generous online pals (you know who you are): thanks for helping to spread the word about my books—meeting you has been a true joy. And to the book clubs who so generously hosted *The Love Wars*, and with whom I had the most exhilarating discussions, thank you! I look forward to seeing you again very soon.

Thanks to Samantha Heller, the world's best and most overused first reader, Sue Ann Heller, Kate Ostrove, Edith Roberts, Raj Bhattacharyya and, of course, Kannon and Dashiell Bhattacharyya, my incredible nephews (who have been blessed with PowerPoint skills as prodigious as their enthusiasm).

And, of course, to Zoe, Gigi and Glen: thanks (infinity times infinity times infinity's worth) for making it all worthwhile.

Finally, two books in particular were helpful to me as I imagined and wrote this novel: *Addict in the Family* by Beverly Conyers and *Beautiful Boy* by David Sheff.

If ever two were one, then surely we.

—ANNE BRADSTREET

If you do not tell the truth about yourself, you cannot tell it about other people.

—VIRGINIA WOOLF

the
never never
sisters

prologue

THE FIRST THING I do is offer them candy. I keep a jar of it, well-stocked, right there on the coffee table.

In my experience, people are one hundred percent less likely to tell a lie with a Hershey's Kiss tucked into the side of their mouth. So while they're unwrapping their chocolate or caramel or whatever, I lob the easy questions at them: How long have they been together? Do they have any kids?

And then, once they've relaxed a little, settled into the beige couch across from my blue chair, I probe: What do they want out of our meeting? If I sense from one of them a certain reticence, as I did that Tuesday morning, I repeat the question.

I've found it helpful, when pressing for the truth, to lean forward and hold eye contact. So I employed this method as I posed the question once more to both Scott Jacoby and his wife, Helene.

"What. Do. *You*. Want?"

Helene—a tiny, feminine woman with the brash voice of a New York City traffic cop—stared back at me with an electric gaze. "To save our marriage."

I'm not sure how I developed this particular niche, but usually the couples who I meet with in counseling sessions aren't in need of mere tune-ups. No one asks me for tips on how to stoke an already ignited passion or to help mediate a dispute so that both parties feel sufficiently heard. My clients come to me in full-on crisis mode, swinging from the broken rope bridge of their marriage—the point at which they'll either let go into free fall or scramble to safety.

Scott was still silent, his arms crossed over his navy suit jacket. I hadn't yet determined whether he was annoyed at having to leave work in the middle of the day or if his body language was a symptom of greater marital fatigue.

He stared across the room in the direction of the photo I'd hung on the wall. It was a picture from my wedding two years before, not that my clients could tell this, because it was of our midsections and taken from the back: my white silk veil, the dark block of my husband Dave's tux, our interlocking forearms. I hoped it was generic enough that people would see in it their own happier times, but Scott's unfocused eyes indicated that he wasn't envisioning anything so hopeful.

"What do *you* really want, Scott?"

Waiting for his response, Helene leaned so far forward in her chair that she appeared to be praying. I've seen a lot of heartache in my office, but it took my breath away—those troubled eyes in the middle of that frozen, perfectly made-up face.

"Scott?" My voice was as gentle as it could be.

Finally, Scott sighed, then rubbed his cheek with his right hand. "I don't know what I want."

"Okay." I took care to sound appropriately neutral. "Take some time. Try to think about it." I pushed the candy jar toward him. It should be said that I buy only the good stuff: Hershey's Kisses, Werther's, Reese's Minis—none of those nubby little mints or hard candies with wrappers in the image of strawberries to help you associate the flavor.

Although I know better than to take it personally whether my clients' marriages work or not . . . I can't help myself. I take it all very personally.

Dave had pointed out the irony of this when I came home one day and declared I was a failure. (I was right on that count; the

Guinetts did not make it.) "You ask them what they want, right?"

"Yes." He'd left out the second part, the "why," so I reminded him. "It's like an oral contract. They commit to wanting the marriage to work in that initial moment and it's helpful later, when things get tough."

"But if you keep having to remind them what they want, how do you know it's still truly what they want?"

"You wouldn't understand," I had said. "It's a very intimate environment in my office." I didn't have a good response right then, but two days later, when I heard his key in the lock, I met him at the door with a spatula. "Listen," I said.

He'd stepped back, out of the range of the spatula, which had dripped marinara sauce in a large splotch in the entry hall. "Listening."

"If people come to me, they want to protect their marriages. There's nothing wrong with wanting to help them—okay?"

He'd leaned down and kissed my head. "Okay."

As I explained to Helene and Scott how we could proceed, that was the undercurrent I tried to convey: that I respected their step toward protecting the sacred and that I would help them as best I could.

I will always remember that—the three of us sitting in the office, clustered around the candy jar, as we pledged to resuscitate their marriage, me just the tiniest bit smug, totally oblivious to the fact that at that exact moment, my own marriage had begun to fall apart.

July

◆

chapter one

ALTHOUGH IT WAS only three o'clock in the afternoon when the Jacobys left my office, I was done for the day. I really wanted Helene and Scott to hire me. I respected their marriage, yes, but I was also salivating at the thought of an additional Tuesday or Thursday session.

Dave had had a brutal few months at the office: seven-day workweeks and late nights. The summer was not unfolding as we'd planned back in February, when we'd optimistically rented a house in Quogue that we'd seen online. Quogue was not one of the scene-y Hamptons towns, and the house itself was just what we could afford—modest and far from the beach, but it looked adorable. Three tiny bedrooms upstairs, a bright yellow kitchen with big white-knobbed fifties-style appliances and a sweeping tree with a rope hammock in the front yard. Dave had been too busy with work, so my mom had helped me narrow down the search. "Charming," we'd both proclaimed at first sight of the Quogue cottage. "That's it!"

Even though my calendar had *Quogue* written across each weekend (as well as the last two weeks in August), we had yet to see it in person. All our friends were already out there, and Dave had pushed me to go alone—*someone* should enjoy it, he said— but he hadn't had a single day off since Memorial Day, and it would've felt disloyal. I didn't want to resent his work schedule; I wanted to fill mine, but it was difficult to drum up clients in the summer months on the emptied-out Upper East Side.

I puzzled over this as I walked the five blocks home from my office, that instead of using my free time productively, the opposite was happening: the less I worked, the less I did. I should have been catching up on billing. I should have been focusing on business development: talks, articles, blogs. By Sixty-eighth Street, I'd resolved to contact my master's program administrators to see whether they knew of any volunteer opportunities. By Seventy-second Street, I realized that I should not be passively waiting for opportunities; I should create one. How hard could it be to write a grant proposal? I would single-handedly bring marriage counseling to an underserved neighborhood. Maybe Mott Haven? By the time I reached my block, Seventy-sixth street, I was imagining being notified of the award I'd receive for my dedication in having started All Hearts, which is what I'd name it. Or For All Hearts.

I was picturing myself approaching a podium in that navy sheath I'd seen online when I pushed open the door to my apartment and was stopped short by the inside chain. I stepped backward to make sure that I'd gotten off on the right floor, because all the hallways in my building were identical, but our neighbor Jake Driver's kindergarten scrawl, *Welcam*, Scotch-taped on the door across the hall, was confirmation: I had made it home.

"Hello?" I called into the sliver of space between the door and the entryway. I could only see the wall, but I heard the TV, the sound of it being switched off and, eventually, the shuffling of feet down the hall and then the pushing closed of the door, a breeze puffing in my face and the rattling of the chain.

Then the door opened and there, at three twenty in the afternoon—or, as he would call it on any other day, "lunchtime"—was my husband, Dave, his face streaked with tears.

chapter two

HE SPOKE FIRST. "You're home this early every day?"

I reached out slowly, put my keys on the entry table. "On Tuesdays, yes."

"Wow. No wonder you have so much time to work out." He turned and walked away from me, back into the living room.

I followed him. "Dave?"

He had slumped down on the couch. "What?"

I controlled my stream of questions—why was he home and, more important, acting like a total asshole?—and sat down next to him. "Did something happen?"

He held up a palm, like a celebrity deflecting paparazzi. "No quack talk, please."

"No, of course not." *Quack talk?*

"I really don't want to get into it."

"Did you get fired?"

"No!"

"You're crying?"

"I was."

"Is someone . . . hurt?"

"No." He slouched down farther. "Not physically. I'm not getting into it."

I stood up. "Okay." I could tell that his diffidence was an act; he was watching me, curious about what I'd do next. If I'd said what I really wanted to say, we would've started fighting, so I worked hard, very hard, to lift my shoulders in a shrug. "Just tell me when you're ready to talk."

What now? I walked back down the entry hall and picked up the bag I'd left in the corner of the hall. My hands shaking, I unpacked my wallet and sunglasses and placed them on random shelves in the entry hall closet. How serious could it be if no one was hurt? Maybe something had happened with one of his clients or there was fallout from an office power play? Eventually, Dave shuffled back down the hall.

"I was suspended from work," he said. "For two weeks. They wouldn't tell me why. I didn't do anything wrong, and I don't want to talk about it yet."

"Okay." It may sound callous, but I felt instant relief. Dave's law firm was a notorious hotbed of internal politics, and being temporarily ousted for a mysterious nonreason seemed in line with the other horror stories I'd heard from Duane Covington, like getting summoned back from your vacation when you were standing in line to board a plane to Europe, like being bullied into signing over to a more powerful partner the client you'd worked so hard to land, like pretending you hadn't billed as much as you had so that same partner could take credit for your work. A suspension explained Dave's reaction (he was a workaholic and would be understandably freaked-out by this) yet was easily remediable. He didn't need to stay with Duane Covington; his clients would follow him anywhere. I waited for Dave to tell me more, but all he did was stand in the hallway with a spaced-out expression that was disturbingly similar to Scott Jacoby's.

"Can we rehash it tomorrow?"

"Of course." I put down my bag. This was a work issue, separate from us, and the best I could do was avoid a major fight by stepping back and listening. Everyone craves being understood. We need it; we work for it; we exhaust our vocabularies to make sure we've properly communicated our viewpoints. But we don't put in one-eighth of that effort trying to understand others. I swear it's physiological, because even knowing this, I'd felt it myself thirty seconds before—an ember in the pit of my stomach driving me to push back at Dave's adolescent sulk.

"I'm sorry for being a dick."

I waved my hand, magnanimous and a little proud of myself for my measured reactions. It wasn't ever easy.

"I'm going to set up an office in the guest room."

"Yeah?" One of the summer projects on which I was already behind was renovating the guest room. Ian, our decorator, and I had a big meeting planned for the following week, and by then I was supposed to have cleared out everything Ian had tagged during our last meeting. "Creating the canvas," he'd called it, because Ian was a person who said such things without irony. "You're not going to work in the office alcove?"

"That's not really an office. It's more like a desk in the kitchen."

"Oh."

"I think I'll need more space."

"Fair point." Dave and I were a little out of our league with Ian; we'd have never been able to command an audience with him if he hadn't just completed a huge job for my parents. I was already on thin ice; last month Ian had not at all been happy when I changed my mind about the window shade fabric. He and I had only just recently reestablished our delicate rapport— a sensei-protégé dynamic that worked best when Ian spouted wisdom and rattled off designer names and I listened, wide-eyed, trying to think of good questions to ask that would prove I'd been paying attention.

I couldn't imagine how long I'd pay the price if I canceled next week's meeting. Nor, I realized, could I explain to Dave that my decorator anxiety meant no home office for him.

"There's a lot of crap in here." Dave had walked to the door of the office. "And what's all this tape everywhere?" He ripped off a long piece from a lampshade and held it up for my inspection.

"It's for the renovation." I opened the closet to a solid wall of boxes that we'd stacked up to the ceiling when we first moved in three years before. Honestly, I'd forgotten they were there. The mess was apparently the last straw for Dave, who slid down along the wall until he was sitting in a heap on the floor.

"Don't worry. I'll get rid of all of it. I'll move the boxes to the bedroom and we can put the renovation piles in here." Right at my eye level was a box labeled in my mom's slanted handwriting: *Paige, Childhood*. Seeing it, I felt a fresh, perhaps overly dramatic, wave of urgency. Like many therapists, I had a keen awareness of the unhealthy family dynamics that I would not pass down to the next generation. There would be no secret-filled box for Dave and me.

"Dave," I said, "we have to air the ugly things."

He saw me looking at the box and nodded, realizing what I was thinking. "It's not like that," he said. "I'm just tired."

So I helped him plug in the cords, clear off the desk and shove into the closet anything that might distract him from his work. After a half hour of item shuffling, we surveyed the room. "This looks good," I said, although it didn't.

"Yeah. Well." He sat down gingerly, fidgeting around before extending his arms like a virtuoso pianist. "I should probably get some work done." And then, before I was out the door, he started typing, his fingers scrambling in constant motion across the keyboard as though they were being chased.

chapter three

WHEN I WOKE up the next morning, Dave had already gotten out of bed. I found him in the living room, his posture incongruently rigid for someone watching television on the couch in boxer shorts. The anchor of the financial news channel—the woman with the last name that sounded like a Mediterranean island—leaned forward, and Dave did too: "FBI agents swarmed and arrested thirty-one-year-old Louis Gallent in the parking lot of his San Francisco hedge fund yesterday on insider trading charges.

"Gallent, who founded the Elmwood Fund last year, is alleged to have received a tip alerting him to massive imminent layoffs at Lifeblood, Inc. Authorities charge that he traded on that information to avoid losses of one hundred fifty million dollars. Gallent, the latest in a string of arrests linked to financier Gerald Rocher, worked for Rocher until 2012. So far it's unclear whether authorities have found any direct link to Rocher, known in some circles as Jellyfish for"—she lowered her eyelids knowingly—"the toxic reach of his tentacles."

"One percent scum." I was trying to be funny. Dave and I frequently growled that expression when his banker clients got demanding. Because it was morning, though, my voice emerged in a croak. Dave, startled, pressed the remote and diminished the screen into a small blip. "So," I said, clearing my throat, "did he do it?"

Dave's brow rose high as if he didn't know whom I was talking about. "Did who do what?"

"What they arrested that guy for—the insider trading thing?"

I hoped Dave would sink against the couch, rub his hands together and provide an impassioned point/counterpoint analysis on the man's guilt. Instead, he shrugged and headed for the other room.

I followed him into the kitchen. "Are you okay?"

"I'm fine, Paige." He scooped out the coffee beans and put them in a single French press, not even asking if I wanted any.

"You seem better than yesterday."

"Sure." He turned on the kettle, took out the milk and slammed the refrigerator shut.

My eyes narrowed at his back. "So when are you going to fill me in?"

His palm wrapped in a death grip on the refrigerator door, he pivoted toward me. I braced myself for the fight; by this point I was twitching for it to be honest—mutual understanding be damned. Then his shoulders sagged. "Now's fine. Let's go out."

"Okay. Bagels and Joe?"

"I'd rather go to the Patty Melt."

"Seriously?"

"Yeah."

"Okay." I shrugged. "The Patty Melt."

◆

The Patty Melt was only three blocks from our apartment, but it was perpetually empty. The last time we'd eaten there, I'd pulled a hair from my hash browns. Long and red, it was so obviously from neither of us that we'd both recoiled, pushing our plates away in silent agreement (I had thought) that convenience aside, we should not let the restaurant's perpetual fried onion smell and tasty-sounding name trick us into even mediocre expectations ever again.

Our waitress, undeterred by the mood of our booth, floated over, her eyes glazed. Her name tag read BELIZE. Ordinarily I would point this out to Dave and he would run with it and I would laugh, corny as it was. *Ketchup, pelize. When you get a chance, pelize.*

"Can you come back later?" I smiled in a way I hoped transmitted that, as Belize no doubt sensed, we were going through something here.

Belize ignored me, stopping nibbling on her pen to gaze up at the light fixture.

"Coffee." Dave pushed his cup forward as though it were the only thing between him and insanity. "Please."

I shook my head. "None for me, thanks."

Belize glided away, hands clasped behind her back like one of Degas's ballerinas. Dave concentrated on stacking two forks, intertwining their tines in such a focused manner that I knew I was going to have to start off the conversation. "What does 'suspended' even mean?"

"I get paid; I work. But I can't go in."

"Why? What happened?"

"I have no idea."

"They didn't give you any explanation at all?"

"Nope."

Belize twirled over, two coffees in hand, and set them down in front of us. I smiled at Dave about the extra coffee, but he missed it, focused as he was on stirring milk into his.

"They said *something*, right?"

He shrugged listlessly. "Not really. Herb told me that they had to do a little investigation over the next week and I needed to stay out of the office."

I frowned at Herb's name. "That's who suspended you?"

"I know." Dave stuck out his lower lip. "It's bad."

Dave thought this was bad because Herb was his mentor. I had grimaced, however, because I was remembering the last time I'd seen Herb. Dave and I had been standing with him and his wife, Brenda, in a tight little cocktail cluster at Denise Bellavoqua's retirement gathering. Egged on by Dave's many questions, Brenda was providing a detailed report of the technical difficulties in the Metropolitan Opera's production of *The Flying Dutchman*.

Dave had appeared genuinely interested in her story. ("Not even remotely," he'd assured me in the cab home.) I had been wondering, vaguely, if I could ever be that passionate about something cultural, when Herb asked how my practice was going, and then the next thing I knew, we were sectioned off against a wall, his body blocking me from Brenda's explanation of how a broken flying wire had resulted in the bass-baritone's sprained ankle.

I babbled on nervously about my work, aware of Herb's glazed eyes locked on my neckline. In the first pause, he said something gruffly. I didn't hear what exactly, but it sounded a lot like *You're a nice piece.* Or *You got a real nice piece.* Neither phrase seemed particularly appropriate. I hadn't had the heart to tell Dave about it.

"Did he seem mad?"

"Not at all. He seemed . . . apologetic. Like he knew it was ridiculous."

"But you didn't demand an explanation?"

"Of course I did, but he said it was best not discussed."

"That's just weird."

"I know."

"Well," I said, "obviously they want you at the firm. If you leave, so do your clients. All it takes is one phone call to—"

Dave clutched my arm. "Paige, you cannot tell them about this. Promise me."

"Why? My parents could fix everything."

"They'll make it worse."

"You have nothing to be embarrassed about."

"No parents, no friends. No one, Paige."

"Why?"

"Just promise me."

"Fine. So then for tonight—"

"What's tonight?"

I waited for him to remember that my parents, about to leave for Nantucket for the week, had insisted on a "farewell dinner."

"Oh god. Dinner." The farewell dinner was not to be confused with the "welcome back dinner" and the "bought new socks dinner." We saw my parents frequently—once every two weeks or so—but instead of just calling it dinner, my mom liked to imbue the meals with a greater purpose. She thought it made everything sound more "fun." Dave didn't even smile.

"So don't go."

"Then they'll know."

"Know what? I can cover for you. I'll say you don't feel well."

He closed his eyes, considering. "Nope." He shook his head. "Nope. I have to go. I always go. Don't I?"

"Yes."

"I can do this."

"Dave, it's not a Navy SEALs mission."

He dragged his top knuckles over the growth on his cheeks, and I heard the sound of roughness, like scratching sandpaper. "You go first, meet them there and I'll come later. We'll say . . .

We'll say that I came from the office and was working late. You think they'll buy it?"

"I think that only a crazy person wouldn't."

This was his cue to say that we were in trouble for sure because my parents were in fact crazy people, but he didn't. It should have been a relief, not having to respond to one of his predictable jokes, but by then I felt a small surge of alarm. Teasing my parents was low-hanging fruit to Dave, basic nutrition; he should have grabbed it, swallowed it whole, his eyes scanning for the next crop.

I leaned back in the booth, watching him as he gnawed on his cuticles, one-day-old stubble spreading over his chin like a rash, and for one horrible, stomach-sinking moment, I thought, *What if he's like this forever?*

I immediately hated myself. "We could fight it, you know. Get in Herb's face, demand an explanation."

"How?" Based on his drooping eyelids, he didn't have much enthusiasm for the idea, but I pressed on.

"Hire a lawyer."

"That was my first thought too. But then I burn the bridge forever."

"The bridge to Herb? You still care?"

"I just want it back to normal. To go to my office and have it be like this never happened." He pushed his hand across the table toward me and spread his fingers out. I put my hand on his. "Are you mad?" he asked.

"Mad? Why would I be mad?"

"I don't know. I wish I had more answers for you."

"Dave, you didn't do anything wrong. It's going to be fine."

He looked skeptical. "You think?"

"By the end of the summer, this will all probably feel like it happened to someone else."

"Thanks." He swallowed and focused on his empty plate. "I was thinking today. My work used to be everything and it's still a big deal, but I now have you. Without that . . . I'd probably be falling apart."

Expressing vulnerability made him uncomfortable, I knew, so I just grabbed his hand tighter. "Hey," I said. "Let's get out of here."

"Yeah," he said. "Get back to work."

"I meant, get *out of here*. Like to Quogue."

He lowered his eyebrows but didn't say anything.

"The house?" I palmed my phone. "I'll cancel my clients if you cancel yours?"

Dave's mouth yanked up into a forlorn smile, and I knew his answer before he said anything. "Dave," I said, trying not to sound accusatory, "you could tell me, no matter what it was."

"I know."

"I mean—" The Patty Melt? The bloodshot, glassy eyes? Both indicated he had something to hide. "Is this like the last time?"

"I told you." He met my eyes dead on. "I will never do that again."

I kept my hand on his back as we walked out of the Patty Melt and stood for a moment on the sidewalk outside. And then, instead of settling into a hammock with divided-up newspaper sections and fresh-baked croissants, we went our separate ways—me to work to wait for my ten fifteen and Dave back to the former guest room to try to convince his clients that he was calling them from a fifty-floor skyscraper in the middle of Manhattan.

◆

Dave had lied to me once before.

On a Saturday night a few months before our wedding, we were out with Stan and Irene Blakesey. Dave and Stan had started together at Duane Covington as first-year associates and were now the only two left from an original group of twenty-three. They had a survivors' bond, Dave had explained to me. It was like being foxhole buddies, you know, without having actually feared for their lives.

Irene, who read restaurant reviews with a religious zeal, had secured us an eight o'clock table at some new Italian place with dimmed lights and dark walls and floors. I could barely see my food, but I didn't even really care because Irene had us on our second bottle of something and was starting to dominate the conversation in a voice already too loud and rising. The four of us went out every few months, so I knew that by dessert, Irene would be doing a fairly decent impression of Jack Nicholson.

"The gravy's not right." Irene was half Italian and called all red sauce "gravy," something that had been an initial source of confusion to me. She dipped in the tines of her fork and held the red sauce up to Dave's mouth. "See?"

Dave was the least likely of all of us to enjoy being spoon-fed gravy by Irene, but he opened his mouth gamely, if somewhat stiffly. "Yeah," he said. "Way off from my childhood in Tuscany."

"Ex-act-ly," said Irene, and Dave mini-shrugged at me and widened his eyes in an expression of *I have no idea what I'm talking about.*

"What?" Irene caught the look and whapped Dave in the shoulder with her napkin. "Gravy is the linchpin. You need good gravy, Davy. Ha-ha! Gravy Davy!"

Dave held up both hands. "I'll take your word for it."

"You *need* good gravy." Irene was insistent. "Try the meatballs. The meatballs are sublime, and you need . . . You need a fun evening, Dave! We gotta do something nice for Dave. All of us," Irene said.

"Why for Dave?" I said.

"We need to cheer him up." She reached out and pushed the forked meatball right in his face. "Poor Dave."

I leaned across the table to scoop some truffle oil risotto from the communal plate. Irene always ordered too many sides. "You mean that they were out of the branzino special he wanted?"

"Yeah, right." When Dave failed to bite the meatball, Irene put the whole thing in her own mouth, talking as she chewed. "You must be pissed."

Across the table, Dave's face had drained of color. "What are you talking about?" I said.

"It's criminal. You've given them *everything*, and they screw you like that. And you can't go somewhere else now. It's too late for that!" Irene's brown eyes softened. "I just can't believe they did this to their golden boy."

Dave shrugged and said something under his breath about not being worried; it would all work out just fine.

"I still don't get it." Only Irene met my eyes.

"Partnership. Of course, it will work out fine—it will." Irene said this primarily to the plate of meatballs before spearing another.

I didn't make a scene, just smiled tightly and looked past Dave's pleading eyes at the couple at the table behind us. The man was talking animatedly, and the woman nodded at him in utter agreement as they tore off hunks of bread and dabbed them in their bowls to sop up the extra sauce. Apparently their table had no problems at all with the gravy.

Dave spilled it all during the cab ride home. Apparently, he'd been up for partner that year. Herb had been assuring him for four years that he was a shoo-in. About a month before the committee made everything official, though, Herb had taken him aside and told him that it wasn't Dave's year. The department's numbers were bad and they needed a sacrifice. He had to think long term: Everyone would notice that Dave was the kind of guy who would take one for the team. They would reward his loyalty and patience if he could just have a little faith.

I could barely compute what he was saying. "Who," I finally asked when we got home, "doesn't tell his fiancée that he's up for partner?" I screamed it so loudly that I heard the words reverberate through our apartment, bouncing off our walls and broadcasting through the space under the front door. For several months afterward I was embarrassed to see my neighbors in the elevator.

Dave said nothing. He stood there in the hall, sad and guilty, as if he'd been as helpless in creating this moment as he was to stop it.

I slipped off my engagement ring, left the apartment and walked two miles down to Penn Station. My parents, wrapped in robes in the front seat of their station wagon, met me at the other end. Even though it was past midnight, they drove me straight to Walmart to buy underwear and a toothbrush.

Dave rented a car and drove out to New Jersey every day for a week. He had been so nervous about partnership that he didn't want to speak about it out loud, he explained. He'd pictured dropping the announcement at my feet like a puppy with a newspaper and was beyond embarrassed when he had failed. Maybe, he admitted, he had planned the dinner as a passive way to come clean. When Irene Blakesey blurted it out, he'd felt only relief.

"It's so uneven," I said. "I tell you everything. And I'm not really looking to have a master-puppy kind of dynamic with my future husband."

We wouldn't, he swore. And we didn't; I knew we didn't. He

begged me to be patient with him. He told me his childhood fears and insecurities that week: his mediocre fourth grade IQ score his mother had carelessly left out on the kitchen table, not quite high enough for the gifted program; the football team he didn't make; the junior high school bully who targeted him by waiting at the water fountain and slamming his face in the spigot and the horrible things his father had said when Dave came home with a gash above his eye.

He was raised, Dave explained, to expect that other people laughed at your failures. It broke my heart, both the fact of it and how fundamentally I understood him.

The following year, when he did make partner, Dave told me all about it: the little snippets of gossip, the passing encouragements from near strangers, the thirdhand reports of what happened in the committee meetings, the promises from Herb. In truth, it was a little too much detail; I could have handled a summary or two, but I was grateful for the opportunity to listen, to model a little unconditional love and support.

I told him it didn't matter what happened. I only wanted him to make partner, I promised him, because it was so important to him.

What an idiot I'd been, taking off my ring and storming out of the house, so ready to throw away my future with Dave. All it had taken to get past the shock was listening for one moment.

chapter four

THE WONDERFUL, WARM, liquid-muscle feeling from my early-evening workout disappeared about five minutes into our family dinner. I felt it leave my body, floating away like a spirit as my father slathered butter on his bread. My dad and I were alone at the table with the chafing silence that accompanies him to all social gatherings when he cleared his throat in that middle-aged man way: sputtering car ignition.

He grabbed another roll. "You'd think I'd have enough influence to spring Dave from the office."

"He's usually stuck working for those clients who aren't, you know, family." Our tired tones would have let any eavesdropper know we'd had this exchange many times before.

"I don't know why he even needs those others. You'd think the guy was ambitious or something."

I aped my dad's smile—half of my mouth pushed up—and lifted my glass. I was a little worried that Dave had gotten lost in our apartment. The real estate agent hadn't divulged that there was a Bermuda Triangle between his office/guest room, the couch and the bathroom, but there had to be one. It was the only explanation for his not having picked up or responded to even one of my four telephone calls throughout the day.

My dad continued the butter slathering and I sifted through e-mail on my phone until my mom's voice floated over to our table from the front door of the restaurant. I could guess what she was doing without even turning around: sweeping in; kissing Mario, the maître d', on both cheeks and asking about his new granddaughter by name in a way that would make Mario feel warm and special; assessing the antipasto table and commenting to whoever was stationed behind it about how something—the sardines, the eggplant—looked delicious.

When I smelled tuberose and powder behind me and felt her lips graze my hair, I was relieved—I was sure our table was more desperate for her stream of conversation than Mario would ever be. She eased into her seat, which was pulled out by my father in one fluid move, and paused. "You look gorgeous."

"Thank you, Mom."

"I wonder." She leaned in close. "Maybe, with that dress—I don't know, a strapless bra? I feel like it would be so empowering to stand against wearing that lady-of-the-night look. Be strong! Just say no to showing your undergarments at dinner."

My dad and I responded to the comment solely with our eyes: his were averted as though he'd accidentally found himself in the women's dressing room and mine were rolled. Still, I subtly patted my twisted bra straps into submission under my sundress. My dad reached out for another roll, but my mom beat him to it, catching his outstretched hand.

"Frankie." She shook her head slightly and removed the butter knife from his hands. "Enough." She sat back, exhausted from the effort of corralling us, and smiled her appreciation at Mario, who had brought her a seltzer and cranberry juice without being asked. He had put it in a wineglass, and if I squinted, it looked like a watered-down Shiraz with a lime plopped in it.

"The usual for everyone?" My mom glanced around the table, and we nodded. I ordered the ravioli special for Dave, and Mario winked an *of course* before sweeping off. My mom lifted her drink and pointed it to the empty chair next to me. "And where is the Boy?"

The Boy—that's what she had called Dave since I first

brought him home, like he was the missing piece: he replenished the number of family members back up to four; he had the whole good job/steady/responsible/respectful thing down; and, most important, he was a "bootstrapper." Dave, just like my mom, had taken on the power of his own catapult, journeying from nothing to something.

"Dave's working late," my dad explained.

My mom nodded her approval. It was "very bootstrappy" to work late. "When do we expect him?"

"Soon." They looked at each other and then at me. "What?"

"Tell her." My dad picked up his butter knife again before putting it down.

She mashed her lips together as though blotting lipstick. "Later."

"What? Just tell me now."

"We got an e-mail." My mom used a spoon to retrieve the lime and squeezed it over her drink. She sat back as though this were a major announcement.

"Um. Congratulations? You're a little behind the rest of us, but it's good you're getting comfortable with tech—"

"Oh, for godsakes." My dad picked up the butter knife again. "Tell her from whom."

"Yes, from whom?" I leaned forward as I awaited their answer.

My mom ignored me and sat up in her seat, her face brightening. "Ladies and gents, here he is." She waved her arms as Dave approached the table.

He bowed. "I'll be here all night," he said. "A funny thing happened on the way to the restaurant."

"Ba-dum dum," said my mom.

"Wow." I'd been expecting Hamlet from act five, and Cary Grant had shown up, showered and shaved. "Nice suit."

He shot me a look, half smile, half warning.

"It is a nice suit," my mother agreed in all earnestness. "Very becoming."

Dave brushed off his shoulders, valet-style. "Thank you, madam. I try my best. Frank, did you get my e-mail?"

"I did, thanks. I forwarded it on to Bill."

"How was work today?" My mom winked at Dave. "They let you out kind of early."

"It was fine," said Dave. "No drama."

"I got you the ravioli." I looked at Dave carefully, searching for a sign that he was the same guy who had frozen at the thought of this very gathering, but his face betrayed nothing. No flinching, no rapid blinking, no quick look to the left, or right, or whichever way it is that liars are supposed to look.

"I love ravioli," he said. "How is everyone?"

"Fine," I said. "They were just about to tell me about some big e-mail they got today."

"No, we weren't." As she spoke, my mom's brow furrowed as though I had completely misunderstood her. "I was just going to ask what you two think about the West Indies for Thanksgiving."

"I prefer turkey," said Dave.

We all laughed a little too hard.

"Right on the beach, complete with a yoga studio and a live-in cook!" She was crowing, as she usually did when discussing such spoils. That's the thing about being invited to the Rich Party in middle age—apparently, you get thrilled every time you look in the goody bag.

"No golf course?" Dave asked. I marveled at the casualness of Dave's teasing little smile.

"I don't know." She shook her head. "Who cares about golf?"

"Would this be the prevailing attitude over the vacation, or would a guy be allowed to go play?" He was humoring her; we all were. Even in a normal world, he'd never take a vacation during the fourth quarter of the year, his busiest time.

My mom laughed. "I'm sure there is a wonderful, world-class—who is the best golf course designer?"

"Arnold Nicklaus," I said, as Dave said, "Donald Ross."

"That"—Dave indulged me with an overly patient smile—"is not even a person." His work phone rang and he reached into his pants pocket, glancing at it to see who it was. "Sorry—work. Please don't wait if the food comes."

"Go, go." My dad waved his hand. "By all means."

As soon as he was out of earshot, I looked between them, back and forth. "What's the big drama?"

"We didn't want to talk about the e-mail in front of Dave."

"So I gathered."

They both looked grim. "It's from Sloane," my mom said.

My dad nodded. "Your sister," he said helpfully, as though I had forgotten all about her in the two decades since I'd last seen her. And I had, largely, mostly because I was shushed anytime I mentioned her name.

As part of my master's program, we had been encouraged to discuss our motivation for becoming therapists. The most compelling explanation someone could give was that therapy had been and remained a powerful tool in his or her own life. I'd tried therapy once, and it had been a total disaster, so I had no idea how I found myself pursuing "the calling," as one professor called it.

My stock line was that I was interested in the "inner workings of people," but it felt like a hollow rationale, as if I believed people could be tuned and wound like pocket watches, which I didn't. I had once confessed this to Beth Fishman, my therapist during the first eighteen months of my program. I had also told Beth about Sloane.

Counseling wasn't mandatory for the students, but the program encouraged us to participate, so I'd copied Beth's name from a creased list that the school receptionist had given me with the inspiring title of "Counselors within Ten Blocks of Campus." I'd had a brief moment of hope that Beth's late and bumbling arrival to our first meeting—the wet hair streaming down her blouse that left dark streaks on her sky blue silk blouse, the endless searching for her glasses in her bag—heralded an absentminded genius. It didn't, as it turned out; she was just distracted.

For the first seventeen months of my sessions, Beth and I chatted like buddies about television shows and our favorite restaurants. I'd regale her with my blind-dating stories, and she'd offer sympathy and incredulity the way my friends in relationships did, but that was about it. Then one morning, she rushed in five minutes late as was her norm, drip marks on her shirt, and announced, "I'm moving to Kansas City."

"What?" I said, completely taken aback.

"Kansas City," she repeated, and stuck out her tongue. *Blech.* "I don't really want to go. My husband got a great job, though. I won't even have to work."

It was the type of admission I had grown to expect from Beth Fishman, and even though I was technically her work, I was not offended. "I bet it'll be nice when you get there."

"It's probably a great place to raise kids, heartland values, the whole deal. Blah, blah-blah, blah-blah. Anyway, you and I have three sessions left, and that's it."

"Oh." There was an intriguing new edge to Beth Fishman's voice. "Okay."

"So let's get to it," she said. "When's the last time you talked to your parents about your sister?"

It was when I'd been home on break from college, having just completed a segment on substance abuse in my introductory psychology course. There had been some dry course reading about the physiology of addiction, with a few disturbing vignettes sprinkled in the materials.

Then we watched the video about Alexis. Happy, sunny, adorable little Alexis, shown in home movies as a preschooler, her tights-clad legs pumping the air on her backyard swing set, and then as a seventh grader, impressed and clear-eyed on a cruise around the Statue of Liberty.

Enter crystal meth. At the point when I got up to leave the lecture hall, Alexis was living in a cardboard box near a highway exit. I murmured excuse-me's, sidestepped chair legs and tried not to glance at the movie projector screen. I did, though, when Alexis literally growled at the camera. She had crazy eyes, and her front tooth was missing. Her father calmly explained to the camera that it felt like she'd been possessed by a demon.

I'd come home from school with so many questions. Maybe I should've waited, but I brought it up at our first family dinner, over my mom's almond-crusted chicken. I posed them rapid-fire: Why did Sloane just disappear after rehab? Where was she now—did anyone know? Why weren't we looking for her? I tried not to think about that one awful night, but sometimes it caught up to me in dreams, and wasn't that type of thing always better discussed?

I expected to hear that they'd been trying to protect me, which I understood. I would counter that I was now an adult, ready to hear details. We never got that far. My mother handled about seven minutes of questions before shutting herself in her bathroom. My father excused himself, albeit more politely, for the safety of his study.

The next morning, my mom took me to the movies and then the mall, where she bought me the boots I'd been blabbering about for weeks. She did not hide the fact that she found them, knee-high and patent leather, as ugly as sin, but I accepted them and her silence on the Sloane topic without further question.

Beth Fishman leaned so far forward during this that I was a little worried she'd topple over. When I finished, she tsked. "They handled that incredibly poorly." I nodded. Beth Fishman was not afraid of making judgments. "But I like what you're doing. You're taking it back."

"Taking it back?"

"It's why you want to counsel people—to make sure they shed light on issues, rather than bury them."

I nodded. It was not a genius connection, but I'd been too close to make it myself. I wondered aloud if I should keep trying to talk to them about Sloane.

"Blood from stone." Beth Fishman shook her head so enthusiastically, a droplet of water from her still-dripping tresses landed on my lap. "I wouldn't bother."

I felt compelled to offer Beth Fishman something in return for allowing me to be her last professional hurrah. When we said our good-byes, I mentioned offhand that I washed my hair at night when I thought I wouldn't have enough time in the morning. It saved a lot of time.

Even though I knew practically nothing about Sloane, I knew this: *she* was the reason why I couldn't abide Dave's silence about this suspension, the reason I spent my days trying to help people access and express their submerged thoughts in the name of family cohesion. Still, when my mom mentioned her name that night at the restaurant, I was stunned to hear someone else say it out loud. It had been so long. "And?"

"She's planning a visit." The waiter slid a plate of fish in front of me, and I lifted my fork.

"Shouldn't you wait for Dave?"

I swiveled to peer through the front window of the restaurant at Dave's body language: hunched and pacing, phone at ear. "He said to start. You're aware, right, that there's no way Sloane's actually coming?"

"I don't know." My mom pressed her fingers against the stem of her glass. "She mentioned a flight."

"For when?"

"Saturday." I glanced at my dad, who leaned back and nodded again, satisfied that the story was being told and that he wasn't the one telling it.

"Let's talk about something else." My mom jutted out her chin toward the door. I glanced over my shoulder and saw Dave coming in from outside, rearranging his features into a can-do grin.

"Why can't he know?"

"Let's just see what we're dealing with first before we tell people."

"He's not people, he's—"

She lifted her own fork and knife and started cutting through her radicchio to signal that she was done talking about it. Dave pulled out his chair and sat down in the silence of us carefully examining our silverware.

"It's still brutally hot out there." You'd have to be listening for it to hear, but his voice had a nervous edge. "What'd I miss?"

"Nothing," I said.

"Don't say nothing." Greens were on my mom's fork, poised upside down in front of her mouth. She had always eaten like someone in a period film, and I had never been sure at what point they'd covered that when she was growing up in the tenement off Flatbush Avenue. "I was just telling your wife about a cute dress I saw."

Dave's work phone rang again and he ignored it.

"You need to get that?" I said.

"Nope."

"Really?"

"Really," he said. "They don't need me right at this moment. They just think they do. Cute dress, huh?"

chapter five

THE AIR OUTSIDE was still heavy with heat when Dave and I walked home from the restaurant. I pulled my hair up off the back of my neck with one hand and fanned it with the other in my best Southern belle impression. "My golly, Mr. Turner. Isn't sundown supposed to promise *some* relief?"

Dave was silent.

I dropped the twang. "We weren't talking about you in there."

"I know." His hands were in his pockets, his eyes straight ahead on the sidewalk. Obviously his lighthearted dinner banter had been an act.

"We were talking about Sloane."

"Your sister Sloane?"

"Are there any others?"

"There's a Sloane at work. In word processing."

"Yeah, not that one." I shoved him affectionately, even though it really was far too hot for contact; in response to my touch, his shirt suctioned to his side. "She e-mailed about a possible visit. They're being really bottled up."

"They probably just don't want to focus on it. Why waste time planning for something that's never going to happen?"

"Maybe." My mom didn't have to divulge the real reason she'd excluded the Boy from the announcement—she was embarrassed, worried that sharing our demons was like showing off a clubfoot on the first date. Dave and I had been married for two years, after all, and only a handful of people really knew about Sloane: the three of us and our close family friends the Rabinowitzes, who had been around that last, horrible year and borne witness, namely by babysitting me for long stretches of time.

Dave's work phone rang. He removed it from his pocket and glanced at the screen before returning it. "When's the last time she was here?"

"My mom has flown to California a few times to try to see her, I think, but the last time Sloane was here and I knew about it was"—I calculated—"twenty years ago."

"How old is she now?"

"Thirty-six."

"I almost forgot she's a real person."

"That's exactly what I thought earlier." She hadn't been a real person to me as much as a rallying cry. *At-ti-ca! Remember the Maine! The mistakes of Sloane Reinhardt!* If I strained hard enough, I could access faint memories of her, normal sister stuff: running through the sprinkler in our old front yard and the time she hit me with a rented tennis racquet at the town courts and wailed over and over, "But it was an accident!" I'd needed stitches under my eye, and she'd spent all of her allowance money on a teddy bear for me with my name stitched on its heart.

This was the one I'd never forget, the one that was crystal clear while the others were hazy: I'd been a babyish eleven, still sleeping every night with a night-light, a pile of stuffed animals and my bedroom door wide-open. I'd like to pretend this lack of maturity was a reaction to family tensions, but I can't; I don't remember sensing them at all.

That night, I was asleep until I heard a crash that made me sit up in my bed, my stomach knotting in fear. I lay back down, but then I heard a clanging and a man's voice—rough, loud. I waited for my parents to do something before I remembered that they were out, which meant Mrs. Chanokowski, the neighbor from three houses away, was snoring on the daybed in the spare room down the hall. I went into Sloane's room, but it was empty.

My clock said one in the morning, so I tried to go back to sleep, but I heard more voices and then laughter. I could tell from the way the light shone up the stairs that it was coming from the living room, so I grabbed a baton—I still hadn't mastered twirling, but perhaps I could swing it at someone—and inched down the stairs until I could peer down.

They were in a circle, five of them—Sloane and four guys who were probably all still in high school. To me, they looked like men: broad shouldered, stubbly faced, hands like cuts of raw meat. One of them was passed out. Another had a little metal canister and a yellow party balloon. He filled the balloon, shot the air in his mouth like I'd seen people do with party balloons and helium, but then instead of his voice coming out like Mickey Mouse, he fell back, gasping and laughing, before crashing into a glass cabinet that broke in pieces around him. He rubbed his head with his hand, and there was blood everywhere.

"Fuck," he said, and Sloane grabbed one of my mom's throw pillows and pressed it to his head before grabbing the balloon. It probably was from a prior indulgence, but at the time I connected her nosebleed to the balloon: first a trickle, then a gush. I shouted out, and when she turned toward my voice, her eyes were glinting and narrowing.

"Fuck," said another one of the guys, and I have since realized that he was being decent, having spotted me standing there in my nightgown and appreciating that it was not an ideal scene into which to insert an eleven-year-old armed with a glitter baton. Sloane didn't seem to care, though. I don't know if my memory has embellished this, but she started to laugh uncontrollably and offered me the balloon.

Mrs. Chanokowski appeared, her hair in some sort of shower cap, swatting the boys with her hands like they were flies until eventually all of them buzzed away defensively. (Not the passed-out one, of course, but he was gone by the time I crept downstairs to find my dad talking brightly and making waffles instead of reading the paper as he usually did in the morning.)

People talk about defense mechanisms like they're a weakness, but spend enough time in the mental health field and you'll recognize them as a safety net. Consider repression: some experts say it's dangerous, that suppressed memories inevitably return to bite you in the keister, as my mom might call it, and that can be true.

I was pretty sure, though, that the acrobatics my mind had done to dim my other memories of Sloane were in the name of self-protection. That image—her possessed eyes, the blood from her nose, the way she offered up the nitrous oxide to me like she was inducting me into some club—kept me from mourning her loss unnecessarily. My family, all I needed or knew after my sister's disappearance, was my mom, my dad and now Dave. Sloane had fundamentally different wiring from the rest of us and belonged somewhere else.

When Dave's phone rang again, we looked at each other, rolling our eyes at the work intrusion, and I smiled permission to answer. He shook his head.

"But shouldn't you? In light of . . ."

He lifted it out of his pocket and shut the thing off. "No," he said. "Sometimes, you just have to draw a line in the sand and not be available."

"At least they still seem to really need you."

"Yeah, I guess," he said, but his expression was sour enough to make me suspect he didn't agree.

chapter six

Vanessa

ON THE WAY home from dinner with the kids, I held out my arm to make Frankie do the Regency stroll—his term, not mine. I'd first seen it done on a BBC production of *Mansfield Park*. One person held out her arm straight and the other linked his arm around hers, tucking in his hand like the spare end of a belt.

"Vanessa." Frankie sometimes, like now, sighed my name instead of saying it. "As we've discussed, life was not better then."

"Yes, it was."

"How?"

"The entertainment, for one. They put on plays and concerts instead of watching those *Housewives* shows. Also, the fashion: Empire waist dresses are highly flattering."

"We wouldn't have done any of that." Frankie held up three fingers, pressing them down as he listed. "You would have been a scullery maid. I would have probably been tubercular. And you know opium would've made a huge appearance."

We strolled in silence after that. Frankie was thinking about work or insurance policies, and I was thinking about whether and when there would be a call from my elder daughter.

There was no logical reason Sloane wouldn't call—you don't e-mail someone after two decades unless you've seriously thought about seeing them—but I'd gone all belts and suspenders to make sure she did. I'd given her my cell and Frankie's cell, and the home line, and even Frankie's office number, because Missy was an excellent secretary, so highly organized that you had to wonder why she'd settled for being an assistant. I didn't understand it—young women really had options these days. Missy should be running the company, not managing Frankie's calendar, and someday she and I would get to the bottom of that. For now, I was grateful that she was still Frankie's secretary and that I could count on her to track us down.

The doorman, Tom, smiled pleasantly as we walked into our lobby. He probably had no clue we had two children. If Sloane appeared in the lobby, he'd buzz her up, thinking she was just a guest. Maybe even one of those bike messengers, depending on how she was dressing these days.

When I first saw the incoming e-mail *From: S. Reinhardt*, my stomach sank and rose at the same time. I dialed Cherie with trembling hands and, together, we shopped it out. I bought a leather handbag—tough, structured, with pounds of hardware hanging off it. I emerged from the store calmer.

What if her voice was cold and frosty, like the last time we'd spoken? How would I handle it? Or what if it was welcoming? Or, god forbid, slurred? There was something animalistic about the way my senses heightened when I imagined the scenarios. The leather bag—all skins and guts—had been the perfect purchase. I'd have to scour Madison Avenue for some feathers too. Maybe a pelt.

But Paige, tonight at dinner, had barely reacted to the news. It was as if I told her I'd bumped into Kirsty, the hygienist from Maplemount Dentistry. No, Kirsty might have inspired a familiar smile; she'd always put together a crackerjack bonus bag, with the different flavors of floss and the toothbrushes and stickers. It was more as if I'd announced to Paige that it might possibly drizzle this weekend. "Can you believe her reaction?" I asked Frankie.

"Hmm?" He was obviously lost in thought about his insurance widgets.

"Her reaction? It was so . . . blasé."

"Better than the alternative."

"Yes. A real relief." We had painstakingly bricked up the drama for Paige, hidden it behind a wall so that she could just grow up normally rather than in the shadow of Sloane's issues. "We'll keep the first get-together just between the nuclears, as quiet as possible."

Frankie, bless him, did not respond. It was ridiculous to pretend that nothing had changed in twenty years, but I didn't want Sloane to feel she'd been replaced, that we'd moved on without her.

When we got home, Frankie got absorbed by his study—I swear that man was going to get fused to his chair one day like that Shel Silverstein poem I read to the kids about the boy who grew into his TV set—and I went straight to the kitchen. The architect had initially installed a computer system to make our apartment "smart." It had been composed of one slim tablet, a PA speaker system and some earphones, and I couldn't figure out the damn thing; anytime I tried to phone anyone or watch *60 Minutes* for that matter, I randomly pressed buttons, but nothing ever happened. So, we'd scrapped the streamlined future. Nothing more high-tech than dimmer lights, we'd agreed, except for the heated floors and towel racks, which were heaven in the winter.

We ended up using the early-model cordless with attached message machine that we'd had for years. The SPAM luncheon meat of phones, it had proved indestructible through being accidentally left in the fridge overnight and once, by a teenaged Paige, outside on the deck during a thunderstorm. By this point, there was something comfortingly familiar about the way it blinked red, as though whatever its news was, I'd heard worse before.

Yet now the steady blink made my pulse, which had just started to return to normal, race. Add in the tunnel vision and the way my feet froze to the spot, and I again thought of animals: fight-or-flight response. Who was I kidding with the leather and the pelts? Those were for warriors. I was the opposite of a warrior, whatever *that* was, passive and waiting, no weapons, just hoping for the best.

I pressed it as if she were somewhere watching me, gauging my commitment by the force of my action. I jabbed my finger on the button as hard as I could, to show how much I wanted her home.

chapter seven

I HAD TWO hours until my first appointment and decided to use the time to organize my office bookcase by color. I pushed aside the azure *Getting to Yes* to make room for indigo *Love Poems and Memories*. Maybe because the blue reminded me of the speckled linoleum at the Patty Melt, it popped into my head as a tidy little thought: I still had questions about Dave's story.

Something—shame? fear?—had kept him from opening up about the whole story behind his suspension. Since the Patty Melt, he'd been hyperfocused on work. "Don't even bother knocking," he'd said.

My phone rang with an unknown number, which was somewhat of a relief from the tension building in my stomach.

"Dr. Reinhardt?"

"This is Paige."

"Paige, it's Helene Jacoby from the other day."

"Hi, Helene. You know I'm not a doctor, right?"

"You're not?"

"I do have a master's in counseling, though."

"Fine, that's fine. We want to come in again."

"Great. Scott . . . too?"

"Yes, he's totally on board. We both felt very comfortable with you and liked your style." I suppressed a smile at her word choice; at that exact instant I was trying to discern which of two book spines had more red in the purple. They thought I had style—wait till they saw the bookcase.

"The thing is—Scott's feeling stressed about work. Do you ever meet on weekends?"

Little did Helene know that this particular summer I would've been grateful if they wanted to meet on Saturday nights. "Yes, if I'm free, I'm happy doing that."

"I'm traveling for work, so how about next Saturday?"

"Fine. Does eleven o'clock work?"

"Great. See you then."

I hung up, feeling somewhat encouraged and energized. Obviously I could still read people—I'd sensed in that first meeting that Scott's discomfort might be related to missing work. Whatever his concerns were, whatever his hesitation, we'd get to the bottom of them. As long as he was willing, I could coax him along.

I stepped back and assessed the bookcase. Objectively, the color progression was far more soothing, key for a therapist's office. I wasn't sure Dr. Max, who shared the space with me during evenings and who owned some of the books, would agree, though, so I opened my one locked drawer and took out an entire bag of gummy bears. I would leave it for Dr. Max with a note with a smiley face. I was pretty sure the sugar would erase any objections.

I don't remember who started the tradition or when, but Dave and I got a kick out of trading terrible pickup lines. Dave was much better than I was, and I sometimes wondered if he'd spent a past life trolling in European discos; he'd lift one eyebrow, lean a little too close and breathe right in my mouth: "I lost my number. Can I have yours?"

Last Hanukkah, he'd handed me an envelope from Murray's

Cheese, promising one cheese selection a month for a year. At first I didn't get it, but on the card he'd written: *Are those space pants you're wearing? Because your ass is out of this world.*

I looked up, and he wiggled his eyebrows and leaned close. "Get it? Cheese of the month? Get it? Get it?"

The cheese usually arrived on the first Thursday of each month, so I checked for it when I got home for lunch. Alas, the box hadn't been delivered, so I went up to the apartment without the guaranteed laugh that we both needed.

Per Dave's instructions, I didn't bother shouting a greeting to him before going straight into the kitchen. He had left his work phone on the kitchen counter, right next to an opened box of cereal and two empty soda bottles. When I opened the fridge to get some water, I felt the phone's long vibrations—a mini earthquake rattling the hundreds of tiny Cap'n Crunches next door.

Four (4) missed calls. The Argentinians, Dave had explained that morning when I'd finally asked who had been calling so incessantly. A blowup on one of their filings—extremely poor timing, yes, but it was what it was. There had been a jolt of something on his face—annoyance or fear—that made me wonder if it was *his* screwup, difficult as that was to imagine.

I would tell him about this exact moment a few months later—my nonchalance as I cupped his work phone in my right hand, slowly typing in his password with one thumb, my left hand still on the fridge. If someone had forced me to articulate what exactly I thought I was doing, I would have said, *I'm helping.* It seemed obvious—to find out who called and report it to Dave when I returned his work phone, which he was probably missing like an amputated limb. I think this was when the questions started to bubble, although they were deceptively tiny, offering no hint of how angry and loud they would become as they roiled up to the surface.

I assumed his password was 4165—our birthdays combined and transposed—our universal code for the ATM, our luggage tags, our online grocery delivery account. I used it as my password for everything, even though I had recently read that you weren't supposed to do that.

Maybe Dave had read the same article, because 4165 didn't work. I tried other combinations: our anniversary; Dave's birthday; Burp, the name of Dave's childhood dog (which said everything I ever needed to know about his family); Hana, the lush Hawaiian coastline where we went on our honeymoon and Dave's favorite place on earth; his initials; his mom's maiden name; my name; my birthday. *Access Denied. Access Denied. Access Denied.*

My phone rang from within my bag, and I knew without checking that it was my mom. "Hold on a second." I pressed MUTE and pinned the phone under my armpit, her tinny stream of conversation still audible as I turned the doorknob to Dave's office. "Here." I stood in the doorway and reached out my right arm, his work phone still in my palm. He jumped from his chair to retrieve it. "You got more calls, and what on earth is your new password?"

"What?"

I grabbed my phone from under my arm. "Paige?" my mom was saying. "Paige. Paige? Hello? Paige? Paige?" I pressed CANCEL MUTE and closed my eyes against the headache that had started earlier in the day. "I'm here. Hold on. Just talking to"— Dave shook his head, eyes wide, hands crossed over each other, and I remembered he wasn't supposed to be at home—"myself."

I shut the door on gesticulating Dave and walked into my bathroom to grab some Advil from the medicine cabinet.

"Talking to yourself? Well," said my mom, "should I be worried? What about?"

"Cell phone passwords."

"Really? I thought you were a better conversationalist than that."

"Thanks for the vote of confidence."

"Are you lonely, doll?"

"No." I shook out two pills into the palm of my hand and gulped them down without water, gagging only a little.

"Sometimes people talk to themselves when they're lonely. You're going to get mad at me, but you know what would help—"

"I can guess—a baby?"

"A baby would give your life purpose. It's the most fulfilling thing."

"Isn't having a baby to cure loneliness the worst reason?"

"If you're sixteen, maybe."

I walked out of the bathroom with the goal of lying down on my bed, only to stub my toe on the two boxes I'd moved from the closet two days before. My mom's pressure to procreate wasn't the garden-variety Jewish-mother type; although I could appreciate her motive—replacement, "do-over"—it was no less annoying.

I had no plans to tell her that I'd started to peek into strollers as I passed them on the sidewalk to see the babies inside, stretched out asleep or grasping fruitlessly at air. Or that Dave and I had both started to warm to the idea of having one.

"Please stop." I rubbed my toe, then switched to speaker phone so I could browse e-mail messages. I usually ticked off quite a few mindless tasks while my mother and I chatted.

"Would you believe I didn't even call to nag you about this?"

"Yeah?" My e-mail checked, I opened the lid of the box containing my childhood mementos. The first thing I saw was my old pink journal. On the cover, I'd written *Paige Reinhardt* in carefully practiced bubble handwriting. The second box was

Dave's, and it had his hallmark lack of organization: an avalanche of loose photos chronicling everything from the bowl-cut years up to law school.

What was the rule about throwing away stuff? If you hadn't used it in a year . . . I stacked the boxes together and with my foot push-kicked them across the floor to my closet. "So, you're not calling to nag me about grandchildren. And I returned your scarf last week. What else could it be? I'm on the edge of my seat here."

She chuckled and then shut off her laugh like a faucet. "She's coming. On Saturday."

"Sloane?" It was odd to speak her name aloud; my voice seemed to belong to someone else at that moment. "As in the day after tomorrow?"

"Yes. Your dad just spoke to her."

I clicked her off speaker and pressed the phone to my ear. "How was she?"

"Fine, apparently. But you know, this is *Dad*."

"Hardly the world's most astute social detective."

"To say the least. She's taking a red-eye from California, so I thought maybe we could have breakfast here the morning she gets in."

"What about Nantucket?"

"Obviously we won't go *now*."

"How long is she here for?"

My mom paused. "He wasn't sure, so we're planning on staying in the city for the time being. I'll put together something little for Dad's birthday."

"Did he get any other information?"

"No."

"He's useless for these types of things."

"I know. But apparently she was asking about you."

"That's . . . new." I was being charitable. In truth, it was a little creepy.

She sighed. "All of this is new, hon. Can you do Saturday?"

"I have clients in the morning."

"On *Saturday*?"

I shrugged into the phone. "I can make it. I just have to leave in time for their session."

"Fine. I was thinking we'd just keep it the four of us."

"It's five with Sloane."

"I meant the four of us—you, me, Dad and Sloane."

"No Dave?"

"It might be a lot to spring on him. I mean, who knows how she'll be? Tired from the flight, probably . . ."

Tired—the ultimate euphemism. "He won't care. He has work anyway."

"Good."

"Is this—you're happy, right?"

"Of course. She's coming home. It's all I've ever wanted." Her voice did a little brassy vibrato on the last few words, like Ethel Merman. "I'll leave you to your conversation with yourself, my dear. The lull of empty chatter."

She'd said the phrase so carelessly, the way you hum a catchy melody, like it meant nothing.

Sloane was somewhere across the country, folding and packing T-shirts, probably smiling to herself about all the havoc she could wreak. And the rest of us would be defenseless, so used to exchanging empty chatter that we wouldn't know how to call out to one another in warning.

chapter eight

THE FIRST TIME I ever saw Dave's "pissed-off" face was about six months after we started dating. He looked so dramatically sulky—pouty lips, stern eyes, eyebrows slanted down—that I thought he was *pretending* to be annoyed about my plans to meet an ex-boyfriend for drinks. (I had since admitted to Dave that I was wrong about that fight; we were still in the early stage and had the roles been flip-flopped, I would have been insecure too.)

Still, that face. I probably found it cute at the time, but I was long over that now. I smiled back to mitigate the flash of resentment I felt.

It was late afternoon on Friday, July 4; Duane Covington and all other corporate Midtown offices had shut down hours before, but Dave, stubbornly, perversely, remained in the office/guest room, turned three-quarters away from me, his arms folded over his chest and his lower lip stuck out.

"So basically," I said, "you'll shower and leave the house for my parents but not for me."

He sighed, deeply and slowly, an inhalation that seemed to take roughly five seconds to travel up through his nose, expand visibly through his chest and be expelled, in a rush of dramatic frustration, through his mouth.

"That's okay." I leaned against the doorframe of his office and tried not to be bothered by the vaguely moldy smell that had bloomed over the past four days. His current diet was Coke, Eskimo bars, Cap'n Crunch and Pink Floyd on a loop—nothing capable of decaying. Was the smell possibly from *him*? "I understand. Not gonna pretend it's not annoying, but I get it."

"So you'd prefer that I fake it with you?"

"Of course not."

"Then schlepping to see some lame fireworks along with five million strangers is about the least compelling thing I can think of to do right now."

"I understand why we can't leave the city for the holiday weekend, even though everyone else has——"

"You could've gone."

"Right. Like I'd desert you now."

"Come on, Paige. It's not about me. You have to stay for Sloane anyway."

"You've been in this room for four days. You need to leave. Just for an hour or two." I desperately needed an evening out as well. "Welcome to tough love, Dave. How many times have you left the apartment since Tuesday?"

He shrugged.

"You've left once."

"I've left twice."

"What was the second?"

"Mail room."

"As in the one in the lobby of this building?" Eyebrows raised, I walked over to his desk, where a newspaper was carefully folded up next to his keyboard.

I pressed my finger hard against the headline about the financial scandal, and Dave recoiled, like his nerves had annexed the paper. "Did you just wince?" I poked the article and kept my finger on it, feeling like a locker room bully. Dave regarded me warily.

"Are you getting your work done?"

"Yes."

"Has anyone complained that you've missed deadlines?"

"No."

"Has Herb said anything new to make you worried this won't blow over?"

"No."

"I am doing my best here not to push you." No response. "But it's time. You. Need. To. Go. Out."

Dave tilted his head to the side for a moment before giving me the briefest nod. Displaying a shred of self-awareness that I had feared extinct, he got up out of his chair and walked past me. Two minutes later I heard the shower running.

My victory was short-lived. Dave emerged from our bedroom freshly shaved and cleanly dressed in a button-down shirt and Bermuda shorts, staring down at his work phone and grumbling about missing a call while in the shower.

I ignored him and grabbed our picnic basket with two hands. I had ordered it in February—right after we put down our deposit on the Quogue house—fueled by fantasies of sipping wine on the beach, our grapes and cheese protected from the sand by a little red checkered blanket. The thing was ridiculously heavy, intended for riding in the backseat of a convertible along roads bordered in sea grass. We were taking the subway; Dave had made clear that if he was going to be so stupid and weak as to agree to leave the house, he refused to be so stupid and weak as to take a car through the July Fourth traffic.

I knew if I asked Dave to carry it, he'd find one more thing to complain about and the night would be totally shot, so I lumbered along as best I could, gripping the ridiculously small handles, the wicker slicing my knuckles, while I tried unsuccessfully to make light conversation.

When we emerged from the Forty-second Street subway station, it was so bright and sunny, I could smell my own heating flesh. As we walked, sweat pooled under the back pockets of my cutoffs and trickled down my legs. I didn't comment on the damp stains at Dave's armpits because he'd found enough to complain about: the crowdedness of the train, the heat and my plan that we should go all the way to Pier 84. "You know we could've seen them just as well on TV," he said, "without having to travel through Hades."

I ignored him, but when we finally got to Twelfth Avenue, I dropped the godforsaken picnic basket, opening and closing and shaking out my stiff fist, and looked around: people in flag shirts, people clogging the intersections, people taking pictures, people in tank tops and bare chests, squinting into the heat.

"Holy crap," I said. "I feel like an extra in *Gandhi*."

"This"—he surveyed the crowd—"is my personal hell."

"Where should we sit?" I tried to find an empty patch, but all I could see were little red, white and blue bodies dotting the ground. I charged ahead, finally finding a two-foot patch of space in the middle of a cluster of several families.

With Dave standing above me, I plunked down the basket and spread out the checkered cloth, placing on top of it the quinoa and three-bean salads and roast beef sandwiches. When I took out the small bottle of champagne and the strawberry juice, I placed it upright and in the center of the blanket. This was supposed to make him smile, but he hadn't even noticed.

Before I met Dave, I'd never taken a sip of alcohol. I felt comfortable enough with him to ask what I'd always pretended to not care about knowing: What did it taste like? (Surprisingly thirst quenching, he said.) What did it feel like to be drunk?

(Fun, he said, or painful; it all depended.) His answers only inspired more questions, and I finally proposed outright that he help me learn for myself.

He bought one bottle of champagne, two pints of strawberries, borrowed a blender from somewhere and made a passable puree. He didn't have much experience with champagne cocktails, but he thought, correctly, that I might enjoy the taste. It's funny now to remember what I pictured before that first sip—some sort of Hieronymus Bosch scene of mass projectile-vomiting mayhem.

I sipped, though, buoyed by his emotional support. Dave had sworn he'd cut me off if I turned out to have an insatiable appetite, but I didn't. We had two strawberry Bellinis each: perfectly enjoyable and perfectly easy to put down. I was free, and Dave had broken the spell.

"Looks good," said our neighbor to the right, who was chewing on a cart hot dog. He and his entire family were, I guessed, from the Midwest—all polite, milk-fed smiles crowned by four identical green foam visors shaped in points like the Statue of Liberty's crown.

"Nothing like a New York street dog," I said, keeping my tone sunny and friendly.

Dave met my eye for a long beat in a way that highlighted my phoniness—did I really believe there was nothing like a New York street dog? Had he ever even seen me eat one? "Hmm," he said. "Maybe I'll get one."

"If you're hungry," I said, unable to keep the steel out of my voice, "why don't you eat some of the picnic I prepared just for you?"

He picked up the container of three-bean salad, eyed it suspiciously and plopped it down. "Doesn't really appeal."

I felt the Midwest family looking at us, curious.

I leaned in close to Dave. "What the fu—" Five feet away the kids sat on their blanket, cross-legged, eyes wide, like Dave and I were performing in Shakespeare in the Park. "What the hell is your problem?"

The Midwest mom, inches from me, drew up her shoulders.

"You know my problem," said Dave. "You've had a front-row seat. And yet here we are."

The Midwest guy cleared his throat.

"Not really. I don't know shit. Sorry." I directed that to the family. "You've totally clammed up. It makes me wonder, Dave. It really makes me wonder." I realized then so simply: it had.

He picked up the champagne and put it down. "What world do you live in that you'd think I'm in the mood for champagne and fireworks? Thank you so much for your feeble attempts at support. I know it's a stretch for you, and I suppose it's the most I'm going to get."

"What are you talking about? I've done everything you've wanted. I've left you alone; I haven't told anyone about your mysterious work stuff. I've stayed in town with you this whole summer—"

"A huge sacrifice. That I never asked you to make."

"That's not fair. Even before your whole"—I pressed my index finger to my lips—"*thing*, I've just been alone, hanging in the winds for months. It's not easy to be totally dependent on your schedule."

"Then don't be. Find something to do. Are you even listening to yourself? How alone *you've* felt. What *you* want to do. Notice a trend?" He was practically spitting out the words. "I know it's an impossible lesson for you to wrap your head around, but not everything is about you."

I stood up. "I don't even know what you're talking about."

"My whole life, Paige, has been ignoring what I want to make you happy."

Arms shaking, I grabbed the wicker picnic basket. I was aware that we had an audience by this point—there was a silence all around us that hadn't been there before. I thrust the entire basket at the Midwest family. "Enjoy," I said, and pushed away through the throngs of sweaty, increasingly drunken people streaming in the opposite direction. I was almost at the subway when I felt a hand on my shoulder.

"Hey," said Dave.

I ignored him and pushed faster through the heat.

"I'm sorry," he said. "Paige! Wait a minute!" And then he ran away to grab the door of an opening taxicab. Five girls spilled out, laughing and readjusting from the journey, yanking up tube tops, pulling down shorts.

Dave held open the door. I hesitated.

"Come on." He gestured that I should get in. "I apologize. I shouldn't have snapped at you. I'll follow you to the subway if you insist, but wouldn't this be better?"

I slid into the back, my eyes laser-beaming ahead toward the windshield. Dave gave the driver our address.

"I'm losing it, Paige." Dave turned to me. "You know how much my job means to me."

"I thought you were fine."

"Not." He cleared his throat. "I'm not."

"No kidding." We were stopped in traffic, and a stream of people passed directly in front of our cab as they jaywalked across the street. "You need to get a grip."

"I know."

"This is a job, Dave. A stupid job. You can always go in-house for my dad. I mean, it's not like we need to worry about—"

"It's what I do."

"Worry?"

"No. The job you just called stupid."

"It's not who you *are*, though."

"It is." I searched his face for signs that he was kidding and found none. "Come on, Paige. Be honest."

"Your job is the most important thing about you? No." I shook my head. "That's crazy."

"It's not. You haven't known me any other way. It's not like you married some . . . guy who paints street murals."

He slumped against the cab door, as if exhausted from his great exposé. It wasn't my truth, though, and this—one-dimensional and hopeless—wasn't my Dave. Had this guy asked me out four years prior, I would have given him the wrong number.

I could see, though, how being so ambitious and devoted could result in Dave's now being completely unmoored, how someone's strengths could, in great concentration, become his weakness, curdling those same characteristics you initially found so attractive.

I checked myself for the unfairness. Had Dave upon meeting me known how frequently I'd make him rehash things he didn't want to, or, for that matter, had he seen me first thing in the morning instead of after an hour of grooming, he probably wouldn't have asked for my number in the first place.

We were past all of that now. We had committed to each other, for better or curdled worse.

"Trust me." Dave's gaze charged into mine as though he knew exactly what I was thinking. "You can't understand what this is like for me."

"I think your perspective is off."

"No, I mean, it's good that you can't. Your life has been simple, easy. I don't fault you for it. It's the kind of life someone should have." His voice broke on the next words. "But I was nothing before this job. Just hard work poured into one goal. I've done everything anyone has ever asked of me at work. And now"—he snapped his fingers, which were in his lap—"it's gone."

I felt cut by his words. Sloane's disappearance and the void that followed had been neither simple nor easy. But how would Dave have known how panicked I now felt about her arrival? It was news to even me. Apparently, there was a leak in the neat little "Sloane" container in my brain. It was like I'd opened up my bag to find that my thermos had dripped milky, sweet coffee over everything inside, leaving it damp and permanently pungent. I put my hand on his leg. "What you've built is not gone, Dave. But even if it were, you can build it again somewhere else."

The cab picked up some speed, edging north on the West Side Highway. Dave fiddled with the seat belt nylon and stared straight ahead. "I feel like I'm drowning."

◆

At home, Dave slouched on the couch and turned on the fireworks. I scanned the shelves of the refrigerator for food, picturing that Midwestern family looking up at the exploding reds and blues, tentatively nibbling at the roast beef sandwiches, weighing the temptations of the food against the likelihood that I cooked with arsenic.

When I heard the booms of the 1812 Overture, I stuck my head into the living room to watch, but Dave had switched the channel to financial news. I tiptoed past him into his office. Not that I wasn't allowed in there—I just thought it'd be easier to avoid the discussion. At his desk, I unfolded the newspaper that had earlier made him flinch. We didn't have a subscription to the *Metropolitan*, and I wondered: if Dave hadn't left our apartment, how had he managed to pick up a copy? I started to read, hoping it could tell me something about my husband's state of mind.

Donald DeFranza was almost home, his key in his hand, about to unlock the front door of his luxury four-story mansion in Englewood, New Jersey, when they swarmed. As his two young children and wife watched horrified from the living room window, DeFranza was surrounded from all sides by federal agents. Before they could touch him, though, he collapsed on the front steps.

"It was crazy," said Byron James, his neighbor. "The feds came up on him and the guy just fainted. He would have cracked his freaking head open, but he fell right over one of the shrubs. Lucky, I guess."

Or not. The first words DeFranza heard when he came to? "You're under arrest!"

Authorities have not yet released many details on DeFranza, thirty-five, the latest Wall Streeter caught in the insider trading scandal hovering around Jelly Rocher of Mission Fund. Some are speculating that he followed the same path of Morgan Bell and Ricardo Lalouse before him: paying contacts hundreds of thousands of dollars for illegal tips and then using that information to line the pockets of Mission Fund executives.

Experts say DeFranza is a bigger catch: "This is potentially huge," said an unnamed source who worked with him. "DeFranza is big, he traded big, and he was a favorite son of the big guy himself, Rocher."

When I went back into the living room with a pile of take-out menus, Dave switched back to the fireworks. "Lots of exciting new shapes this year," he said.

"Such as?" I tried to inject some enthusiasm into my voice.

"Watch and see."

I stood above him for a second before sitting. "I'm sorry for forcing you out tonight. It was selfish."

"It's okay," he said. "We both sucked."

We rarely bickered, Dave and I. I'd listen to couples air grievances all day and tell them that conflict was natural in the face of living so closely with someone. There had been times I'd go home and wonder—where was ours?

I'd asked him that once and he'd shrugged. "I've fought with other girlfriends. You and I just get along." It did make sense, that some people were more compatible than others—*liking* each other in addition to loving each other—or maybe it was a testament to my insistence that we try to understand where the other was coming from, as annoying as Dave might say it was in the moment. Whatever it was, I was grateful. I hated arguing.

Dave sorted through the menus with feigned interest, and I joined him, picking up one from the roast chicken place. I stared at the red drawing of a waving, headless chicken and thought of the newspaper article I'd just read.

The image that had stuck even more than the poor guy fainting in the shrubbery was DeFranza's wife at the window, watching the arrest from inside. Had she always been aware that she'd made a deal with the devil? That the four-story manse in Jersey was funded at least in part by stealing and lying? Had she tried to persuade him against breaking the law, or encouraged him, crossing her fingers that they wouldn't get caught?

Had she been floored, unable to link the scene playing out to the decent man she knew?

And, more important, what on earth did she do now?

chapter nine

Vanessa

PEOPLE WHO SAY money doesn't buy happiness are idiots; money *literally* buys happiness. Take, for example, the Saskatoon berries I had express mailed from the Pacific Northwest. It took twenty-four hours from the time I realized I needed them to the minute I held them in my hands—the shipping costs were astronomical and I will take them to my grave.

When the alarm went off at five in the morning, Frankie sat up in bed. "What happened?"

"The Saskatoon berry jam needs attention."

"What?"

"The jam that is currently *in* the slow cooker and must come *out* of the slow cooker. Flavor: Saskatoon berry."

"Ness, get a hold of yourself." This was rich coming from a man who, upon making it big, bought four versions of the exact same suit. *Yes, Frankie. I'm the one who doesn't know how to relax.* "Are you having a breakdown?"

Frankie must have been thrown by the word "Saskatoon." He didn't accuse me of having a breakdown the night before when I discussed the menu: schmear and bagels, frittata, fruit salad and crumb coffee cake. There were only four of us, and it would've been understandable if he'd questioned the sheer volume. He didn't—because all of those words, unlike Saskatoon berries, were familiar to him.

I'm not trying to sound like a sexist, but it's a matter of

wiring. Fathers are incapable of remembering details the way mothers can. Sloane had tried Saskatoon preserves once, at the Museum of Canadian Wilderness, and had loved it so much, she'd insisted on a Saskatoon cake for her seventh birthday. I improvised: red food coloring in vanilla cake mix, with canned Saskatoon jam (from the museum gift shop) spread between the layers. An instant hit.

Frankie, not recalling any of this, was nervous enough to follow me out of the bedroom and into the kitchen. It was still dark outside, and we both squinted when I switched on the track lighting. "Frankie, I promise. I'm fine." I bent down to try to preheat the oven to four hundred fifty, which was difficult because my glasses were in the other room. "I just want to meet her halfway. More than halfway."

"That should be relatively easy, given that we bought the ticket."

"Because we *insisted* on it, as we should have." I glared at him a bit. Frankie's inner compass veered cheap, although through the years I'd gently nudged him away from drying up into a complete miser. "She's putting herself out there. You don't reach out and take the time to visit someone unless you really want a relationship."

"You don't know what she wants out of the trip."

"And you do?" I lifted the washcloth off my bowl of rising coffee-cake dough and stuck a finger in. Nice and springy.

He scratched the back of his head. "I guess I'll go shower."

I shouted after him, down the hall. "Your outfit is hanging on the back of your closet door."

I picked it out not to be bossy, but because I knew that left to his own devices, Frankie would wear a suit and send entirely the wrong message: formal and about to leave for the office, not dear old dad enjoying weekend breakfast with his family, remembering fondly the time we tried the Saskatoon berries.

Frankie really was wrong to be worried. I had been stressed at first, but now that Sloane was hours away, I felt good. I was about to hold in my palm what I'd dreamed of for years.

chapter ten

MY MOM OPENED the door at eight o'clock, not in her usual morning robe, but fully dressed—leggings, a black button-down shirt and espadrilles. She smiled, the expression tense and brief. "Was the Boy hurt about not coming?"

"No. He understands." When I'd left that morning, Dave had shaken his head in sympathy. "Good luck," he'd said in a tone of voice that could be described only as one part pity, two parts relief.

I put my head close to my mom's. "How's the scene in there?"

"Great." Again, the smile. "She got here about five minutes ago, and she's in the kitchen getting coffee."

"But how does she *seem*?"

"Really great. Come see." She put her hand on my back and pushed me down the long hall.

Sloane was leaning against their kitchen island, one leg crossed over the other, a mug of coffee in her hand. The teenager—stringy, sullen—had morphed into a ropy, sulky woman with crow's-feet deepening her olive skin and a few threads of gray in her long onyx hair.

"Hey." She nodded dismissively and I felt myself shrink back to my stoop-shouldered preteen self.

"Paige is so excited you're here!" My mom pulled me closer to the island and stepped toward Sloane, only to retreat like a kid playing in the surf. She clasped her hands together and separated them and hung them at her sides before finally anchoring herself in the work of ripping foil covers off platters of lox and bagels. As she did it, a grin hinged crazily over her mouth, like a child performer who's been coached to *Smile! So it looks like you're having fun!*

"I am." I looked right at Sloane, not because I wanted to, but because watching my poor mom was making me nervous. "What made you visit?"

"Paige." My mom folded a sheet of tinfoil in half, smoothing down the edge. "Let her settle in. She just got off a plane."

"It's okay." Sloane shrugged, twisting one of the pieces of lank hair around her finger and pulling. She needed a better bra. "It had been a while. I thought it was time."

"Right." Talk about a nonanswer.

"How was the flight?"

"Fine." She drained her coffee cup and looked around for the pot for a nanosecond before my mom swooped in with a refill.

I went over to the cabinet and fetched a cup. "Where's Dad?"

"He's on a call. For work." Sloane's voice was even, and I couldn't tell if there was a slight edge of mockery.

"But he'll be out in three minutes," said my mom.

"He'll be out in three minutes," repeated Sloane, glancing at her watch as though she intended to hold him to that. "So, how's life?"

"Good."

"You got married?"

"Yeah. Two years ago." We didn't know Sloane's exact address when the invitations went out, and after much debate and some fruitless Emily Post research by Lydia the wedding planner, ultimately ended up scanning Sloane an image of the invite through an e-mail that might or might not have been hers. She hadn't sent an RSVP.

"Congrats on that."

"Dave is wonderful," my mom said. "You'll love him."

"I'm sure." Sloane raised her eyebrows and nodded.

It was my turn to ask about her life, but I was afraid of the answer—inclusive of angry words, no doubt, like "rehab" and "benders" and "dealers" and "fault" and "blame." Most certainly, her response would rip off the thin veneer of civility we had established so far. "Are you still in California?"

She nodded, willing to cop to that, but didn't supply any additional information, like, say, a city or even which general area within the state. My dad, looking a bit burdened, walked into the room, wished me a good morning and ignored everyone else as though we were his usual breakfast crew. He grabbed the paper off the island and sank down in his regular chair at the table, unfolding it before him.

"Franklin," my mom's voice sounded in warning. "No. Paper. At. Breakfast. Today."

"Christ on a crock, Vanessa." He didn't even look up. "I heard you the first fifty times. I'll stop when we eat."

"On a crock?" I said. "Did you just make that up?"

"I remember that," said Sloane. "You reading the paper at the table every morning. You still do that."

"That's right." My mom brightened as if Sloane had recited an ode to family in iambic pentameter. "That's exactly right. He reads the paper every morning."

I did not point out how pathetic it was that our family tradition, the thing we could all reconnect over, was my dad ignoring us in favor of the news of the world. Although, to be fair, the way he read the newspaper—as though it offered a sound and sight shield to everything within a two-mile radius around him—probably was unique.

I sat down and then Sloane did, and my mom walked to the table with a large bowl of something red and gelatinous. With obvious pride, she placed it next to the bagels.

"What's that?" I bent my head closer, sniffed.

"Saskatoon jam!" She said this happily, like it meant something.

"Oh," I said. "Yum, yum." My eyes met Sloane's, and she made a funny face, jam skeptical. I had to bite down my smile. Sloane and I would not be bonding at my mother's expense.

"You've changed your hair. You've got that whole"—Sloane moved her hand in a circular motion parallel to my face—"blond thing going on."

Blond thing? "Um. Yeah. I've changed a bit since puberty." It came out sharply enough that the three of us looked around nervously. Sloane grabbed a bagel, slowly spreading cream cheese with one side of the butter knife, and my mom rushed into the uncomfortable quiet like the cavalry.

"Paige is a therapist now."

I felt my eyebrows descend, low enough that their wiry translucence branched into my field of vision, reminding me I was due to get them done.

"Wow." Sloane's voice was monotone—not overtly aggressive enough for me to respond in kind.

"Marriage counseling," said my mom, speaking again for me.

"A marriage counselor." Sloane smiled benignly, and my mom smiled too before tittering nervously.

"O-kay." The tittering had apparently annoyed Sloane, who jerked away from both of us.

My mom and I exchanged a glance, and my dad tried to fill the silence. "So where are you staying?"

"We're staying downtown," said Sloane. "With a friend."

If anyone else noticed the "we," no one said anything about it.

"You know we have a lot of room here. We'd love it if—"

"I can see," said Sloane, turning around and taking in the vaulted ceilings, "but it's very comfortable where I am. This place is insane, though."

"It was just luck." My dad cleared his throat. "I had nothing to do with it."

"That's not true, Frankie," said my mom. "If you hadn't done such a good job at the bank to begin with, Brent never would've poached you from them to work at Moonstone. If you hadn't done such a good job working at Moonstone, it wouldn't have been ripe for the offering."

She always said it like this, as though my father had caused the boondoggle, his one sure step leading to the next—*this is the dog that worried the cat that killed the rat, that ate the malt that lay in the house that Jack built.*

It was sweet that she saw him as a superhero, but in reality, my dad's life as in-house counsel at a bank had been identical to his life as in-house counsel at Moonstone, down to the allotted weeks of vacation and pay grade. He hadn't gone there to strike oil; it was just what had happened.

Sloane swiveled her head as though at an open house, and my parents watched her like nervous sellers.

"What do you want to do when you're here, Sloane?" My voice must have been too sharp again, because one, two, three, their faces whipped toward me.

"I have some plans."

"Anything interesting?"

"Um, some tourist stuff."

"Like . . . what?"

"I really want to check out some of the *SummerEyes* sculptures. Have you gone yet?"

"No, not yet." I tried to catch my mom's eye. Coming to New York for that particular art installation was kind of like going to Hawaii for the films. New York's latest public art project, the *Eyes*, was the misbegotten plan of some artiste wunderkind who'd spent taxpayer dollars commissioning one hundred

sculptures of eyeballs in parks all over the city. He'd been pillo-
ried when his pièce de résistance—an overbudget giant unblink-
ing bloodshot papier-mâché pupil just north of the zoo—was
blamed for causing its fourth panic attack. "I don't know if I'll
ever make it. They're supposed to be terrifying, actually."

"I don't know." Sloane shrugged. "Some of them sound worth
checking out."

My mom leaned forward tentatively, hoping to bond over the
artistic merit of the *Eyes*, and I felt a surge of protectiveness
toward her and a stab of anger directed at Sloane. It was difficult
to tell which was stronger.

Sloane offered to walk out with me, but I managed to duck the
invitation by agreeing that of course we should all have another
breakfast on Monday, but I had to leave for a session. I darted
out as they continued to discuss their calendars, which were surprisingly complicated given that my mom didn't have a job and
Sloane was here on vacation.

I was in the elevator, praying for the doors to just close already, when a hand waved through them. They receded and
Sloane pushed her way in, muttering something under her
breath about never getting out of there. Then, a little more
clearly, she asked which way I was headed.

"Up to Sixty-eighth Street."

"Good," she said, checking her watch. "You can come with
me to meet Giovanni."

She was sufficiently declarative to render me defenseless, so
I followed her out of the building. As soon as we were on the
street, she pulled a single cigarette and a lighter from the pocket
of her shorts. I smelled the smoke, dry and corrosive, and fanned
the air in front of my face, but Sloane was undeterred by my

discomfort. Halfway up the block, her cigarette burning from her lips, she pointed. "There."

Two men stood, waiting, the heat outlining them in hazy waves so they looked like something out of a mirage. When we got a little closer, about twenty feet away, one still appeared as if from a mirage. He was built like an Adonis in perfectly broken-in jeans—broad shoulders, brush of blond hair, a T-shirt that both clung and draped. Jeans. In ninety-five-degree heat. Obviously, he wore them because knew he looked good in them. Which meant he was an ass.

"And Giovanni is?"

Sloane dropped her cigarette and stomped on it, speaking softer and sounding shyer than I could ever have thought possible from her. "My fiancé." I stopped right there on the sidewalk, incredulous, as Sloane leapt forward and ran smack into the arms of the guy next to the Adonis, the one at whom I hadn't even bothered to glance.

They hugged and murmured at each other—probably more about my parents: *Did you survive? Yes, I managed even though they hung me by my thumbs*—and I caught Adonis's eye. He smiled, and I blushed and looked down.

A hand touched my shoulder. It was the fiancé, who had made up the distance between us, his other hand holding Sloane's. "Paige?"

Sloane moved closer to him until their whole bodies were entwined. "Giovanni?" I said. He was not what I'd have dreamed of for a life partner for my sister; instead of a skanky ratlike creature, Giovanni was like a gangly, friendly version of the little prince: curly hair, huge Bambi eyes, about half an inch shorter than Sloane and I were.

"Hi!" he said, and, hand still on my arm, leaned forward to give me a squeeze. "So great to meet you."

"You too," I said, my eyes falling back to the nameless Adonis as if felled by gravity. He had that same smile on his face. Beautiful but simple, I decided. It was always the way.

"We brought something," Giovanni said. He fished into the beige tote bag slung over his shoulder and brought out a box, a brown ribbon quartering it into four uneven sections. "For you."

"Me?" I wondered how he had known that I was going to be appearing at this block at this time for the presentation when I myself had had no clue. "Thank you."

"Open it."

"Yeah, open it," said Adonis.

"Um. Okay." I tugged off the ribbon and lifted the box. Four fat truffles sat in paper. They were beautiful, sure, but as it was a little after eight thirty and already sweltering, they seemed inappropriate. I could tell Giovanni was about to urge me to taste the chocolate, so I made some happy exclamation about how I couldn't wait to have some *after lunch*, and shut the box quickly.

"It's from her store." Giovanni removed his hand from around Sloane's waist, only to clamp it down on her shoulder. They needed to get a room.

"You have a store?"

She nodded. "I manage it."

"She runs it!" Giovanni was almost crowing, and Sloane and Adonis started to laugh and shake their heads as though Giovanni's exaggerations were a familiar comedy to those in the know. "It's the best chocolate."

"It is pretty good," Adonis said.

They watched me expectantly, and I saw no way out of opening the box and nibbling one—something toffee with dots of nuts all over its square top. I pretended to be in heaven, but really I was preoccupied taking it all in: the candy box, the open smile on everyone's faces, Sloane's hand in Giovanni's back pocket, the friendly street corner Greek God endorsing the chocolate. None of it was what I expected.

When my eyes clicked with the Adonis's for a third time, I wiped my hand on my skirt before sticking out my hand. "I'm Paige."

"I know," he said. "For days all anyone's been talking about is meeting you."

I assumed he was making fun of me. "Yes," I said drily. "My exploits are the stuff of legends."

I sensed something from Sloane and Giovanni—worry? Giovanni said, in an apologetic tone, "Percy's one of my oldest friends, so I call him first whenever I'm coming to New York." Had they feared they'd offended me? It was so far from the truth, I felt like I'd been flipped into upside-down world.

"It's fine," I said. "Nice to meet you all."

"We're going to breakfast, if you want to come," Giovanni said. "Please come."

"Yeah," Sloane echoed with sufficiently less enthusiasm.

I checked my watch deliberately. "I've got clients coming, so I should run."

"Clients?" Percy said.

"I'm a marriage counselor." I braced myself for the questions. People loved talking about my job—they were fascinated by others' marriages, but Percy just laughed, his mouth opening far enough that I could see the luminous white tops of his back teeth.

"Honestly?" said Giovanni. "That's pretty funny."

"It's a real job," I said defensively. Now that I really was offended, no one seemed to care.

"Of course it is," said Percy. "It's just that I'm a private investigator. I should give you my card so you can send the suspicious ones to me when it doesn't work out. We can work like an assembly line."

I wanted to say something smart and snappy to put him down, but I couldn't come up with anything aside from assembly lines being why Detroit was in financial ruin. I wasn't sure that was accurate, or even logical, so I noted to myself that he wasn't quite as good-looking as I'd originally thought. Then I smiled my phoniest smile and told Sloane I'd see her Monday before walking away as quickly as I could.

Slouched in my office desk chair, I listened to Helene's cancellation voice mail message. No explanation, just an apology and a halfhearted request to reschedule to July 8. I could call this one from a mile away: the Jacobys were never coming in for another session.

I pushed against the desk with my bare feet—sorry, Dr. Max—and returned a phone call to my friend Lucy who was out in the Hamptons.

"When are you coming out?" She had started every phone call this way since leaving the city six weeks before.

"I don't know, Luce."

"What's that? Tomorrow? Tomorrow's great!"

"I can't. Sloane's here."

"Bring him along, whoever he is."

I had to laugh. "Sloane's my sister."

"What?! The crazy one?"

"She's not crazy. She has substance abuse issues."

"So how's the visit going?"

"It just is. Not much to report from here. How are things at the beach?"

Her voice got muffled. "I'm on the phone. Yes, but I'm on the phone." Then louder. "Paige, can I call you back? We're trying to leave in time for the farmers' market so we can barbecue later."

"Of course." I had to admit it sounded nice, but there was nothing stopping me from doing the same thing in the city. I could go to the Union Square farmers' market, buy some fixings and plan my very own barbecue. Then I could invite over my distracted mother and Sloane, intense and sulky. And surely Dave would be delighted to cohost—he was in top form this week, a hint of color having just returned to at least one of his cheeks. Stove-top corncobs and mildly depressed mindless chatter on the seventeenth floor. Fun, fun, fun.

I opened the box of Giovanni's chocolates and stuck an entire round truffle in my mouth. What I should do was go home to my husband.

I bit down and caramel oozed out over my tongue.

Not bad. I stuck in another one and tasted the tang of passion fruit sharp behind the smoothness of the chocolate. Not bad at all.

I knocked on the door to Dave's home office. "I'm baaack," I sang, opening it a crack.

He was better today, still in the same gym shorts and T-shirt, but he appeared happy to see me as he turned around in his chair. "How was the big reunion?"

The Jacobys' absence was still fresh on my mind, so it took me a while to realize he meant the get-together with Sloane. "Fine, I guess."

"Do you think she's using?"

I shook my head. "She seemed very with it. Not entirely pleasant, but with it. And she has a fiancé."

"Really?"

"His name is Giovanni."

"What's he like?"

"He gave me chocolate."

"So he essentially bought your soul?"

"Ha." Something was still bugging me about the Sloane visit—like a little divot in a manicured green lawn. "Don't you think the timing of the visit is odd?"

"Summer?"

"After Moonstone's public offering. All of a sudden, my parents have gone from worrying about the mortgage to being loaded."

"That happened three years ago."

"Right, but still . . ."

"So, what are you saying? She waits three years to contact them, meets Giovanni of the boxed chocolate and then all of sudden becomes a grifter?" I shrugged. "There's this song, by Styx, I don't know if you know it, but it's called—"

"Please stop." The first time Dave had done this, we'd been in a cab after our fourth date, heading to my apartment. I still hadn't decided what was going to happen when the car stopped there, whether he'd be coming in with me or not. At dinner, as on the three dates prior, he'd done everything perfectly: made the right reservations, ordered the right appetizers, whipped out his credit card before I even had a chance to reach for my purse, lifted his arm to conjure cabs from thin air. He'd asked me questions about myself, he'd made witty jokes, spoke about current events in a way that made them feel accessible and like I wasn't a moron for not getting each reference.

Something was stopping me, though, from falling all over him in the cab, as cute as he was. Did I like *him* or just his collection of attributes and achievements? He was practically my mother's wish list for me in human form.

We smiled at each other in the backseat. I didn't want the lightness of his brown eyes to lure me, so I stared out the window on my side of the cab. About two blocks up, a runner made his way up Madison Avenue in the dark. His body bobbed with each step, his gray sweats flapped loose around him, his ears were covered by headphones so large they looked like Princess Leia's buns. The guy was booking it, sprinting full on in a way that made me want to cheer for him, and next to me, in perfect unison with the runner's steps I heard a soft voice: "Bum. Bum ba bum. Bum ba bum. Bum, bum, *bum*."

"The Eye of the Tiger." After we stopped laughing, Dave kissed me, right there, and with that spontaneity, I knew any hesitation on my part was ridiculous. Why question that we locked together like a jigsaw puzzle? My supportive family jutted out where his was just a curved indent, and his ambition was rock solid where mine tended to wilt. This was it: game over, as though every other guy I'd dated had been a rehearsal.

His repertoire for sound-track humming was usually eighties pop: "Hit Me with Your Best Shot" to stave off a fight, for example, or, as cringe-inducing as it should have been but wasn't, "I Want Candy" before fooling around. In the past year, he'd aired out this Styx one before—"Too Much Time on My Hands."

"Not funny," I said. But it was. It always was.

I would never have admitted to any happiness that Dave was suspended, but there was something cozily indulgent about the two of us being home together in the middle of a workday. I realized how much I'd missed just having him close by, sharing the same space, and instead of going back to my office, I decided to stay in and unpack those boxes from the closet.

I started on the easier box, Dave's, piling the photos into two groups, Dave before me and Dave after me, with the thought that maybe I could organize them or even put together one of those bound books for his birthday.

I hadn't seen one of the pictures before—Dave hiking, probably about age seventeen, based on how beanpole-skinny his legs were—but the rest were familiar: him at twenty-eight, smiling in front of the keg on the porch of the beach house he'd rented; the shot of earnest, save-the-world Penelope, his girlfriend from college, standing awkwardly in the middle of the quad, her hair pulled back severely. I'd first seen it years before, clipped inside a greeting card of a cartoon hand holding a fist of posies. I'd opened the card to read the inscription: *Thank you for loving me like that.*

"Excuse me." I'd pushed the card at Dave from my cross-legged position on the floor, surprised that such a buttoned-up-looking girl wrote *that* message. "How exactly did you love her to inspire this card?"

"Like this." Dave had stuck out his hand formally.

"Yeah, right," I'd said.

He'd replied, "Really. I swear," before putting his arms around my waist and lifting me onto the couch. End of discussion about bland Penelope.

The box also contained several photos of Gemma, Dave's drop-dead gorgeous girlfriend from law school, who was obviously a romantic counterreaction to poor Penelope. That one didn't seem to hate posing: pursing her bee-stung lips, hair strands across her face, stretching her hand up (midriff exposed) in the one where she tried to touch the WELCOME TO TEXAS sign.

I had always pretended to be slightly suspicious of her—how

does a man get over someone that beautiful?—but Dave had never made me feel insecure about an ex, and I'd long before subscribed to the nauseating theory that all of his ex-girlfriends had turned him into the man I met.

Also floating in the box was our wedding announcement from the *Times*. There'd been a massive snowstorm the week before our wedding with airport and subway closures. All of the details we'd sweated over evaporated like steam. Our band: canceled. Our guest count: halved. Our flowers: botched and sparse.

Some style section reporter had called us up afterward for an article about the storm's impact on area weddings. I'd been quoted: "It ended up being a perfect day. And the good news is that if we can get through the stress of that week, we can handle anything that marriage brings up."

I put the clipping aside to show Dave. Then, stall tactics over, I regarded the second box. *Do it quickly,* I thought, *like ripping off a Band-Aid: just open the lid, pull out the journal, flip to the first page and read:*

Dear Me,

So, Dr. Pressman is making us write letters to ourselves. But you knew this already because you're me.

Love,
Paige

I could still conjure the image of Pressman's waiting room in precise detail in my memory: the walls were light brown and ornamented with generic beach paintings, one of which had footprints imprinted on it, recalling that Psalm about the Lord carrying someone through hardship. I used to stare at it, wondering if Pressman was a closet Jew for Jesus. I had all but ignored the tiny little pencil sketches of a bunny and an old lady hanging on the wall to the right of his door.

One day, though, I thought I heard the door opening and glanced at the bunny. Instead, there was a duck, his long ears transformed into a beak. I looked again and found the bunny. I was tickled and continued to challenge myself, to see how quickly I could trick my brain into thinking it was a bunny. Then a duck. Then a bunny again.

I stared at the old-lady sketch next. Her hooded eye could be an ear, her hooked nose became an elegant jawline—and suddenly before my eyes, she was young and dressed to kill. Now I felt left out, as though I'd missed something very crucial.

The second I perched on his mustard-colored couch, I told Dr. Pressman what I'd finally noticed. Then I prodded him. "So. Which one is it?"

"Which one is what?" Like some first-draft Lewis Carroll character, Pressman answered every question with a question.

"Which is the real one—the duck or the bunny?"

"What does that mean—the *real* one?"

"I don't know. I guess which is the main one, the one the artist sat down to do first?"

"Hmm. Paige." He pressed his index fingers together and stuck them directly up to—but not in—his nostrils, unfortunately a gesture he used many times during a session. "Why do you want to know?"

Pressman had been a horrible therapist, at least for me at twelve. I wish I'd answered his questions with more questions: *I don't know, Dr. Pressman. Why does anyone want to know anything?* Instead, even though I hadn't stopped wondering, I dropped the topic.

Under that top notebook was a pile of more of the same brand. I counted them. Nine. I certainly hadn't written enough to fill that many, so whose were they? I flipped through them so quickly the words appeared to be jumping across the page. By the third notebook, I identified the handwriting as my mom's, although the loops and curls on the page were springier than the flatness I was familiar with, as if the spirit of her script had been eroded over time.

I had barely recalled that my mom had gone to Pressman too, and that there had been a place and a time that she'd talked about what happened with Sloane. Here was evidence that she'd had opinions and feelings during those months, some tangible enough to put into words and deep enough to fill reams of notebooks. It felt like a slap, a betrayal.

Perhaps that's why I felt entitled to read them.

chapter eleven

I talked about Frankie too much today. Was wondering with Pressman whether it was possible to heal as a family with Frankie not in the sessions. Pressman shrugged, told me to write down a memory of him.

"What memory?" I said.

"Any memory," he said, pressing his finger to his lips the way he does when he wants me to be thoughtful. "Whatever memory you want. See where it takes you."

My Memory

I left in a great rush. Summer payday Friday, squeezing into an elevator so full with people I didn't even realize he was in it until, holding open the door onto Lexington Avenue, I saw the glint of his glasses, the bob of his head a few people back. He nodded at me, pressing himself against the door to relieve me from the duty of being a doorstop. I smiled my thanks and walked down Lexington. I was about to cross Thirty-sixth Street when I sensed someone standing next to me at the corner. "Where are you headed?"

"Oh, hello, Mr. Reinhardt." I probably smiled my good-employee smile and maybe batted my eyes. "Macy's." I omitted mention of my plan, which was to buy an expensive lipstick. "You?"

"Penn Station," he said, holding up a small bag. "I'm headed to the beach for the weekend." He picked up his pace and I kept up with him. This was the longest conversation we'd had. "Six thirty train."

"Do you go out there a lot?" Of course he did, I thought. Of course his summer was full of beach weekends. It was disappointing because I'd always assumed he was lonely, but in an appealing way that I could remedy.

"*My cousins do. On the Sound. I have to go at least one weekend each summer.*"

"*Have to?*"

"*They have a seven-year-old and a one-year-old. Have you ever spent the night with anyone that young?*"

I shook my head. "*Cute?*"

"*Horrible. Miserable. Loud.*" *But we laughed, and it got us past the mental barrier that he was my boss, and we talked all the way to Thirty-fifth and Broadway until we heard the sirens. He grabbed my arm, pulling me back from the street corner as a fire truck raced by, skimming close enough that I wondered what would have happened had he not been there.*

Apparently—who knew?—if you are already a bit soft on a boy, having him save your life will only fan the flames. So it was then I noticed Frankie's eyes up close—sparkling, long-lashed, lovely eyes. (Where have these lashes gone, I wonder? I know where the hair is going, the waistline, the muscle tone, but the lashes? Do they retreat into the eyes with age? Sad if so.)

I melted a bit, and then reminded myself we worked together, and I looked away quickly at a mother pointing down the street to her toddler. "*See the fire truck,*" *she was saying.* "*Fire truck.*"

"*Fuh truh,*" *said the toddler.*

"*That's it! That's it!*" *She clapped.* "*Fire truck!*"

"*Hope nothing's happening at Macy's.*" *He was joking, but the fire truck was there when we rounded the corner, parked right in front with its lights still rotating. There was a crowd gathered at the gilded entrance doors, and Frankie pushed ahead of me, putting his hand on my shoulder to stop my forward motion.* "*Let me check what's happening.*"

"*Don't you have to catch a train, Mr. Reinhardt?*" *I remember that calling him that felt like a dissonant chord, oddly formal after our friendly conversation.*

He ignored me and pushed through the crowd, and I stayed right behind him, peering over his shoulder to see the scene. Two firemen were talking to a uniformed security guard. My first thought was how over-heated they must be, all of them in their dark uniforms, hats trapping sweat and heat. Then I saw the man on the ground, motionless. The security guard was gesturing and pointing at him, saying something, and one of the firemen crouched down next to the man, shouting. He stopped, plugged his nose and waved his hands in front of him dramatically to show how badly the guy stank. Comic relief. A titter of laughs ran through the crowd as it realized this was not a real emergency.

Frankie, five inches in front of me, turned around. "It's just some drunk," he said, and true, there were customers streaming in and out of the store, some of them looking down and hurrying away, some of them ignoring completely the small but growing scene a few feet away. "I guess no need to worry."

I stepped closer. I had seen the man's bald spot, the purplish hue of his pate around the bristly white hair, and when I looked closer, body parts began to click into place like collected clues: the bearlike slope of the arms, the distended belly, the dirty shirt. It could be him. He hadn't been home in several days.

"Any ID?" said one of the firemen, the one who had crouched down, now upright again. The second fireman reached out idly with his foot and stepped lightly on the drunk's shoulder, rocking him back and forth. He didn't budge.

"Haven't wanted to get close enough to check." The security guard waved his hand in front of his face. "Alls I know, one of the customers com-plained about a half hour ago. So we called yous."

"Miss," said one of the firemen, "can you step away?"

"But it might be—," I said. "I might know him."

They exchanged looks, and as I approached, the smell—fetid, as though a quart of milk had been poured onto a fire—was overwhelming. The man was facedown, and the fireman put out his foot again, ready to turn him onto his back by rocking him with his boot, but the second fireman reached out, stopping him. With great effort, he leaned down and used his hands to heave the man to the side so his face was visible.

I recognized the face to an extent: swollen, fleshy, broken blood vessels. Open mouth, cracked teeth. An unfamiliar number of cracked teeth—the two front ones were missing. And this guy had dark bushy eyebrows and dead blue eyes, staring openly past me until the fireman thought to close them with his hands. Immediately after which he wiped his palms on the front of his pants.

It was not my father. It was probably someone else's father and now, of course, with the wisdom of years, I realize that it was also someone else's son, someone else's baby, but in that moment, I was sickened with relief at not having to do whatever came next—the administrative part of things that would no doubt start by explaining to the firemen, this crowd and Frankie that my father had met his last moments in front of a crowd of gawkers at Macy's. Three summers later, after my father had disappeared for good, I wondered whether the Macy's scene would have been preferable to the facts I was ultimately left with: found on Horatio Street by sanitation workers after being severely beaten.

"No," I said, backing through the crowd, my desire for that Macy's lipstick completely dead. "I don't know him." I looked at Frankie, who was watching me with concerned eyes. "I don't know him."

He nodded, silent.

I smiled bright and false. "Have fun at the beach."

"Hey," he said. "Hey, you want to do something?"

"Now?"

"Now."

He took me to the movie Manhattan. We went out to eat. We didn't talk about the drunk in front of Macy's. We talked about work and Woody Allen and the food until he looked at his watch and realized that he was in danger of missing the last train and keeping up his seven-year-old nephew (now a twenty-nine-year-old accountant, certified after four tries at the exam!), who *always stayed awake until he arrived. He raced outside to a pay phone but not before hailing a cab and paying the driver for my fare all the way back to Brooklyn. He patted the roof after closing the door and leaned into the open window. "It's too late for the subway."*

There's no doubt that the moment forged something between us. There was little room for pretense afterward, and I wonder if that set up me and Frankie unfairly: Have I been too grateful? Have I found too much meaning in his kindness? The day felt like I'd shown him everything—I'd been quivering, naked, raw—and he'd stayed.

But I wonder what would've happened if I hadn't kept step with him on that corner. What if I had hung back and taken my time?

If that moment was what sealed my bond to Frankie, what kind of foundation is that?

chapter twelve

Vanessa

I'D ASKED SLOANE for her number at that first breakfast. Twice, actually. The first time, she didn't hear. She was tired. Overwhelmed. Taking in her parents' luxurious apartment after a twenty-year hiatus from our lives, she appeared somewhat stunned. She probably thought we'd made a pact with Satan.

Conversation loosened up during the meal, so I asked for her number again. An entire wall slammed down in front of her eyes. I could practically hear her internal alarm screaming: *Perimeter breached! Perimeter breached!*

I held my ground. "I just don't know how we'll make plans if we can't get in touch." I was proud of myself for not backing away. I've understood Sloane since birth—since her gaze first burned up mine with those dark wise eyes. (They say that newborns are blind as a litter of puppies, but not Sloane. That kid knew what was up from day one.) That doesn't mean I knew the right methods to reach behind her bravado, of course, but I never doubted that it was there.

Paige, a mite tone-deaf, excused herself in the middle of this fraught moment. Sloane's eyes followed her, and she shouted the phone number at me and ordered me not to overuse it before rushing to the elevator after Paige.

"Scraps," Frankie muttered, but he'd remembered the last four numbers and I the first three. Once we got it safely written down, we looked up the area code. (Oregon? When was she in Oregon?)

"They need to spend more time together," I said. "We have to help them along."

"Okay," Frankie agreed with me, but he was already looking down the hall to where his suit was, empty and waiting for him. I nodded permission. I felt strong; I'd already figured out how to proceed.

They were close enough in age that they could be friends, like Cherie's kids were, always dating each other's roommates and hanging out in one big group. Socializing, telling one another the things they didn't tell us. A pack.

♦

I waited until Sunday morning before calling Sloane and when I did, a man picked up. Had she given me a fake number? I had expected hostility but hoped we were beyond the lies.

"I'm sorry. I'm trying to reach a Sloane Reinhardt," I said. There was a pause, and the next thing I knew, her voice was in my ear.

"What."

"If you're not doing anything today, I wanted to invite you on a shopping trip. I mean, you wouldn't have to actually buy anything if you didn't want to. You could buy something, of course—I'd be happy to treat—"

"I have no interest in shopping with you."

"This was Paige's idea." I would work this like the *Parent Trap*—tell Paige how much Sloane wanted to be with her, tell Sloane how much Paige wanted to be with her . . . and poof! Reservations would melt. "It could be fun."

Her voice softened, I swear, for a moment. "I can't." And then it was flinty again. "Bye."

"See you tomorrow, then." As I hung up, I started worrying about who the man was, which of course, having borne witness to Sloane's high school years, I had very good cause to do.

chapter thirteen

"WHEN YOU HAVE kids, make sure you have a daughter." My mom always said this at least once during our shopping trips. "So you can do this."

"I'll put my order in with the gods." It was my standard response. Neither of us ever mentioned the obvious possibility of that daughter being an estranged junkie, in which case she'd most likely not be game for grabbing a chicken salad at Barneys every few weeks. I supposed there was also a fifty-fifty chance of winding up with a daughter like me, though, someone who lived for the shopping day tradition to an almost pathetic degree.

Lunch was my favorite part of the routine, even now that my mom insisted on going to the floors with the expensive designers and buying without regard for price. "Don't even bother looking at the tags," she'd say, waving her hand as I imagined Marie Antoinette did after her line about letting them eat cake. I loved the meal despite my mom's constant dieting, which was always the wacky, demanding, all-in variety, requiring the deletion of at least one layer of the food pyramid. Earlier she had handed back her menu with a packet of dried something and the request that the waiter mix it with rice milk. He had bowed his head deeply and apologized; no rice milk. No almond or cashew milk either, so the two of them negotiated and settled on soy. When he brought her brown shake along with my summer salad, she made me swear I wouldn't tell anyone. "I'm really not supposed to have soy," she whispered, as though she were about to dig into an entire chocolate cake.

I traced a cross above my heart with my index finger, and she winked in response. We felt off our normal groove; I'd been working to click us into track since we first met up in the shoe department. They were showing dreary colors for fall—mustard and purplish gray and brownish green—but we tried them on anyway, slipping cutoff pantyhose over our toes and pausing in front of low mirrors, exaggerating our attempts to see the style.

The whole morning I'd been thinking about that raw journal entry, which was, to say the least, a new perspective on my parents' we-met-through-work story. I had tried to process it, rereading it in my mom's voice. The tone and cadence were familiar, just not the darkness or the ranting looseness. It was pure, uncalculated: a confession. "Did you hear from Sloane today?"

My mom dabbed her lip with her napkin in a manner befitting a duchess. "She said she had plans all day."

"Oh? When did she say that?"

"I called her this morning to invite her."

"Really? Shopping is pretty clearly not an area of interest for her." Yesterday, Sloane had looked like an eleven-year-old camper—slogan T-shirt, cutoffs, stubbly bruised legs. Plus, it was *our* thing, my mom's and mine.

"It's not really about the shopping."

As if I didn't know that. "What're they doing instead? Seeing those sculptures?"

"They?"

"Her fiancé."

"Her who?"

"Fiancé. Yep. I met him." Her face darkened just a touch, as though someone somewhere had twisted an old-fashioned tint dial on us. "You're allowed to talk about this stuff, Mom. You can show surprise that she's engaged."

"I'm not surprised. She has a whole life. She's a grown woman."

"You're not hurt that you didn't know?"

"I thought she seemed really good, didn't you?"

"Sure." What I tried to convey with my raised eyebrows was this: *That wasn't an answer, but if you're not going to ask, I'm not going to tell.*

"When she was talking about the exhibit yesterday, it made me remember how she'd do these nature paintings. She did this whole project when she was eight using fruit slices as stamps. And do you remember the plays?" I shook my head. "To be honest, they were a little lacking as entertainment: not much plot. Just elaborate dress-up and long monologues."

"About what?"

"There was a heavy *Peter Pan* phase. We had a small dog costume, so you were usually Nana the sheepdog."

"I don't remember that."

"You were so young. You'd kind of wander around the stage. She did the whole production, soup to nuts." She leaned forward and sipped through her straw. Daintily, but this was always her Achilles' heel—it was nearly impossible to channel period fine dining while using a plastic straw. "She's a creative soul, your sister."

"To me, she seemed kind of weird. I mean, I know she's your prodigal daughter and all, but . . ." I laughed, and she didn't join in.

"I'm sure it was hard for her. To be out of touch for so long and then just come back in. We don't even know what she's been through."

I nodded. "Of course."

"I know"—our eyes met—"that this is an upset. Be welcoming, though, tomorrow at breakfast? I think it will go a long way. She really wants to spend time with you."

"Okay."

"You're my good egg, you know?" She cupped my jaw with her hand, and I leaned into it. "My easy breezy."

"Mom, remember when you gave me those boxes? When you moved?"

"Sure."

"How carefully did you pack them?"

"I don't think I did. I think Betty handled your bedroom and the hall closet, all that stuff."

"Yeah, because I went through them yesterday morning when I was clearing out the closets for the renovation." I felt clunky, but I was desperate to edge us closer to talking about what she'd written. "I found my journal from Dr. Pressman."

My mom sipped again. "He was pretty good, actually. You never knew what to write, though. You were always asking me."

"Well, apparently you didn't give me a good answer. I skimmed through, and if you didn't know what they were for, you'd think the big issue in my life was whether or not I'd get a part in *A Chorus Line*."

"I don't remember that." She frowned. "I don't remember you trying out for *A Chorus Line* in sixth grade. Isn't there a lot of talk about tits and ass in that?"

"We sang it as 'pride and class.'"

"I guess that works."

"Ridiculously. Pressman had you guys do it too, right?"

She arched one eyebrow. "Do you really believe that Dad wrote letters to himself in a journal? It was all I could do to make him go to the sessions."

"But you wrote them?"

She shook her head. *I don't remember.* I could tell from the shift in her eye that we were about to loop the conversational cul-de-sac.

"Did you write about your father?"

She looked down and stirred her shake with the straw. "Probably."

"What was his name?"

"Paige?" She let go of the straw and put her hand over mine. "We don't need to keep his memory alive."

"Do you know where they are?"

"Know where what are?"

"The journals."

"No." She said this with finality—her mouth shutting as soon as it possibly could in a way that settled it for me: if I wanted to learn more about the lost years, I was on my own.

"I don't really remember anything from that year," I said.

"Good. It's better that way."

"I don't remember Sloane much at all. What was she like as a kid, aside from those bursts of creativity?"

My mother sighed. "Serious. Focused."

"Give me more examples."

"Listen, the best thing we can all do is get to know her again. It's a blessing, Paige, to not remember the bad. I wish I didn't."

"That dark, huh?"

She was silent.

"Why?"

She didn't say anything, just pretended to admire the yellow bag of the woman at an adjacent table. "Do you like that one, the maize?" She pointed her head toward the table.

It was the same ugly color we'd seen in the shoes, and I frowned in its direction and shook my head.

◆

The front door slammed behind me, and as I put down the shopping bags in the hall, Dave emerged from his office. "I just had a great talk with Herb. I feel good." He indicated the shopping bags. "Whoa. You did some damage."

"It's for you, actually. For back-to-work when it happens." He bent down and peered in the bags, holding the sides apart with his fingertips. "All shirts and ties."

He slipped his hand inside the neck of his shirt and mimed a beating heart—*thump, thump.* "No one's sweeter than you."

"So, what's the latest?"

"Herb told me they're not concerned anymore. It's almost over."

"That's great." The phone rang and I ran to check the caller ID. "It's Lucy. Did he say anything else?"

"No. Go ahead—take it."

"Do you mind? We've been playing phone tag."

"It's fine. I'll finish up my stuff." He went back to his office, leaving the bags in the hall, and I picked up the phone.

"Hi, Lucy."

"So, when are you coming out?" she said.

"Ha-ha."

"You sound so far away," she said. "Oh wait—I have to give Antonio directions. Sorry, I'll call right back."

"Who's Antonio?" In that moment before she hung up, I heard a splash and a peel of laughter, and I pictured her outside by her parents' pool. I could be there now, sunbathing on one of the landscaped rocks, its warmth soaking through my towel, my toes dipped into the water. I'd visited her there every summer since college until this one.

When the phone rang again, I raced to pick it up. "Who on earth is Antonio?"

Silence.

"Luce?"

Pause. "Is this Paige?"

"Yes."

"Hi, it's Brian Lochlyn. From Dave's office. We met at that dinner last year? The one honoring female corporate lawyers?"

"Oh yes. Brian." What I mostly remembered was that more than half of the speakers had been men, but I could conjure a vague recollection of a pale associate at our table with a bright green bow tie, talking earnestly about the firm's "mommy tracking" options. "Sorry. I was expecting another call."

"From Luce," he said helpfully. "I gathered. Am I tying up the phone?"

"Not at all. How are you? Happy belated Fourth of July." I walked the phone down the hallway to Dave's office door.

"To you too, you too. Is Dave there? I just missed his call, but his message said he was at home."

"He is. I'll get him."

"So, how's he doing? Is he hanging in there?"

"Yeah, he is. He seems to be working very hard, getting a lot done."

"And you? Are you holding up?" Brian, I could tell—by the paste of empathy squirted on top of his words like a line of mustard on a hot dog—had probably been one of those student-counselor types in college.

"I'm fine." *Why wouldn't I be fine, Brian?*

"The allegations are crazy. It's just a matter of clearing them up. Sitting tight until then." Brian was undeterred by my silence. "Everyone who knows Dave knows he'd never do anything like that."

"Do anything like what?"

Brian paused, then gulped audibly. "Like, just, I mean, anything to get suspended. He's so ethical! I mean—"

I heard the creak of Dave's office door swinging open and muted the phone. "It's Brian Lochlyn," I said. He reached for the phone, and I held it just out of reach. "You guys close?"

"Not especially."

"So why's he calling?" He reached again for the phone, and I clutched it to my chest and stepped back.

"What are you doing, Paige?" He moved toward me. I again moved just out of reach, and then he raked his fingers through his hair and frowned to show his frustration. "He's my liaison. I'm supposed to run things through him during the suspension, you know, when I have to keep a low profile, and if you don't give me the phone, I swear I'm going to flip. There's a deadline, and I know you're just trying to be funny, but, Paige, this is not the time—"

I held up the phone and he snatched it out of my hand, shutting the door behind him. I sat there, on the floor in front of his door, trying to listen to his conversation, but all I could hear was the low rumbling of his voice, measured and professional.

chapter fourteen

THE CONVERSATION AT our second family breakfast was gunning and stalling like a driver learning stick shift. "So," Sloane said, breaking an especially awkward pause, "how was shopping?"

"We wish you'd come with us." My mom gave me a pointed look.

I chimed in. "Next time. For sure." I supposed it was strange—my mom and I hanging out together yesterday while Sloane had been only blocks away.

Sloane stood up abruptly. "I've got to smoke."

We all stared for a minute, unprepared for such urgency, especially surrounding a habit that had been shunned at all Reinhardt events since Great Uncle Richie's death from lung cancer fifteen years ago. Had I made a similar announcement, my mom would have brained me, but she just smiled apologetically and asked, as though it were a huge imposition, "Do you mind doing it on the patio?" Sloane shrugged and slid open the door, and my mom spun toward me. "Go keep her company."

"Aren't you worried that I'll breathe in her secondhand smoke?"

"Just stay, you know, to her side."

"Okay," I said, incredulous. "Here goes your little sacrificial lamb."

Their patio—one thousand feet of outdoor space—was large for New York standards, and it took me a while to spot Sloane, sitting in the shade with her legs tucked under her, using a crumpled tissue as an ashtray.

I walked slowly to her bench. "Is it okay if I sit here?"

"Of course," she said. "Wait. You want the shade?"

"Thanks."

"I know it's insane to add more heat to this situation. But, you know . . . addictions. So"—she inhaled and exhaled, shooting the smoke out of the side of her mouth away from me—"when do I get to meet Dave?"

"I don't know. My mom—I mean, Mom—thought it might be nice to just have us four at first. Is that why you're not including Giovanni in any of this?"

"Um, no. I didn't want to expose him."

"We wouldn't hurt him, you know."

Sloane yawned and ran one hand through her hair by way of response. "So where is your husband now?"

"Working."

"What's he like? Tell me everything." Her words were flat as dehydrated fruit, all the juice sucked out.

I was trying not to think about Dave, because doing so launched a jittery little twinge right in my gut. Last night, I'd waited outside his office. When he hung up with Brian, I'd knocked on his door and blurted out what Brian had told me—"those crazy allegations." "What did that mean?" I'd asked.

"I have no idea," Dave had said.

I had persisted, and Dave kept repeating that he had no godly clue. Who knew why Brian Lochlyn did any of the strange things he did? Brian was not someone to take seriously. Didn't I remember that awful dinner we went to a couple years ago—the one honoring attorneys of color? We had that important black judge at our table, and everyone was so busy sucking up to him, except for good ol' Brian, who just wouldn't shut up about his thoughts on affirmative action. It sounded vaguely familiar, jibing enough with the memory of the women's dinner to lead me to conclude that Brian was the firm's most socially awkward associate, if not the world's. Still, even if I could accept that Brian had misunderstood those crazy allegations, I didn't like how the facts were emerging piecemeal, as if Dave were showing me an impressionist painting dot by single dot. I should have understood the big picture by now—seen how the random dabs of color were actually water lilies.

On the other hand, I was grateful for Dave's steady reemergence. That night in bed, his hands reached out, pulling gently at my pajama bottoms before snapping, a little urgently, where the waistband met my skin. I'd turned toward him, trying not to act as grateful as I felt. It was the first time we'd been together since the suspension, and I'd hoped sex would cement our connection, or at least make things feel normal.

Back to that other hand, though, it hadn't.

I turned my head away from the smoke. "It's boring."

"Boring?" Sloane cupped the edges of a crumpled tissue and tapped some ash into it. "Harsh."

"Wrong word. It's just hard to describe the person you know better than anyone. I can't sum him up with pithiness."

"How long have you been married?"

"Two years."

"And what's he do?"

"He's a lawyer."

"Like Dad."

"He's so not like Dad." I stared her down. "In a thousand different ways he's not like Dad."

"What does that mean?"

I couldn't help but smile. "For one, he emotes."

She laughed. "I see. How else?"

I nibbled at the rough edge of a fingernail. Dave was the original man with a plan. *Of course we'll be together,* he'd said, both explicitly and through his actions when we started dating. Why bother with games or courtship? I'd been wary, wondering to Lucy if he was as deluded as the naked emperor who'd believed he was clothed in gorgeous thread. He wasn't. He was just mature.

I kept quiet. Never in my life—not even before that year—had Sloane ever shown this much interest in me.

"You always were kind of shy, huh?" I bit off the edge of the nail. I was not particularly shy. It was just that her questions felt like fingertips drumming on a bruise. "You look different, though. You're all, like—polished."

"Um, thanks."

"It was a compliment. I mean, it probably came out wrong, but it's good on you."

"Thanks."

She breathed out smoke again, nostrils flared, and but for the slightest bit of concern in her eye, she looked just like a dragon.

After breakfast, as I walked to work, Brian's phrase repeated in my mind in a deranged parrot's voice: *Crazy allegations,* squawk, *those crazy allegations,* squawk! I tried to ignore it as it hummed during my single session of the day (the Hoestlers) and again when it popped up as I fine-tuned the bookcase organizing. I tried to beat it out of my head as I ran the park loop after work, but I couldn't.

Determined, I knocked on Dave's door as soon as I got home. He raised his head and asked, eyes imploring, "Do you know how hard it is to do a closing from outside of the office?"

"I don't."

"It's like trying to juggle while handcuffed. Like trying to peel a grapefruit with your freaking toes."

So I let Dave work, reassuring myself that I would find a better time to talk to him soon, and drowned out the chanting—*crazy allegations*—by blaring a reality show about therapists and their screwed-up personal lives. Halfway through it, I drifted off to sleep.

♦

Scott Jacoby alternated between jumping up and sitting down in my office, making quite a scene. "She got suspended." He leapt to his feet. "Suspended! For insider trading!"

Helene had also gotten suspended? She sat on the couch next to Scott, her feet resting rather calmly on the carpet. My eyes were too heavy to drag up to her face. How could I help the Jacobys if I couldn't make eye contact? Should I address the woman's feet?

I recognized her flats, tasteful black napa leather with a peep toe large enough to showcase her two biggest toes, which were painted with a very familiar glossy oxblood polish. My eyes yanked up, and my mother smiled at me, somewhat pityingly. Where was Helene? "Where's Helene?" I said.

"Don't worry about it, hon," my mom said.

"Sham*Wow*!" Scott jumped higher. "Sham*Wow*! Sham*Wow*! Sham*Wow*!" He screamed it louder and louder until his voice swallowed up the room.

My eyes sprang open. "*ShamWow is for the house, the boat, the car, the wet sweater, the dog. No other towel's gonna do that. See what I mean? All I can say is* ShamWow!" The TV flashed light across the dark room: infomercial hour or, as the clock read, two thirty in the morning.

My throat was parched, and my heart pounded in that way

it does in the aftermath of vivid dreams. Dave wasn't in our bedroom, so I got out and walked to his office, opening the door without knocking. His back was to me, his leg jiggling up and down as he focused on the screen, editing a document.

"Are you suspended for insider trading?"

"What?" He looked amused as he turned around to peer at me.

"Have you done anything illegal?"

"No."

"You swear?"

He glanced back at the computer screen for a second, then at me. "No."

"You don't swear?"

"I meant no, I have not done anything illegal. What is this?"

"The Brian thing is bugging me."

He sighed. *I explained the Brian thing.*

"I don't think you've ever fully told me what happened."

"Probably not. I don't really know what happened, Paige."

I'd been leaning against the door, but I stepped into the room then. "Just tell me about that morning. Walk me through it." He turned back toward his computer screen as if he were watching a star-crossed lover board a departing train: *There's a place for us . . . somewhere a place for us.* "I wouldn't ask if it wasn't important."

He got up from the chair and stretched back his arms. "Okay."

chapter fifteen

EVERY WORKDAY MORNING at roughly eight fifteen, Dave shoved his keys in his leather messenger bag, slung that bag over his shoulder and set out for the twenty-block walk to work. I'd accompanied him a few times, so I knew that throughout the walk he was largely distracted by thoughts of the day's deadlines and calls. His ultimate destination was the General Motors Building on Fifty-ninth Street, a skyscraper set off from Fifth Avenue by a plaza that sat squarely in the middle of a major Manhattan artery: diagonal from Central Park and directly across the street from the New York Plaza Hotel.

That morning, as always, he strode across the plaza, ignoring the fountains, the small crowd gathered around the morning news program being filmed there and the tourists waiting for the toy store to open. He walked quicker than some of the joggers streaming into the park, passing through the security turnstiles and not pausing until he turned right into one of the elevator banks designated for Duane Covington, LLP.

He had worked at the firm for twelve years and inevitably bumped into someone he genuinely liked. That morning he saw Stan Blakesey and, as always, Dave brightened, and they gossiped about fallen comrades until Stan got off on seventeen.

When the elevator doors opened on twenty, Dave walked down the sunlit hall to his office—a four-hundred-square-foot perfect rectangle in the northwest corner of the building with park views. Dave was proud of his office, especially after Herb had confided that his assignment had been a matter of some delicacy. It needed to be large enough to acknowledge Dave's substantial rainmaking contributions to the corporate practice, but not so large as to piss off his more senior colleagues. All in due time, Herb had said.

As soon as Dave plopped down in the chair to log onto his computer, Herb himself knocked on his door. Getting visited by Herb was strange enough—usually Herb did the summoning—but the tentative politeness of his knock made Dave half rise out of his seat. When Herb shut the door behind him, Dave knew something big was happening.

Herb asked Dave how his summer had been going. The two often spoke several times a week, so Herb knew damn well how Dave's summer had been going. "Fine," said Dave, trying to be casual.

"Good," Herb said. "Do you mind coming up to my office?"

The two of them clipped up the internal stairwell, Herb setting a fast pace and Dave keeping step and wondering if all this secrecy meant a spot had finally opened up on the compensation committee. It was one of the most prestigious at the firm, and Dave had been gunning for Richard Abbott's spot, since Abbott was rumored to be decamping to another firm.

Hedda Brynn, the human resources representative, was already sitting in Herb's office when they got there, her legs crossed tightly and a folder on her lap. Dave greeted her and asked, with concern, if this was about her son. The kid was a tennis player, nationally ranked in some teen tournament. Dave had spent some time talking to him at the last family retreat and felt a connection. Perhaps he was in trouble and had asked for Dave, even if, as Dave pondered this, he doubted whether a seventeen-year-old would really need a good corporate lawyer.

No one said anything and Dave was about to ask more

questions, but Herb, now safe behind his desk, leaned forward, hanging his head sadly. "Dave, buddy," he said, "you're the subject of an ongoing investigation, and you need to stay out of the office until it's cleared up."

A joke, Dave thought. He looked at both of them, half smiling, but when their faces stayed serious, he got that it wasn't a joke. His brain frantically sorted through his cases and his associates. "Is it the Pinkus Farms matter?" he said. "The work Noah's doing on Arkat? Is it—"

"Dave." Herb patted the desk gently. "That's all we can say. But I know in my heart"—Herb palmed his chest—"that you're as squeaky clean as they come. So let us go through formalities here, and you'll be back as soon as we can clear up everything."

They agreed that Dave should maintain productivity on his matters. Ideally, Herb explained, he'd work at home. Ideally, they could keep his inconvenience to a minimum. The firm would supply whatever equipment he needed. Then Herb accompanied him—first, back to his office, where Dave packed up a Bankers Box, and second, down to the lobby, where a town car was sitting on Fifth Avenue, waiting to take him home. Dave wondered whether he had passed the car, sitting empty, waiting for him, twenty minutes before, on his way into the office. As soon as he buckled his seat belt, he started to cry.

When he finished talking, Dave sat silent for a few minutes on the couch. Then, rather abruptly, he got up.

"Are you going back to work?"

I was surprised at how relieved I was when he shook his head and held out his hand. I followed him to bed and we tucked into our sides at the same time; then he reached out his hand for mine across the middle of the bed. Within seconds, I felt his hand go slack and heard his breathing slow with the unbothered sleep of the innocent.

Dave's report had been convincing and detailed, but my eyelids sprang open every time I tried to close them. I felt like he was lying.

But why wouldn't he tell me truth about this?

It was hard to breathe in that position, so I released my hand from the weight of Dave's and sat up. I snuck to my closet. One of the blue notebooks had a pen—a twenty-year-old Bic, its blue top streaked white with tooth marks—stuck in the spiral. I selected that one and flipped past my mother's scribble, stopping at the longest entry I could find.

chapter sixteen

Frankie was grumbling right up to when he dropped us off at the car dealer. I slammed the door on him rather than say for the fifteenth time that morning that Sloane earned it, so let's just be happy about that fact. Let's not waste our time bitching about a thing. It's only a thing. We can provide it; it makes her happy: everyone wins.

He kept at it, though. Since when does seven months of playing by the rules get someone a car? A car? You think I ever got a brand-new car when I was a teenager? Seven months of sobriety means she gets a later curfew, a new sweater. (I think his real problem was with the color: mint green. Cars, Frankie thinks, are silver or black. Maybe—if it's a Ferrari or a little sports number—cherry red.) "What did Pressman say about the car?" he asked. "He can't think this is a good idea."

Slam dunk for me. "Ask him yourself," I said. "Come to a fucking session and ask him yourself."

Frankie shut right up—he has made clear his position on journaling. We get it, Frankie. We all get it. Men don't show their feelings.

I haven't actually told Pressman about the car. I'm not scared of his disapproval, but I think he's getting fixated on what he calls my "Guilty Feelings." He's very disapproving of these Guilty Feelings. "Vanessa," he said last week, "I don't want your Guilty Feelings to run the show."

I was touched (it's the closest the guy has gotten to expressing a direct opinion); too touched to tell him that as a mom, I have nothing but my Guilty Feelings. They are my touchstone. If you don't feel guilty, especially when you know it's your goddamn fault, that all your kids' problems can be traced to your bloodline, you're not doing your job.

I don't think Pressman has kids. I don't see any evidence of them in the driveway—no basketball hoop, no swing set. The only hint of his life outside the room with the couch is the bad cooking smells through the vent. I was talking with G. in the waiting room about the car thing, and we both started to sniff at the air—there was a starchy, overcooked, heavy odor overpowering the room like those waves of smell in a cartoon.

"Potatoes?" G. said.

"Sauerkraut," I said.

"Boiled beef? No." G. sniffed. "Broccoli, first steamed, then boiled for twenty minutes, then microwaved."

"What's his deal?" I asked.

G. pointed toward Pressman's closed door. "Based on the smells, I think he lives alone with his housekeeper-cook, a refugee from the Marriott prison institutional cooking services who dresses in one of those black-and-white maids' uniforms and walks around with an ostrich feather duster."

We laughed way out of proportion to how funny it was, but sometimes a joke just hits right. I needed at that moment for Pressman to be reduced to a goofy caricature. I don't know why, I just did.

We had one minute left. One minute before the start of the hour, when Pressman would open the door for G.'s session. I didn't want him to see me still there, so I started to leave.

"About the car," G. said, "I think you should go with your gut. You're her mom, and if you know she's in a good place, that should be conclusive."

I do know she's in a good place, a much different place from where she was last year. For one, the company she keeps. G. told me that a parent who was halfway paying attention would have been able to take the temperature from G.'s group of surrounding friends at any given moment, to tell whether G. was using or not.

Jeremy is a relief. Not just because I know the dad's a pediatrician, but just look at him. The button-downs and baseball caps. He shakes my hand, calls me Mrs. Reinhardt. He looks me in the eye. He's on the swim team. He talks about movies and early-morning practices and algebra tests. No room for monkey business with all those late-afternoon practices. What's that phrase I heard Sloane say? "His body is a temple."

Last year, one of the things I kept coming back to was how much easier it would be if Sloane were a boy. Not that boys can't get abused that way, but something about my skinny little daughter out on the streets at midnight met me at the place of my greatest fears. I felt as if all the caution I'd used in my own life—calling cabs when I couldn't afford them, wearing flats so I could walk fast late at night when leaving work—had been prematurely spent.

It's not like I wanted to give her a car last year, to be used by those greasy hoods she hung out with. Who knows what would've happened in it? Now it's a different story entirely. And even if I do have Guilty Feelings, that's not why she's getting one; she gets the car because it's Sloane's birthright as a regular suburban daughter who turned sixteen and whose parents can, with a little extra budgeting, afford it.

chapter seventeen

I WAS STILL sleeping, my face pressed against the notebook spiral, when my phone rang. "Mom?"

"Hon, talk me through something." She was using her rushed party-planner voice, so I assumed she was calling to brag about something like the thread count of the napkins for my dad's party later that night.

I checked my watch. Theoretically, clients were due in my office in three hours. But because it was the Jacobys, I wasn't holding my breath. "Sure."

"Do you think Sloane will be okay tonight, with all the people?"

I exhaled. *This!* This, I realized, was one of the reasons why I hadn't stopped reading the journals, as maddening as they were. They rambled. They were out of order. They required constant flipping through pages and indecipherable initials. But still. They were a missing piece to everything else that we couldn't discuss: my grandfather, Sloane's adolescence, why she—steel-nerved, tough, frank, bossy Vanessa—dissolved around Sloane. "I do. I think she'll be fine."

"Did you ask her to bring Giovanni? Because I don't want to bring it up without her telling me about him and—"

"Mom. I haven't talked to her either."

"It's a lot of people for her alone. She's meeting Dave. She's seeing the Rabinowitzes again. I could tell Cherie not to come."

"Isn't it more celebratory for Dad if they're there?"

"Come on. He doesn't care. And what if she needs to smoke?"

"You did not just say that. You're going to cancel Dad's party so your daughter has enough time to smoke?"

"I guess not."

"It's not that many people. It's"—I calculated the guest list in my head: Mom, Dad, me, Dave, Cherie and Darren Rabino-witz, and, of course, Binnie and her husband, Michael, who happened to be Dave's law school friend and was incapable of discussing anything that wasn't about work or baseball statistics, and Sloane—"eight people. She can handle it."

"Would you look after her?"

"Of course. Every forty-five minutes, I'll take her for a smoke break."

Dave wandered past me into the bathroom and did a double take when I said that. "Sloane," I mouthed, and he nodded, pointing to the shower to indicate his destination.

"Thank you, my dear," my mom was saying. "That relaxes me plenty."

"You're joking, right? *I* was joking."

"Bye, sweetie. Oh, and I did something funny."

"What?"

"It's a surprise. You'll see tonight."

I stood there after she hung up until I heard Dave turn the water on, and then I darted for an empty trash bag. Since his suspension, things had gotten a little gross in the orbit of his personal space—no time, he claimed, no time—and I'd been sneaking into his office whenever he showered, just to pick up the empty bottles and wrappers, to clear the crusty cereal bowls and spoons. It made the smell in there a little fresher, even if I always felt like I was doing community service—shuffling around the room, white bag in one hand.

I patted the papers on his desk, listening for the telltale crinkle of a Pop-Tarts wrapper buried by books and documents.

There, faceup on his desk, was his work phone, the automatic lock function disabled because of a book corner pressing down on its keyboard. *Hey,* the message he'd been typing read. *Good point about the collateral. But I happpppppppppppppppppppppppp.* I released the *P* key and picked it up, and there the thing was, in my hands, unlocked and innocent. No need for a password.

The water flow turned quiet. Dave, three rooms away, was done with his shower, reaching for his towel, pressing it against first his face and then his shoulders. I toggled to the call log and back to the e-mail screen. There was no time to really read anything, but it was immediately apparent: Dave had been in touch with more people than Brian the Moronic. And wasn't that the whole point of having a liaison? To not contact these others: Maya, Nell, Matt, Jack? The door creaked and I dropped the thing back on the desk, walking clear out of the apartment and down the hall barefoot to the trash room. Technically, it was a waste of both a garbage bag and a trip—there was only one Eskimo bar wrapper and a paper—but I went anyway, slamming the door hard when I left.

Why wouldn't he tell me the truth?

Scott Jacoby's eyes were bleary and red, possibly from crying or possibly from smoking pot. (I've learned the hard way that disengaged and sad can read very much the same in my office.) Now that he wasn't in his work clothes, he kind of looked like a pot smoker—shaggy blond curls pushed back with small oval sunglasses on the top of his head. Plaid shirt. Droopy khaki shorts with paint splotches. We hadn't gotten beyond pleasant greetings before Scott started twisting and turning in his chair as though what he *really wanted*—to the point of obsessive distraction—was to crack his lower back.

Helene, on the other hand, was dressed for a tuna-salad luncheon at the Junior League: green pastel collared shirt and pencil skirt. Kitten-heeled shoes. I got a little knot in my stomach at that. It sounds superficial, but sometimes people who dress like they want different things in life actually do.

"Okay to start?" I asked.

"What you said, last time, about what do I want?" Scott's voice was soft, and I nodded to encourage him. Sometimes, by the end of my sessions, I felt like a bobblehead doll. "That's irrelevant."

"How so?" I said.

"It's about compromise and sublimation." The red eyes were from crying, then.

I nodded gently. "Like, what?"

He shrugged. "I'm basically being asked to ignore and forget."

"Can you give me more details?" He shrugged again. "I ask *what you want* because I believe that, as a foundation, you both have to want the marriage to work, even if you don't see how it can. Do you?"

"Yes."

"And then," I continued, "once you remind yourself that you want it to work, if you learn how to *reflect*—truly understand where each other is coming from—it won't feel like compromise."

I admitted to them, because I'd seen skeptical expressions such as theirs before, that I knew *reflection* sounded cheesy, but it was effective. If you can concentrate on listening to another person—without your own viewpoint getting in the way, without judging or discarding or thinking of a response—for the simple purpose of taking in someone else's reality, you start to understand her.

"How do we do it?" said Scott.

"You'd listen to Helene, try to repeat the essence of what she said in your own words and repeat it back to her. Then vice versa."

"I'm ready," Helene said in that get-down-to-business voice. "Let's start."

Scott started pulling at an imaginary string on his pants leg. "Scott?"

He stopped fidgeting. "Yeah. Reflection. I get it."

"He's fine," Helene said. "Right, baby?"

"I'm fine." Scott cleared his throat. "But don't you want our backstory first? So you can decide who's right?"

"That's not what I do, Scott."

"I know." He removed his sunglasses from the top of his head, shook out his curls and put the glasses back on.

"If there's something you think I should know, tell me," I said.

"Tell her." Helene sounded tired. "Just get it out."

"Not to just get it out," Scott said. "Because it matters. Paige, you're not saying the past doesn't matter, right?"

"It's a tricky balance—to not hide the past but also not get stuck in its axel, so you keep rotating around the same cycle. I can listen, sure, but know I'll be trying to keep you both on track to move forward."

They both looked satisfied with that and then, in polite, worried fragments, they told me what they hoped to get over but weren't sure they could.

◆

They'd been married for ten months when Helene said she wanted out. "A full-on breakdown freak-out," she'd called it. It had nothing to do with Scott, she swore, and everything to do with her father having left her mother when Helene was nine years old. Married at twenty-eight, Helene saw it unfold like a movie reel: she had put all her eggs in one basket, that basket would break and she would relive her mother's mistakes.

She left Scott suddenly and moved to Seattle to be with Paul, a high school boyfriend she'd reconnected with on Facebook. She and Paul were together for one month. That's how long it took for Helene to realize that she'd made the biggest mistake of her life and move back to Manhattan to immediately start trying to win back Scott.

It had taken time and setbacks and many conversations, but Scott had eventually forgiven Helene, or so he thought. Two months before that day in my office, they'd moved back in together. One week after that, he got out of bed to get a glass of water and saw Helene on the computer in the living room, catching up on Facebook. She had long before unfriended Paul, but the next morning, Scott broke out in hives.

"No more Facebook," Scott said, and Helene agreed. "No Facebook."

But then a few weeks later, she came home at ten p.m. after going out for work drinks, and Scott flipped out. It kept happening: Scott falling to pieces, Helene bending to meet him, until they called me.

Instead of looking vindicated after sharing the story, Scott looked sick. "I don't know that I can ever get over it."

"We'll figure it out." Helene said this with confidence. "I'll do whatever you need."

Scott stood up, flipped his sunglasses over his eyes. "Unless you just can't." After he left, the door shut softly behind him—a sigh, not a slam.

Helene stood up slowly, two spots of red streaking her cheek-bones. "E-mail me some times for next Friday, okay?" she said without looking at me. She didn't wait for a response before leaving. I wondered if she was going to look for Scott and try to persuade him to keep at this work of saving their marriage, or just let him be.

chapter eighteen

THE SOMETHING FUNNY my mom had promised for the party was, in fact, pretty funny, which was not standard for my mother's predictions. She had selected a photo of my dad from twenty years ago in which he was waving at someone, right palm up, and made it into one of those life-sized cardboard photos. It was positioned right at the entryway with a sign around its neck that read FLAT FRANKIE.

Dave started laughing. When I didn't join in, he poked me in the shoulder. "Come on. That's hilarious."

"It is." I didn't have high hopes for the evening. All he'd wanted to talk about in the cab ride over was Sloane: What time would she get there? How would she act? How should he talk to her?

"She's not a bear, Dave. You don't have to clap or wear bright clothing or something. Just say hello."

"Like she's a normal person?"

"She is a normal person."

"Are you kidding me? Angry, fucked-up and here-under-suspicious-circumstances Sloane?"

"Start with hello."

He held up one hand, smiled fake-brightly and said, "Hello," awkwardly with a frozen smile on his face.

I didn't laugh. "Has Brian been better?"

"Brian?"

"Your liaison?"

"Better at what?"

"You were talking about what a crappy liaison he was. Has he upped his game?"

In his pause, I anticipated another Brian story—how he'd blabbed about alcoholism and gambling at the Native American Lawyers dinner, or made a speech about moneygrubbing and Palestinian rights at the Hillel Club. Instead, Dave jerked his head to the side like he had water in his ear. "He's been fine. He's adequately performed his job."

"Meaning you've been fine not talking to anyone else at the office."

"Paige?" He squeezed my shoulder. "It's a-a-l-l working out."

I knew I'd overplayed it; instead of feeling like the wronged party, I was the hysterical nonsensical one.

I high-fived Flat Frankie and forced myself to laugh. I was choking on the ha-ha's when one of the waiters my mom had hired for the evening arrived to usher us to the patio. He was wearing an outfit remarkably similar to mine: white pants and a green jacket with a mandarin collar.

Walking behind him, Dave stopped to whisper in my ear. "Do you get an inside line on the color scheme?" I faked another smile and pulled my own jacket closer.

"Paigey Turner the Page Turner!" Darren Rabinowitz knew I hated my married name, knew I didn't use it, but its appeal was just too great for him to pass by. He was fond of phrases like "Where's the party at?" and "Happy Turkey Day!" and would utter them in his fifty-nine-year-old booming voice. Once, two summers ago, he'd called Cherie his "boo."

"Hi, Darren. How are you?"

"Good, excellent. You? Looking lovely as always."

"Fine, fine." We pressed our cheeks together. It was funny, the things I knew about him—the testicular cancer scare, the money he'd "borrowed" from my parents during the real estate bust seven years ago that now no one expected him to repay. I didn't even want to know the things he'd been told about me. Cherie, I assumed, did with my stories what my mom had done with Binnie's, dutifully reporting in on everything from my late puberty (sixteen—cause for some concern at my house) to when I got dumped the morning of the senior prom.

He had probably learned these things over a salad and roast chicken at their dinner table, half listening, occasionally offering judgments. Yet he and I never discussed any of it and never would. It was always this—phony reassurances that all was fine, fine, as the other one thought, *Yeah, right.*

Cherie kissed me, murmuring something in my ear about what a weird, weird week it was. I nodded before wishing my dad a happy birthday and then saying hello to Michael Oster, Binnie's husband. He absented himself from the cluster with his in-laws and planted himself next to Dave as if staking a claim, no doubt relieved Dave was there to buffer the steady, slightly nagging chatter of Cherie, Michael's mother-in-law. Binnie floated up, kissed Dave's cheek and managed to slightly lift up the corners of her mouth in my direction.

"Dave, we were just talking about summer homes. The Rubens bought one in Amagansett, on that block where that old tree fell last June." Binnie and Michael had the forced repartee of actors playing a married couple in a commercial for floor cleaner—all talk of broken washing machines and benign gossip and changes in the teaching roster at little Barclay's preschool.

"Oh?" Dave looked interested, and I couldn't tell if he was pretending.

"So, what's up?" Michael said. "Why haven't you been out east for even one weekend?"

"Work," he said. "Lots and lots of work."

"What are you guys drinking?" I stepped in to change the subject for him.

Binnie held up her glass. "Pomegranate and coconut something."

"Oh, because of the——" I gestured at the burgeoning bump in Binnie's midsection, which would be her third. Hopefully, this one would be as blond and precocious as the first two, or heaven help us all.

"No." Michael held up his drink. "Apple juice infused with ginger. It's a dry party."

"You know"—Binnie gestured with her glass vaguely in the direction of one of the chaise lounges—"thanks to——"

Sloane sat alone on one of the chairs, wearing the same T-shirt and cutoff shorts she'd worn all week. Her knees were hugged up to her chest, and although she had a cigarette in hand—a tiny little orange light that burned in the darkness and I assumed was the reason for her exile—she looked like a ten-year-old who'd been stashed at a kids' table.

I walked over. "Hi." I sat down on the chaise next to her, surprised when her features relaxed into relief for half a second when I did. "You having fun?"

"Well . . ." She fluttered her eyes beneath her lids for a moment. "No."

"Hi." Dave was right behind me, hand extended to Sloane. "I've wanted to meet you forever. I'm Dave."

"The husband." She switched her cigarette to her left hand and shook with her right, unfolding from the little ball she'd been sitting in. "Hello."

"The husband." He plopped down next to me, depressing my cushion with his weight. "So how does it feel to be back? Is it weird?"

"A little, maybe."

"Must be. Seeing everyone after twenty years, watching people age in flashes like Rip Van Winkle. You've got a great family, though."

"Dave." I pushed against him with my shoulder so he'd shut up.

Sloane sucked on her cigarette, which was back in her right hand. "I hear you're part of the family business?"

"What?" Dave seemed taken aback.

"You're a lawyer."

"Guilty. I'm at a firm in Midtown."

"Neat. How's married life?"

"Married life?" He watched her for a second, and I thought he was trying to figure out if she was challenging him.

"She's about to embark on it," I reminded him.

"Oh, congratulations." He put his arm around my shoulders and kissed my cheek. "It's the best. I'm the luckiest."

"Aw," Sloane said in her monotone. "Sweet."

"Hello!" My mom rushed over, leaned down to kiss Dave's and my cheeks and stood over the three of us, hands clasped. "Look at this: the kids—all together." She beckoned to someone with the crook of a finger on her right hand.

"I'm getting to know my new sister." Dave's head bent up toward my mom. "Right, Sloane?"

"Right."

"Excellent."

"Hi there." My mom spoke loud enough to address a stranger ten feet away who was wearing a dark suit with four cameras around his neck. "Can you get a picture of these three?" I did a quick estimation of the party's hired help–to-guest ratio: four to one. "Not just one, actually, but as many as you can." She leaned closer to him, put her hand up to cover the side of her mouth and said, conspiratorially, "I don't really care about anyone else's picture, actually."

He nodded and winked, and she pulled my arm, whispering, "Get up!" and smiled gently at Sloane. "Over there, by the view. Paige, oh my god, you're dressed like the caterers."

"I'm not." I glanced down. "This is emerald. They're wearing . . ."

"Emerald. They're wearing emerald." Dave put his hand on my mom's arm. "That life-sized picture of Frankie is so funny. What did he say when he saw it?"

"Oh, he couldn't believe how much hair he used to have. Get together, you three."

Dave put an arm around me and one around Sloane and hugged us toward him so closely that I could smell the minty spice of his deodorant. I smiled into the flashes, having no hope for the resulting images: Dave's smile the only genuine one and Sloane's outfit awkwardly casual compared to ours.

"Oh," my mom responded to someone's signal across the patio. "Dinner's ready!" She hurried away, and the three of us moved over to the outdoor table, the photographer dutifully recording our steps.

"I feel like I'm walking the red carpet," said Sloane under her breath to no one in particular.

"Casual, I promise," my mom had sworn during the planning stage, and yet there were seating cards, designed, I was certain, to offer both protection and proof of Sloane.

My mom had placed us at my dad's end of the table, which

was always the quiet side. The kids were next: a spectrum from Reinhardts to Rabinowitzes, with Dave and Michael the bridges. Beyond them were my mom and Cherie and booming Darren, the constant, spirited yammerers.

Normally, I would have fought against being shelved with the duds and would've pushed into Dave's conversation or leaned over to chat with Cherie, who could converse for hours about anything from the cleanest way to remove a splinter to the difference between seltzer and sparkling water.

I stayed silent, however. So did Sloane, even though my mom kept trying to draw her into the conversation. Sloane's and my eyes met once, and I interpreted her glance as an admission and acknowledgment that we were each having a less-than-fantastic time.

The toasts started, as they always did, right after the singing and the cake. Darren went first—with a golf story that was as generic as it was loud—something about my dad going par three and the green or the sand. Cherie, who did not technically give her own toast, kept butting in to Darren's: "Why aren't you talking about the time we went to Mexico?" and Darren would boom, "Okay. We went to Mexico." And Cherie would say, "Not like that. Tell the funny parts," and Darren would say, "You tell it, then," and she would.

Michael and Binnie together recounted the Orlando Motor Inn incident. (That vacation had happened before Binnie even met Michael, but by now he'd heard enough about it that he'd probably forgotten he wasn't there.) The story was that we'd all gone swimming in that fluorescent blue pool and when we got out, dripping wet, there had been no towels. My usually mild-mannered father apparently found this unforgivable and expressed his displeasure in such a volcanic way that we were all still discussing it.

Dave rose with raised glass, bouncing a little on the balls of his feet. I was surprised by how self-conscious he was as he told my dad he was "the best dad I know." Dave was usually a smooth public speaker, and it wasn't like he was covering unexplored territory: Dave's own dad had spent the majority of Dave's childhood sitting in a Barcalounger, flipping the remote and grunting for corn nuts. Dave talked to him about twice a year.

I wondered if Sloane was thinking the same thing I was—that Dave probably appreciated our father more than we did. Involuntarily, I smiled at her—my lips twisted in a guilty grin. Wonder of wonders, she smiled back.

Dave sat down, which meant I was up. I watched Sloane pick at the loose fabric of her place mat. She couldn't have known that toasts are de rigueur at Reinhardt parties, and if she had, it's not like she had stories to share.

I willed Sloane to look at me. She didn't, so I leaned over her mat and put my flattened palm down on it, raising my other hand like an orchestra conductor: *Rise!* She furrowed her brow, but I did it again until she pushed back her chair and slouched to a stand.

I'd written a poem for the occasion, albeit an awful one—the worst stanza of which rhymed "hardworking lawyer" with "moral as Tom Sawyer." It had occurred to me, as I watched my dad puff out sixty-three candles, that Huck Finn, not Tom, was the moral one. Wasn't that the whole point of the thing? Now Huck Finn—that would have introduced a wealth of rhyming options.

I raised a juice glass and waited for Sloane to do the same. I had no clue what to say, so I said something about how he worked hard enough so the rest of us didn't have to. I said how generous he was, although really, I don't know if he was intrinsically. (I'd always suspected that if my mother had met an early and unfortunate death, my dad would have done a full-on "Father of Cinderella," and we'd have been pulled into the embrace of a wicked stepmother. I left that part out of the toast.)

Then Sloane mumbled something about how nice it was to be celebrating with everyone together in one spot. It wasn't much, but when she spoke, it was like that pivotal moment in *The Elephant Man—I am not an animal; I am a human being!* Everyone gasped and sprouted tears, and Sloane waited until after the kissing and the aws died down to give me the most potent grateful glance I've ever received.

She cares, I thought. *She actually cares under there.*

My mom, the anchor of the toasts, pushed out her chair. "Frankie," she said, "I've done my share of stupid things." Everybody laughed. "Hey—you all don't have to agree so readily. But the first smart thing I did was marrying you. The second smart thing I did was stay married to you."

"Surely, you've done more than two smart things?" Darren boomed this.

She pretended to think, holding up one finger as if counting, scratching her head, hamming up her head shake. "Not really. I think two. Not that I'll admit that ever again."

She waited for the laughter to die down before continuing, looking at the Rabinowitz end of the table. "Here's the thing about Frankie. Last week I asked him what he wanted for his birthday, and he told me to pick out a nice piece of jewelry for myself." Her voice wavered, and instead of continuing, she blinked, hard, her face caught in that ugly spastic moment heralding tears. I held my breath, uncertain what would happen next.

"That's probably because he likes to play dress-up when you're out of the house." That was Cherie.

"Maybe." She raised her glass, and I could see her returning from the precipice of wherever her toast had been leading her.

"Didn't he ask for fishnets last year?" Darren said loudly.

"And coral red lipstick," said Cherie.

"With that P.S. that you were out of L'Air du Temps," interjected Michael, obviously pleased with himself at joining the repartee.

Sloane sighed—shoulders rising, face blank. The effect was that of someone who wanted to roll her eyes in disdain but couldn't even manage the effort.

My mom's expression had hardened into default: a mask of *Been-there-done-that*. She wagged her finger at my dad. "And you never did have a good explanation for my missing false eyelashes."

My dad nodded, as though saying, *This isn't really funny, but sure I'll play along*.

"Happy birthday," she said. "Here's to another sixty-two more years."

"Here, here." We all raised our glasses. Where had she been going, I wondered, and what did she mean by marrying him and staying with him—as though those were two separate decisions? I'd always thought I'd understood my parents' marriage.

For good reason, my mom had been looking for someone stable and secure. I loved my dad, but I'd counseled couples like my parents, where you saw it so clearly—one of them was just hanging on for the ride of his life.

Later, when the caterers were clearing plates of cake and everyone was getting up to go inside to the couches for more fruit drinks, I leaned across the table to Sloane, who also looked like she was lost in thought. "It's almost over."

"What are you doing tomorrow?" she asked as though she hadn't even heard me.

"Going to work."

"Want to meet me for lunch?" She swept her eyes around the patio. "Just us."

"Sure," I said. "Why not?"

chapter nineteen

SLOANE WAS WAITING at the noodle place she'd picked, a tiny restaurant in the East Village with two long tables in the middle of a rectangular room.

"Hey." As I squeezed onto the bench in the small space across from her, the woman on my left wordlessly inched over.

"It's kind of like eating on a bus, but they're supposed to have the best noodles in the city." Sloane passed me the menu, a cream card about the size of a photograph that announced in tiny rounded gray type: NOODLES WITH CHICKEN, NOODLES WITH VEGETABLES, NOODLES WITH BEEF. "I hear they get pretty"—she slammed her hand against her palm, *chop-chop*—"so I already ordered for us—one of each kind. Okay?"

"Good." I looked around the restaurant, wooden and austere in a modern way—low ceilings, prison gray walls. "How do you even know about this place?"

"I don't remember. Online? That's where I get most of my scoop. But it's a legend; I've wanted to try it forever."

"Online?"

"I read a lot of reviews."

"For food?"

"Food, art, travel. We have a blog."

"Wow."

"Nothing big. Just posting about culture."

"You also have the chocolate shop?"

"The blog isn't a big deal yet. We have, like, only three advertisers so far. The shop is my full-time job. The owner's a friend, so she's given me a little ownership percentage, and I manage it. Artisanal chocolates and wines."

I nodded. "Cool." The wine part begged questions that I didn't want to ask, so I focused on the waiter, who was hoisting a tray of three steaming bowls of noodles and cramming them all in the little space between us. There was a collective wriggle as our neighbors pushed aside their water glasses and napkins.

Sloane pulled out her phone and snapped pictures of the dishes. Then, she separated two chopsticks, rolling them together and using them to lift a portion of noodles, slick with julienned vegetables, onto both plates. She pushed one over the table to me. "Try this first."

She chopsticked a bite-sized amount and carried it to her mouth. "Ohmygod," she said, swallowing. "That is incred— What? Why are you just watching me? What?" Her face sagged. "I'm being really bossy, aren't I?"

"No. I mean, yes, I suppose you are, but it's fine."

"It's not. I've changed, I swear. I'm not as bossy as I was when we were little."

"Oh. Okay."

"You don't remember?" I could tell from the blank moment between us and the way she put her chopsticks down that she felt something—hurt?—about it. "You used to tell on me constantly."

"To Mom?"

She nodded, mimicking a high-pitched voice. "*Mommy, she's bossing me.* You always called her mommy. It made you sound much younger than you were."

"I *was* young."

She shrugged. "Still."

"What did she do when I told on you?"

"Always, always, always took your side."

"I sound so annoying."

"I thought you were, but in fairness, I *was* bossy. Still am. So says Giovanni."

"I wasn't thinking that—the bossy thing. I was just wondering when you'd eaten here before."

She shook her head. "First time."

"You have some serious noodle mojo, then."

She smiled. "Noodle Mojo. That's not a bad title for a post."

I tasted the noodles. "These are insanely good."

"I know. Try the beef."

I handed her my plate. "Serve it up."

"So I enjoyed meeting Dave last night."

Something must have crossed my face, because she put her chopsticks down again. "What?"

I shook my head.

"I swear, you made a face when I mentioned your husband. Not a good sign." She smirked in a not-unfriendly way, and I tried to smirk too, but something happened, and my mouth jerked up too far. Soon my chin was quivering and my eyes were tearing.

"You want to talk about it?" Sloane picked up her chopsticks.

I dabbed my eyes with the small black cocktail napkin, and Sloane propped herself up on the table, her elbows two sharp compass points. "What is this about?"

"It's not really my . . . secret to tell."

"Telling me is like talking to a wall." I couldn't help but look pointedly at her chest, which was as flat as mine, and she flared her nostrils in impatience. "I meant I'm not a gossip. I'm not going to tell our parents or the Ridiculobinowitzes or whoever. I can just listen."

Plus, who would believe her if she broke my confidence? Sloane didn't exactly have a good track record for honesty, although I did believe her right now, the way she was staring at me almost encouragingly from across the table. My problem, I realized, would seem to her like child's play, like my dad's complaint about the lack of towels to the workers busting their asses at the Orlando Motor Inn. I still remember their faces, eyebrows aloft, straight-line mouths: This *is your problem*? *Cry me a river, vacationing white man.*

I started at the beginning with Dave's suspension and told her everything up to his work-phone lie the day before. "So, what do you think?" I leaned back, anticipating her reassurances that I had a great husband and shouldn't look for trouble. I expected them because that's what my mom would've done; it's what Lucy would've done; it's what Dave would have done (setting it to Bob Marley, of course—"Three Little Birds"). It's what *I* would've done had I been on the other side of the table.

"Oh, he's lying to you."

The way my stomach went into free fall when she said it out loud—I knew it was the truth. "How do you know that?"

She shrugged. "Common sense. There's no way someone gets suspended from work without knowing why. No employer would do that, not even, like, evil congloms. Thinking anything else is just plain denial. Why do you think he got suspended?"

"I don't know."

"Come on, you must have an idea—what do lawyers do to get suspended? With them it's all about ethics, right? Maybe he messed with confidentiality? Or was a little too buddy-buddy with a judge?"

"He's corporate. He doesn't really work with judges."

"Well, what, then?"

I avoided her eyes. "I don't know." Dave had denied it and I had tried to believe him, but the certainty came to me in a rush: he was involved in the financial scandal that was all over the news. He had to be. I had something more probative than factual evidence or his admission: how well I knew him, and how much sense it made given his sleazebag mentor and his burn to succeed and please—so molten hot that I was sure in the wrong hands it could be shaped like glass. I forced my gaze to Sloane's and tried to appear like there weren't fireworks exploding under my skin. "Let me think about it."

"The question, even more than what he did," she said, leaning forward, "is, do you care that he's lying?"

"Of course."

"Why?"

"Why?" I sat back and considered. How could I not care?

"I mean people have relationships that work for a lot of different reasons. Yours might be able to withstand some murkiness surrounding his . . . work situation."

"No."

"Why?"

"We don't lie to each other. That's not who I thought we were."

"And that honesty about everything, that's crucial to who you are as a couple, even if he's lying for a good reason?"

I considered this. I had lied to Dave before: about how many bikinis I actually owned before buying a new one, say, or that time I went to one of Lucy's parties and flirted with Matt Mossy, the curly-haired star of that Broadway show about rock stars. He'd kept bringing me mojitos before finally serenading me softly with his biggest number, "Take Me Home Tonight, Little Mamacita." He ended it by putting his hand on my shoulder and saying, with a perfectly straight face, "Seriously. Take me home tonight." From his confidence, I could tell the line usually worked for him. The exchange was indelibly etched into my memory, and I wanted to giggle every time I saw his picture, but I'd never told Dave. But Mossy had been nothing. Whatever this was—and certainly if it was something involving insider trading—I would've told him. I couldn't *not* have told him.

"Yes." I had to respect Sloane's technique. She was the anti-Pressman, forcing me toward an unwelcome thought. "That honesty is crucial to who we are as a couple."

She nodded, satisfied. "Have you just asked him?"

"I can't." I couldn't tell her that I had and didn't believe his response.

"So then . . . you could look into it yourself?"

"Jesus, no."

"What?"

"I sound like one of my clients."

"What's wrong with that?"

"Um, they come to me because they have marital problems."

"Not to sound harsh, but I think you have marital problems too."

"But not like them. Trust me, it's different. Dave and I are . . . fine in the ways it matters."

She slurped a noodle into her mouth. "You know who you should call? Giovanni's friend."

"Percy?"

"Right, I forgot that you met him. Percy. As in Percy Stahl of Stahl Investigations. He'll help you."

I dropped the noodle that was refusing to wrap around my chopsticks and aimed at another one. When you really thought about it, there was nothing shocking about the idea: people hire experts all the time—to fix their computers, decorate their apartments, even strengthen their marriages. As I always told my couples, knowing when you need help is a sign of wisdom. Even if doing so forces you to confront the fact that your spouse just might be the next Bernie Madoff.

Sloane sensed that I was considering it and gave one final push. "I guess it depends how much it bothers you," she said. "Not knowing the truth."

◆

I stopped home before returning to work. Creeping into the apartment in slow motion, I eased the door closed behind me and slid my feet across the wooden parquet like a cross-country skier. Dave's door was open a crack, and I lurked in the hall, listening to him talk about interest rates.

As I'd awkwardly hugged Sloane good-bye, I pretended that I was still making up my mind about what to do. Normally, I'd run big decisions past Dave first, but because I couldn't do that, I had come home hoping for a sign that he was lying to me. I wasn't picky—I was prepared to take anything, and as I listened to him on the phone, droning on about percentage points, I figured this would do. It was proof that when I wasn't home, he sat alone in the office with the door wide-open, doing his job—his highly technical, somewhat boring, not-in-the-least-bit-shady job.

I skied back down the hall and shut the front door with a slam to announce my arrival. Peeking in his doorway, I waved. He made the "I'm on a call" motion, pointing exaggeratedly to his ear. I tried to look surprised and retreated.

A few minutes later he met me in the kitchen, where I unscrewed the top of an aluminum water bottle over the sink. "Hey. How was lunch?"

"Good, actually. Sorry for the interruption." I turned on the faucet.

"Actually, I'm in the middle of something. Is it okay if I get back to it?"

"Of course."

"So, see you . . . later?"

"Yeah, about six."

He retreated back into his office and I followed, watching as he shut the door behind him. He did it slowly, as if maybe I wouldn't notice if he was very quiet about it. I noticed, though. A closed door to seal me off.

There was the sign.

chapter twenty

PERCY'S OFFICE WAS supremely well air-conditioned, a necessary step, I supposed, for someone who chose to summer in heavy denim. His receptionist, a young Asian woman with her hair piled in a knot on the top of her head, was on the phone, so I stood for a moment, enjoying the breeze. I hoped she'd offer me water too, but she just nodded and pointed me into his office.

Percy's door was open, and as I entered, he got up from behind his desk, smiling and holding out one hand. He was wearing jeans again. Based on the frayed fabric on the thighs, they were the same exact pair.

"Good to see you, Paige." He pointed to the couch against the wall, and I sat. On the small table in front of me was an iced coffee with a tuft of paper covering the top of the straw, like a chef's hat.

"It's for you."

"Thanks."

Percy retrieved his own coffee from the edge of his desk and sank down on the other side of the couch, turning his body toward me. "I know you."

I froze, my hand midway to the coffee. "What's that mean, you know me? Like, my type?"

"No, I know *you*. You run around the park loop."

"Yes." I shifted nervously. No one except Sloane really knew where I was right now.

"I couldn't place you when we met last week. I thought you looked familiar, but then I realized it."

"You run there too?"

"Me?" He pointed at his chest. "No, I just track your loops through my binoculars from behind the bushes. Your time is really getting better." I stared at him and he smiled. "Just trying to lighten the mood. I run too."

"I've never seen you."

"My shoes aren't as bright as yours. You've got those hot pink shoes and I noticed them once on this bleak gray day and then, you know how it goes."

"How does it go?"

"Once you see something, you start noticing it again and again."

"That's true."

"Tell me about it. It's a premise that pays my rent."

"Oh, speaking of that, feel free to charge me for this consult. Giovanni said—"

He held up his hands. "You're Giovanni's family, which makes you sort of mine too. Please. Take the coffee."

"That's a very expansive definition, but thanks." I took the coffee and sipped. "I've met Giovanni once."

"Regardless."

"He seems nice, though. How do you know him?"

"We grew up in the same town. Same school, same class, same T-ball team."

"Where?"

"Ohio."

"How do you get from Ohio T-ball player to New York private investigator?"

"Oh. Steroids." I started to laugh and he did too. "So," he said, "how can I help?"

"This is confidential, right?"

"Of course."

I told him everything, starting with last Tuesday. When I tried to articulate my vague sense that Dave was lying about something, Percy nodded, which made me feel vindicated. "You think he's lying too."

"I don't know about that. I generally think there's a lot of value in someone's gut sense."

"So how do we get from gut sense to hard facts?"

"Roll up our sleeves, pay attention and sort through information, until eventually, hopefully, we'll get a sense of some leads to follow. But I can't promise you answers. It's not like investigation is magic."

"Great sales pitch, Percy." I looked around. "You know, your office seems awfully quiet . . . no phones ringing, no interruptions with urgent business."

"I held my calls." He shook his plastic coffee cup to distribute the milk. "You know what's tricky about this?"

Annie, the receptionist, opened the door and half stepped in. "I know you said not to interrupt, but it's Gunston." She was a whole different creature standing up: miles high and dressed in an asymmetrical drapey black top over skinny jeans. True skinny jeans, as in designed for someone with thighs the circumference of razor clamshells.

"I'll call back."

She nodded and shuffled away in her ballet flats.

"You timed that, right? Just so I'd think you were busy."

"Yep. She comes in whenever I press the panic button under the couch."

"What's her deal?"

He looked confused. "Her deal?"

"You meet with a lot of people who suspect their spouses of cheating, right?"

"Among other things."

"So, presumably they're feeling unattractive and undesirable, and then they're greeted by someone who looks like she moonlights at a *Vogue* photo shoot?"

"Who cares about their feelings? What about me? It's a tough market, and I've got to stand out any way I can."

"Seriously?"

He ducked his head conspiratorially. "I've sort of made it my niche, having employees who look as though they moonlight as models. So what if they can't file and don't know the databases? I met Annie, actually, when I was waiting outside the tents during Fashion Week. It's true I'd been there five hours before someone would actually talk to me, but I knew that if I stared down enough of them, I'd nab one. In an ideal world, she'd dress like a Robert Palmer's girl every day, but unfortunately she insists on a casual Tuesday. Which is today." He crossed his arms and settled against the couch. "Bummer, right?"

A silence passed between us.

"You're kidding."

"Yes. I'm kidding. And she's a fashion designer, by the way. Very talented, but her ship hasn't come in, so I'm employing her in the meantime. But I can tell her to wear a Groucho Marx disguise for those clients you're so worried about."

"I think it would make them feel better."

"I have to tell you, Paige. You're the first client to make this point."

"Maybe I'm just the most honest."

He sipped his coffee.

"Where were we before your whole Robert Palmer song and dance?"

"I was about to tell you what's tricky with this."

"Everything. I feel like I'm looking for *why* he would lie as much as the *about what*."

"Well, that, sure, but from a practical point of view, there are corporate considerations. We'll need information from his employer, which will be difficult to get."

"How would you recommend getting past that?"

"There are things we can do. Not a guarantee, just fact gathering."

"Like?"

"Off the top of my head, putting a recording device in his office at home or looking around in there. Let me think about it and come up with a plan that doesn't, you know, obviously run afoul of the law."

"Okay."

"Do you have any sense of what this is about?"

"He seems really distracted by this ongoing financial scandal. He's a loyal person and his clients are bankers, and although I'm probably imagining things, I've been wondering about whether his allegiance to his firm would—" I didn't want to say it out loud.

"Do something that could get him in trouble."

"I don't know. Maybe."

"That doesn't seem to fit to me," said Percy. "Why would they suspend him for that? I think they'd just fire him."

"Maybe he didn't do something big, but was peripherally associated with something that went bad?"

"Like how?"

"I don't know."

"And you're sure you want to know?"

"What do you mean?"

"A lot of times, the feds don't even arrest people. They don't have enough information; they're waiting for bigger fish. So what if you find out something, and then it's just between the two of you. Is it worth it to know?"

"I want to know. So just keep in mind that whatever it is might involve some sort of insider trading issues."

"Okay. And you want me to help you?"

I nodded.

"I'm pretty booked up this week with all our runway shows."

I sighed. "You're hilarious."

"But I'll make some time. How about we talk again on"—he paused, pencil lifted in the air—"Tuesday? We can meet, go over a proposal. . . ." He trailed off. "You're going to go crazy waiting, right?"

"Not at all." I was relieved to have some days to consider the next move. "Tuesday is perfect."

Sloane had asked me to call her when we were done, so I dialed her cell phone as I walked to work.

"That's great!" She sounded a little too thrilled. "Good for you."

"Sure, I guess."

"What are you doing tomorrow? We can get together and strategize."

I had, as usual, wide stretches of availability, but Sloane's enthusiasm chilled me a little, as if someone had yanked the shades up and sounded the alarm when I was used to waking naturally. "I have plans with Mom tomorrow," I lied. "Any interest?"

"No. Thank. You." She said each word like a schoolmarm.

"So Saturday, then? Breakfast at Vanessa and Frank's."

"Right." She barely stifled a yawn. "Catch you then."

chapter twenty-one

EVEN THOUGH HELENE had left me a confirmation voice mail, I didn't expect either of them to show up for their eleven thirty appointment. I'd had couples storm out of my office before—it was the nature of the business—but Scott Jacoby's exit had felt more desperate than angry, as though he wanted to stay but couldn't find a good enough reason.

I halfheartedly waited and occupied myself with my latest project, an article for *Healthy Marriage!* about ways to reconnect. It was my first assignment for them and the whole thing felt trite, but I'd just read an article in a trade magazine, the gist being that today's marketplace demanded you get your name out there. Now, *Healthy Marriage!* Tomorrow, the morning shows!

It was harder than it sounded, distilling what I practiced into sound bites. For a minute, I blinked in time with the cursor while gathering my thoughts, then wrote:

Ways to Reconnect

1. Plan activities. Divide up a weekend: Saturday one person chooses what to do and on Sunday, the other one gets to! Keep an open mind and remember: the most important thing is to share the experience, even if it's something you end up laughing at later!
2. Bath time. Dim the lights, play soft music, draw a bath to take together. Bubbles optional.
3. Something else.

4. Another one.

5. These are horrible. Have Dave and I ever done anything remotely like this? *No.* We took a bath that one time at the bed-and-breakfast upstate, the one with that gassy dog stretched out in front of the fireplace, but we barely fit in the tub. Dave's legs kept knocking against the side. Hardly a recipe for reconnection.

6. How about this one? Catch your husband in a lie. A harmless, seemingly meaningless lie.

7. What does he do each day? How is he filling the hours? If you sit down with a pen and paper, you can't reconstruct more than thirty minutes of your husband's schedule, which is something you've never thought about before. At least sixty hours per week are unaccounted for—most of his waking time.

8. You could ask him to account for it—not every minute, just to the half hour, but you'd sound like a loon. And even if he agreed to answer the most detailed questions, would you ever be satisfied with the response? Trust issues. That's what you'd say if a client babbled all of this nonsense. You've never realized before why that might make a client respond, "No shit, Sherlock."

9. Shelve all those heavy thoughts and meet random guy. A cute one, whose eyes are so sparkly they drive you to star metaphors.

10. Flirt with same guy. Yes, flirt. Call it like it happened. (Admiration of how he looks in jeans) + (the giddiness of well-timed sarcasm) = *Flirtation.* Normally, you'd be scrolling through your contacts to fix him up with someone. Funny. You haven't done that yet.

11. *Without* your husband's knowledge, ask that same guy—the one you're not about to fix up with anyone else—to help you find out if your husband is lying to you.

12. Ah, you've really set it up perfectly now, haven't you? Just you and Mr. Sparkly-Eyed Comedian, putting your heads together on a very secret project. What could be inappropriate about that scenario?

13. Retire your remaining dignity! Retire your remaining—

When my phone rang, I jumped to pick it up.

"When are you coming out?"

"Lucy!"

"Wow. I'm touched by that reaction."

"I'm excited to hear from you. Where are you?"

"At the beach. You?"

"Work."

"Watcha doing?"

"Writing an article on ways to reconnect with your spouse. For *Healthy Marriage!*"

"*Healthy Marriage!*" She gasped. "What a coup! No, seriously. Did you make that up, or is that a real magazine?"

"I think it's mainly for waiting rooms."

"Read me one of your tips."

"All right, here goes. Number one: Plan activities together."

"Brilliant!"

"Yeah. It's a little pat."

"Here's how you stay together: you get over whatever it is that's driving a wedge between you."

"Consider yourself quoted in *Healthy Marriage!*"

"Fine, but obviously I need to talk to my agent first. What's their circulation—about three billion?"

"I'm intrigued, Luce. You're saying whatever the problem is in a marriage, people should—"

"Act like grown-ups and work out your problems without involving the rest of us."

"Are you thinking of anyone in particular?"

"Yes. My father and Meryl. And, yes, I'm aware they're my hosts and I should be gracious, but I would prefer for them not to fight in front of the rest of us."

"Give me an example."

"Like the other day, my dad told Meryl he was on the phone

with his brother, but Meryl checked his phone and it turned out he was on with my mom."

"His ex-wife."

"Right, and Meryl got all mad, and he said that was why he didn't tell her, and in the process they dragged us all into it."

"So you wouldn't have a problem if Jeff lied to you?"

"Not about something like that, no."

"Hmm. What if Meryl found a bloody knife out behind the shed?"

"Who are you treating—Agatha Christie characters? At this point, I'd advise her to wash it off and return it to the kitchen."

"No, seriously, though. I have a client now who's mad because her husband lied about something that happened at work. A corporate malfeasance type of thing."

"Do you have to decide whether to turn him in?"

"No, that's only if he's going to hurt someone. This is like a minor thing. Victimless." I realized that wasn't strictly true, but it sounded better than the alternative.

"Tell her that you can't be together for so long and share everything with one hundred percent accuracy. It's just not possible. Ask her if she's ever kept anything from him. I'm sure she has."

"I suppose." The security buzzer rang, and I glanced toward the monitor's aerial downward view of the Jacobys, their blurry black-and-white images clustered together as they waited for the door to unlock. I couldn't be sure given the graininess of the image, but it appeared as though they were holding hands. Still squinting at them, I told Lucy my clients were there and I'd call her back soon.

Once in my office, Scott considered the nearly empty candy jar.

"I'll refill it." I poured in some Hershey's Kisses and offered the open jar to them.

Scott reached in and pulled out a Kiss and when Helene declined, I surprised myself by reaching in, unpeeling one and popping it in my mouth. It had been four years since I'd instituted the candy jar. Four years and this, I realized, was my first indulgence. It was delicious. "So"—I tucked the Kiss into the side of my mouth and tried to sound professional—"you guys seem different. What am I picking up on?"

"Nothing," Helene said. "This is just us, how we usually are. I mean, how we were."

"Scott? Last time, you seemed rather unhappy."

"I'm fine," Scott said. He started to clam up again, fiddling with his watch strap instead of making eye contact. I wished, as I had before in this office, that I could open people like doors— bend them at the hinges to see what's inside, close them back up without disruption.

"You seem not so fine."

"Yeah."

"Can you walk me through what happened in between last week and this week?"

"I got tired." Scott finally locked into my gaze. "Of being mad. It's so much easier when we get along."

"I understand. Your regular dynamic is comfortable for you."

"Nice reflection. Two points." He smiled thinly.

"You still feel the same—that you want to work on things between the two of you?"

"Yeah."

"I would press for you to really think about—and tell Helene—what you need, what you're asking for. And the same for you, Helene."

"I read an article last week," Helene said. "What do you think about journaling?"

The Hersey's Kiss had melted to a flat chocolate pad on the

back of my tongue. I swallowed it whole before answering. "Journaling?"

Under my desk, in my bag not ten feet away from Helene, was one of my mom's journals. I had been reading them daily, casually. In slow or weak moments, I'd pull one out, try to decipher the chapters. I'd read it in my office, in a cab, lying in bed at the end of the day. Had Dave and I been talking as we normally did, I would have joked that my mom's confessionals were my new Bible, but he had been too distracted to notice, and if I was truly honest, I wanted to keep them to myself.

"Too pedestrian, right?" Helene frowned. "The article made it sound good—like there was something about the act of writing your truths that made it easier to communicate."

"I think it's a great idea."

Scott managed a weak "Okay," and for the rest of the session, Scott and I popped Hershey's Kisses as the three of us set up ground rules for journaling. The Jacobys would alternate taking turns writing as much as they wanted, but they agreed to commit to two entries before we met again on the twentieth.

"What should we write about?" Helene asked.

"Anything you want," I said, before remembering Pressman stroking his beard. "But if you need guidance, you could write something about trust. How you get to the point where you share that with someone. Is it earned or given? Is it static or kinetic? What does the word mean to you?"

They ran a little over the hour, and when they left, I neatened up, collecting the tiny little scraps of foil Kiss wrappers for the trash, moving back the magazines and chairs.

I didn't have any more clients and had several hours left in the day before I wanted to go home, where, frankly, I was less comfortable than I was used to being. I returned behind the desk and stared at my computer monitor, at the joke of a "Ways to

Reconnect" article. One by one, I deleted the ideas until there was nothing on the page but a blinking cursor.

At a loss, I opened my mom's notebook at random to a short entry. Just two words:

I can't.

I can't what, Mom?

I dog-eared the page for later and returned to my keyboard.

Ways to Reconnect

1. Start a couple's journal that you can pass back and forth between each other! Tell each other stories that you've never shared before.

Somewhere out east, I was sure Lucy was gagging.

chapter twenty-two

I WAS BARELY paying attention later that afternoon as I turned my key in the lock and set down my bag in the hall. When my foot slipped on a piece of paper, I noticed an arrow drawn on it. It led me to another arrow, which led me to another. I followed them through the kitchen and out the swinging door to our little round table.

Our cheese of the month had arrived. Dave had picked up the box downstairs, unwrapped all two pounds of it and set it rather nicely on a cheese plate I didn't even know he'd been aware we had. He'd lit the tall candles on the table and was pouring something sparkling in our long flutes.

"What is this?" I didn't mean to sound ungrateful, but I felt like I'd walked into someone else's life.

"We have a d'Affinois." Dave pointed in his best impression of a fancy waiter. "Prized for its top-to-bottom buttery creaminess. To its left, a cream-filled burrata, fresh from, drumroll please, the bucolic pastures of New Jersey, and finally, ma'am, to round out your palate, right over here, a sweet, tangy English Tickler cheddar from Devon. And do you have a library card?" He slid across the wood floor on his socks right up next to me. "Because, baby, I would love to check you out."

"Um, no."

He patted my head. "Yeah. I could do better. Let me think—"

I crossed my arms over my chest. "Are we celebrating something?"

"How unbelievably great and understanding you've been for the past few weeks."

"Like when I dragged you to the fireworks?" If he was trying to make me feel guilty, it was working.

He made a face. "Come on. You were trying to help." I thought of his earlier accusation, that I was tone-deaf, selfish. I hadn't disagreed. I still didn't. "I made us reservations for next Saturday."

"Where?"

"It's a surprise."

"Oh." It struck me that I should hire an investigator more often; it was catnip for our marriage.

"But it's somewhere really good. I had to, you know"—he made a mock-sinister face and rubbed his thumbs against his fingers, humming "Money, Money, Money"—"to secure it all. So—save the date."

"Okay."

"I'll have to meet you there, though, because . . . I'll be coming from work."

"Whoa, for real?"

He slow-nodded. "That's right. Just got off the phone with Herb. Monday."

"All cleared?"

Slow nod again. "All cleared."

"That's great!"

"Yep."

"Back to your office just like before?"

"Like nothing happened." He smiled and wiggled his fingers sideways from his head down to his chest: *Magic!*

"So what did happen?"

He shrugged. "Don't know. Don't care."

"They still didn't tell you?"

"Nope. I'm moving on."

"You don't want to know more?"

"Nope."

"I can't understand that."

"I don't want to look back, Paige. Let's just—what would your mom say—cleanse ourselves of it."

"Would she say that?"

"Um, yeah. You've never heard her say that? Most important, though—"

"Yeah?"

"Cheese of the month has arrived!" He handed me one of the glasses and clinked his against mine.

"Cheese of the month!"

"Let's taste it."

"Okay."

"And then go out and get crraaaazy."

"Okay." I put the glass on the table. "Or. How about renting a movie?"

"Naw, let's go out." He shook my shoulders with his hands. "Didn't you hear me? I said crraaaazy."

"A movie! We can sit on the couch, getting lost in the burrata."

"Getting lost in it?"

I smiled in what I hoped was an inviting way. "The movie can be one of those awful violent ones about people's limbs being hacked off. *Saw Ten*."

"We can do better than that." He shook his head, but I was already starring in the performance of *This Is the Best Idea Ever!*, moving the cheese tray to the coffee table and microwaving popcorn and exalting about how great it felt to get into pajamas after a long day. *(These are so comfortable—oh, how I love an elastic waistband.)* I was nearly hysterical with phony glee, but Dave seemed unperturbed, like this was expected behavior from me.

We settled into the couch, nestling together like batteries. I was self-conscious of every move—reaching to the coffee table for the cheese, shifting my weight, gasping at the violence. On the screen, an eighteen-year-old blonde was handcuffed to the ceiling, a chain saw dancing at her feet as she shrieked. I wanted to look away but couldn't.

The bottom button on my shirt was loose and with the jittery fingers of my free hand, I worked it, twisting the threads out until it slid off the frayed string, tiny and pearlized. Pulling it off was tremendously satisfying, so I tested the others. They were all secure, so I fiddled with the one that had detached, turning it over and over in my fingers and pressing its four tiny holes into the flesh of my thumb, as if by rubbing it enough a genie would emerge and help me escape.

It worked. Dave's work phone rang. He first craned away from me and next got off the couch. Then, after I pressed PAUSE, he finally embraced a full-on Joe Businessman's pace around the room, so focused on the call that he had no clue he was almost shouting.

After five minutes, I put my bag over my shoulder, went into our bathroom, locked the door and ran the water. I pulled off my clothes, took out the notebook and opened it to the page I'd dog-eared earlier. When the tub was full, I dipped a toe in and, holding the notebook carefully so as not to drop it, slipped down into the warm water and started reading.

◆

I can't.

chapter twenty-three

It's been two months.

G. and Pressman were both telling me the same thing—independently, not in a joint session or anything: Journal it, journal it, journal it.

I didn't want to; it wouldn't help.

Pressman thought it would. He thought it might help me get dominion over my Guilty Feelings, which he perceives have multiplied like the Mickey Mouse brooms in Fantasia. He said just that—used the poetic image—and now all I see are splintering, marching Guilty Feelings. Gold star, Pressman.

But then G. said, no. Not to help. To remember just how difficult the path is.

How difficult the path? I said, "What kind of gobbledygook is that? Trust me, I remember."

"You do now. But you didn't. You were feeling like it was smooth sailing, like the struggle was over. That's not realistic," said G. "That lowers your guard. If you ever feel like that again—the false sense of security—you can go back and read it. To remember: There's no beating anything. There's just struggle."

So.

In the weeks prior, we had argued about whether she had to keep going to Dr. Cassat. I was so strong, sticking to my position. This is a lifelong battle. You've got to have safety nets. "I know, Mom," Sloane had said, jingling the car keys in her hand, nodding importantly. "You're right." She gave up so easily.

We expected her home right after therapy. Twenty minutes late—I was not worried. She probably went to watch Jeremy practice. She'd been doing *that a lot, which was great—exposure to all that healthy exercise, all that treating young bodies like temples.*

At five thirty, I called Dr. Cassat and left a message. She called right back. "But you canceled today."

"No, I didn't."

"You did." I heard the wind waft of pages turning. "Here it is. You left a message earlier today with my receptionist that Sloane had a meeting with the school counselor."

I hadn't, but I knew who had.

I called the school. Sloane signed out right after her free period at around noon. I called Jeremy's house. His little brother answered. No, he wasn't there, and when his mother called back, she didn't sound worried. (See? It's different with a boy. You can be stupid like that.)

Frankie, the police, our neighbors, a few of those hooded greasy boys whose names I'd pretended to vaguely remember (but really knew cold). I called them all. I called Cherie to pick up Paige.

When Frankie got home, he stayed by the phone, and I grabbed my keys and wallet (empty) and drove around and around until finally, I found myself in Newark, stopping periodically at pay phones to check in and ask if Frankie had heard anything useful. He hadn't, but the third time I called him, he reported the following items missing: our VCR, my diamond earrings, his camera, several china figurines from Frankie's mother and a glass bowl. (The camera was at a pawnshop. The figurines are still missing, most likely smashed to bits when Sloane realized they were worth crap.)

You would think I wouldn't have slept that night, but I must have. I had that dream, the same one from when she was little.

The two of us, me and Sloane at the station, staring at the display board, waiting for our track to be announced. I don't know where we're going, but I watch intently, and when the number comes up, spinning like lotto balls, we stampede to catch our train. The doors open for a split second, long enough for her to drop my hand. Only for a second—one minute I had her; then I didn't—I lost that tiny hand, and then the doors closed, and I watched helplessly through the platform as we sped away and she stood small, alone and confused.

Always in the dream there is not just the sense of loss but the confusing powerless aftermath: the moment where I think, what now? Do I run through the long cars of the train, screaming for the conductor? Do I get off at the next stop and retrace my steps? In the dream, there's no point. It will be too late. By the time I do anything, she will be gone—taken, toddled onto the tracks, slipped through the cracks.

There is no recourse.

It wasn't a stress dream, I understood that night. It was a premonition.

I knew she was dead. I just didn't know how—alone or with someone? Overdosed? Stabbed? Raped? Car crash (my preference)? She had realized in the last moments that she didn't want to die. She had cried out for me. She hadn't.

So that I remember how difficult the path is, I will report the gist of my conversation with Officer Stanley, who called at the start of his early shift patrolling Eastern Ohio's portion of I-65:

Someone had "found" Sloane outside the Plainville truck stop, not quite by the trash cans, down the hill a little, where the woods started. She was alive, passed out, under the influence of something. ("Heroin, ma'am, would be my guess, based on her behavior.") Would we like to come and get her?

I told him to arrest her and we flew out, Frankie gripping the wheel of the car on the drive from Toledo, the frequent stops at pay phones. There's an amazing number of logistics involved; as if the situation didn't suck out your soul, you have to somehow conjure the fight to work: mobilize the contacts, parse through options, get the best experts, plead for a bed.

Had these superparents journaled? I wonder. They, the ones with the answers? Because they didn't seem to have forgotten the struggle. How many of them were still doing it? I didn't ask; they did not volunteer.

Major Victory: we got her a bed at Gentle Breezes, an ongoing rehab program in the desert of New Mexico. I think Frankie and I might have high-fived, enjoyed a brief moment of achievement before we remembered that we were celebrating getting a bed at an ongoing rehab center for our child. It indicated some seriously deflated expectations.

We found Sloane, bruised hands, egg lump on forehead, long ribbons of scratch marks on her arms. This is what she said to us when we found her: nothing. Not one word during the motel stay and the flights and drives, although she did try to tell the flight attendant that she wanted a Coke, and her voice came out a thick rasp.

I have two other memories to not forget:

1) Gentle Breezes told us she needed to start her stay in detox.

2) She turned her back when I tried to kiss her good-bye.

Fuck you, Jeremy. For claiming to have blacked out and not remembering anything. For returning to school a week later like you'd just been on a road trip. For your inevitable swimming scholarship to Stanford.

When we get her back, I'll never let her out of my sight.

I leaned over the side of the tub and placed the journal, open, on the floor so that it could dry. I'd inadvertently dabbed drops of water on it, magnifying the twenty-year-old ink in some spots and making it look as though tears had plopped onto the page. It made sense if you already knew the sad ending: Sloane had not returned; she'd slipped away until this July.

chapter twenty-four

DAVE WAS WAKING up when I stepped out of the bathroom in the morning, towel wrapped around me and tucked under my arms. He sat up in bed. "No lazing around?"

"Another family thing." I slid on my watch. I had gone to bed feeling okay, but when I woke up, my first thought was *Are we really just supposed to go back to normal now?* I'd felt a stab of venom behind my rib cage, like a cramp. Or maybe it was guilt.

He hummed. "We Are Family." Honestly, I didn't even feel like smiling. I felt like slamming my weight against a punching bag.

"Can I come?"

"You're not playing catch-up with work today?"

"I can do it after. Unless you don't want me to come." He laughed as though this would never be a real possibility.

"No, of course I want you to come. I didn't tell you about it because I assumed—"

"I'm teasing." He swung his legs out of bed and grabbed a pair of shorts from over the chair, pulling them on. "You'd want any buffer for the family stuff these days, right? I don't take it personally. You'd probably love for Bert to tag along to shield you from all that tension." Bert was our doorman. "And your mom? What's the story there—why does her personality completely alter when she's in Sloane's presence?"

"Hey there, Columbo."

"Why am I Columbo?"

"Because your observations are a bit late in the game. It's gotten much better between everyone."

"Really? Just in the past few days?"

"Really."

"What was it about anyway?"

"It was about her addiction." I said this in a tone of voice like *Duh.*

"I know that, but I mean why does your mom act so scared around her?"

"How should I know?"

"I dunno." He found a T-shirt in the pile of clothes on the chair and shook it out. "Weren't you there when it all went down?"

✦

"Dave!" My mom literally jumped up and down in one place with joy at the surprise of his presence. "I'll set your plate."

I wanted to hug her after reading the last journal entry and reached out, but she was already halfway to the kitchen, where I heard the pull of drawers, the clanking of silverware. Dave's work phone buzzed, and he paused to pick up while I followed her in.

"Where's Sloane?" I said, and she pointed out to the patio. "I'll let her know we're here."

Sloane was standing by the balcony, facing the East River, watching a boat drift toward New York Harbor.

"Dave came with me." The words rushed out.

"Where?"

"Here. This morning."

She turned her head to try to see into the apartment and then peered at me. "You look a little tweaked."

"I am. He's going back to work. He's been cleared by the firm. Whatever that means."

She looked at the pack of cigarettes on the table. "Want one?"

I had to smile at the thought of my mom peeking out to see me smoking. At this point, she'd probably give me a double thumbs-up: *Great work making Sloane feel comfortable, honey!* "No, thanks."

"So tell me what happened."

"I came home yesterday, and he told me the whole thing is over. He's going back on Monday. He still doesn't know what happened, and he doesn't want to." Her expression—hooded eyes—called bullshit. "I know."

"If you want to call off the investigation, it's no biggie. You can just move forward, forget about the questions."

"What would you do?"

"Why does that matter?"

"Just tell me."

She patted my leg and tapped ash into a ceramic bowl.

"Hey," I said. "You have a real ashtray."

She took a drag. "Vanessa. She bought them yesterday."

"Them?"

"Three. The presentation was this morning, right after I arrived. Gift wrapping, a small card. It reminded me of Hanukkah. Remember Hanukkah? Or has it gone in the memory void with everything else?"

"We still do Hanukkah. You should come this year. You and Giovanni. We do the whole shebang, the dreidel and the latkes. It's weird because there are no kids and for some reason, it's still a lot of fun."

"Paige."

"I don't know." I imagined doing nothing. Then I imagined

sneaking into Dave's office and bugging his phone, which would involve a healthy amount of research to do properly. Neither seemed like a good option. "Can you cover for me if anyone comes out here?"

"Of course."

I pulled Percy's card from my wallet and dialed his cell phone. He picked up on the first ring.

"Hi, it's Paige."

"Are you in a bad spot?"

"No."

"You're just whispering a little. It's hard to hear."

"Dave is going back to work."

"Okay." Pause. "So we'll cancel?"

Immediately I realized that if I canceled, I'd wake up angry every day, without knowing why. And then in the evenings, I'd sit on the couch and systematically pull the buttons off all of my clothes. It would be a twenty-first-century version of that chick-in-the-yellow-wallpaper story, slowly going mad while her husband went off to work with a whistle and a spring in his step. "No."

"Okay."

"I'm not calling to cancel. But it seems to me there's a bit of a lost opportunity with him back at work."

"Yeah. I see your point. It'll be harder to access his conversations and stuff. Well, that's okay. We can figure it out."

"What I'm thinking is—should we try to get in there before?" Sloane cocked her head in approval, bit her lip. *Nifty idea.*

"Get in where, Paige?"

"His office. The firm. Should we try to get in there before he starts on Monday?"

"No, I don't think that's necessary."

"But if I could. If I—" My mom slid open the door to the

outdoors, and Sloane stubbed out her cigarette as if mad at it and bounded over. She said something to my mom, and they both went indoors, my mom meeting my eye and pointing at her watch, then miming spooning food into her mouth—time to eat. "If I could get in there without a big production, what do you think of that?"

I pictured Dave's office, what it would take to get in and look around. Not much. I'd done it once before without Dave. He had been at home sick, cramped up with a stomach flu on a Saturday night and in urgent need of a document. The messenger service had quoted hour-long delays due to rain and no one else was around to help, so after much bellyaching (literal and figurative) and back-and-forth, I volunteered. I insisted I could manage it, shrugging off Dave's explanations of how I had to press his key card against the turnstile just so. "Different from a MetroCard," he kept saying, his voice weak and raspy.

"I think . . ." Percy talked slowly in that way people do when they've slipped on the kid gloves. "That is one of the worst ideas I've ever heard. We're supposed to meet tomorrow."

"Yes."

"So sit tight. We can think of something then."

"Okay." Sloane pushed open the door to the patio and gestured that I should come in; I gestured that she should come out instead.

"What did he say?"

"I asked him if I should try to break into Dave's firm tonight, and he said no."

"Seriously?"

"This whole thing is making me crazy."

"I like that idea. Can you do it?"

"I think so."

"I totally would."

"Percy said not to."

"It's your life, not his. No one's going to care about it as much as you."

"True."

"Plus, it's sort of his fault anyway. He's the one who scheduled your first real meeting tomorrow."

"Come on. It's not Percy's fault."

"So." She raised one pointed brow, and I instantly wished I could do the same. "How would you do it?"

"Borrow Dave's key card, go to his office, look around, leave."

"Hmm."

"Suggestions?"

"What about the office of that woman you told me he met with?"

"The HR person?"

"Exactly. Maybe she has notes or something."

"Good idea."

"You should totally do it."

"Maybe I will."

"Check you out." She grabbed my shoulder, and I smelled the whiff of tobacco on her fingers. "Nerves of steel. Oh, and if they ask inside, you were calling the acupuncture place."

"The what?" But she was already pushing open the door to go inside.

♦

"Dave and I didn't know you were doing acupuncture." My mom looked at me, impressed, as I pulled out my chair and spooned some yogurt into my bowl. Dave shrugged with an I-just-pay-the-bills face that I knew my father would appreciate. "So what'd she say?"

Sloane's expression was neutral as usual. "She said she has some openings tonight."

"Tonight?" My mom frowned. "She's open on Saturday night?"

"Yep."

"I wish I could go," said my mom. "Not that I'd invite myself along but . . . we have plans anyway. With Cherie and the Weavers." My dad blinked once slowly and sighed. *Not those bloody Weavers.* My mom ignored him. "Oh!"

"What?" I said.

"How does everyone feel about boats?"

"About what?"

"Boats!"

Sloane shrugged. "Extremely whatever."

"Well, Dad and I were thinking about something fun we could all do—you know, while we're all together. Someone he knows through work has a boat."

"It's bigger than a boat, Van. It's a yacht."

"We thought we could rent it for the day for all of us?" No one responded. "Great! And Sloane . . ."

"What?" It was a short, sharp syllable.

"Why not invite your . . ."

"Invite Giovanni." I had no patience for the awkward moment that was brewing. "You should."

Sloane's shoulders mini-jerked noncommittally.

"We'll set it all up, then." My mom paused. "Does it work?"

"Does what work?"

"Acupuncture."

"Mom, I don't know yet."

"I've heard it does. What are you doing it for anyway?"

"Seasickness," Sloane said, straight-faced.

"She's kidding," I said, jumping in to stave off the hand-wringing and hair-tearing. "Tell her you're kidding."

Sloane lifted one shoulder. "Curiosity."

"What?" my mom said.

"That's why we're doing acupuncture." Sloane's eyes were innocent. "To cure curiosity."

When I choked on a grape, Dave patted my back. "You okay?" he said, but no one had seemed to have any problems with Sloane's explanation.

chapter twenty-five

Vanessa

LUCKILY, CHERIE AND Darren had gotten to the restaurant first. I made Frankie slip his credit card to the maître d' to avoid any future awkwardness—the last time the Weavers had insisted on a whole long discussion about the bill: who drank what and who didn't get an appetizer and who'd tasted a tiny sliver of someone else's meat dish. We needed three calculators and an abacus to get out of there.

Pride is so silly. If I had known someone rich during the many, many years I was "financially challenged," as Frankie called it, I would have let them pay for everything.

"Listen." I put my hand on Cherie's arm. "Pretend we're taking you out for your birthday."

"My birthday is in November."

"I know it is. To avoid a scene. About the bill. Like last time."

"Oh!" She dipped her head, playing bashful. "Well, thank you very much."

"Many happy returns." I smiled.

"What time do we have to leave for the play?" Darren chewed an ice cube.

"No idea." Frankie grabbed his water glass with his full hand and gulped. What was it with those two? As if we'd arrived from the desert instead of a town car.

"We have plenty of time to eat," Cherie said. "What's the issue?"

"The play is always at eight," I said. "Every Saturday night performance we've ever gone to, the play is at eight. How does this not sink in?"

"It's not about having time to eat," Darren explained. "I'm trying to figure out if it will have cooled down when we have to go outside."

"No," I said. "It won't have cooled down. It will be miserable. Anyway," I said, directing this to Cherie, "guess where they are."

"Who's where?" Darren said.

"Where?" Cherie talked over him.

"Acupuncture. Together. On a Saturday night."

"That's great!"

"Great? That's weird," Darren said. "Who goes to acupuncture on a Saturday night?"

"Bonding sisters," Frankie said.

"Oh—Paigey T. and Sloane?" Darren nodded, supportive. "That is great."

"They're spending a lot of time together."

"Wonderful," said Cherie. "But just you wait. It will start to hurt your feelings at some point—how little they want to be with you."

"Aw." Darren reached across the table and rubbed her shoulder. "Poor mom."

"I'm sure." I sipped my sparkling water. It would never hurt my feelings to be left out. Like I said, pride is silly. Plus, this was my victory, and it had been so *easy* to bring them together.

If I'm being honest, being Sloane's mother has somewhat exhausted me. Just the mental hoops I've jumped through, the constant uncertainty: Do I give her space? Do I fly across the country in an attempt to track her down? Where does my life end and hers begin? The answers are never as clear as they seem in self-help books.

Therapists love to tell you that you're not responsible for everything. This is crap; there is no overestimating the importance of how a parent's behavior affects a child.

People who grew up *with* parental support can't know that without it, childhood feels like being handed a novel with the first three chapters ripped out and then directed to participate in class discussions. I know this because I've experienced both.

The partial-novel thing—sixty pages ripped out—happened to me in eleventh grade with *Oliver Twist*, and while I eventually read the whole thing, to this day whenever anyone mentions Charles Dickens, I feel lost and stressed.

The growing-up-without-parental-support thing happened from birth. I conjured an imaginary little brother, Al, and clung to him straight through junior high. On a daily basis, I'd help Al get ready for school. I'd tell him when the farina was cool enough. We'd play solitaire, Al and I. I'd nag him to do homework. (I'm glad there was no Al, though. That hint of comfort and companionship might have turned us placid. We'd have wasted our energy licking our wounds instead of planning an exit strategy.)

Sloane has always pushed back from whatever head start I try to establish for her. It kills me—how could she not understand how much easier it could all be? I have longed to give her the CliffsNotes I've given to Paige: *this* is what a good husband looks like; *that* is the education you need; *this* is what life can be. Instead, it's as though she barely scanned the back cover of the anthology I had printed just for her, and then, for no reason at all, threw the whole thing in the trash.

But I can appreciate that Sloane has used all that anger at me to propel herself forward. She's so pissed at her lot in life that she's managed to stand alone, just like I did.

She doesn't see the connection between us, but it's there: she's my path not taken into darkness, the positive to my negative. Maybe she and I can never peacefully exist; maybe Sloane needs to pull herself away from me because without the string tension I provide, she'd fall slack.

chapter twenty-six

THAT SUMMER I was not so distracted by what my mother hadn't divulged that I'd forgotten one of the things she had: when you're doing something bold, trick yourself into thinking you're doing something ordinary.

She had taught me this before my first day of first grade, when we'd moved neighborhoods into a new school district and I didn't know anyone. I don't remember Sloane—she must have been off somewhere stamping her fruit. What I remember is my mother turning around from the front seat of our wood-paneled wagon. "This is very brave what you're doing," she said. "New things are hard, but you want to know the secret to making them easy? Act like starting school is just no big deal, and you'll fake your brain into thinking it's true."

No big deal is what I thought when I fished through Dave's wallet, left out on the counter in the kitchen, to lift his Duane Covington ID.

No big deal is what I thought when I knocked on the bathroom door a little before seven thirty and told him I was heading out.

"Getting closer to cracking the case?"

I pulled on a cardigan to give myself time before asking, "What?"

"Why Sloane hates you all so much. You were wrong about the tension, by the way. From what I saw at breakfast, things are not better."

"I wasn't wrong. She's changing."

"Granted, she doesn't seem to hate you. But your parents"—
he shivered—"you could cut that with a knife. Maybe she'll tell
you why. Maybe you can ask her tonight at acupuncture."

"I think we each get our own room."

"Oh, Paige." He whistled a song I immediately recognized—"My
Lovin' (You're Never Gonna Get It)." I was sure he was trying to
be cute, but it made me want to give him the finger.

The first time I broke into Duane Covington—with Dave's
permission—I worried through the whole thing. What if I
brought home the wrong document? What if the security guards
caught me and gave me a hard time? What if I bumped into
someone who knew I didn't belong there? The worry was for
naught—getting in was easy; I appeared to fit in so much that
the guard didn't even raise his head when I passed through the
turnstile. I'd wandered through the spookily empty firm until I
found Dave's office, grabbed the fifty-pound document and
lugged the thing home, triumphant.

No big deal, I thought, as I walked down Madison to Fifty-
ninth Street. Duane Covington's lobby cast a cool white glow
through the glass wall of windows. From across the plaza, fifty
feet away, the dark-uniformed security guard looked like one
character typed on a blank sheet of paper—one ominous character. Dave was suspended, I remembered right then; the mag-
netized ID card I'd lifted from his wallet earlier, which now sat
curled up in my sweaty palm, might not work. I could use it, and
the light box lobby would swarm with dark-uniformed guards—
an alphabet soup. I almost turned around.

I was sure the security guard noticed that my smile was lop-
sided. I was sure he heard my heart beating as I palmed Dave's

photo and held the card just so against the blinking red light on the turnstile. Waiting. Waiting.

He rustled, and I shifted the card to the right a little.

Magic.

The turnstiles opened and I walked quickly, sighing, now cool enough to pretend to be an overworked associate drawn into the office on a Saturday night. I was in, and that's when I thought, *No big deal*, and started to believe it.

I took the elevator up to the twentieth floor, to the office of Hedda Brynn, human resources director, the one who had been in Dave's meeting. It had been easy to find out—a quick flip through the pages of Dave's directory.

The double frosted-glass doors separating the elevator banks from the offices were locked, so I pressed Dave's key card against the black thing blinking with a stern red light: Darth Vader's mezuzah. There was a click, the red dot turned an inviting green, and I was in the hall, the low fluorescent lights illuminating the corridor to a dull shade of gray.

Hedda's hallway was empty, and only one other office light was on, the occupant's jean jacket draped on the back of her chair. I pressed down on the long, matte silver doorknob until I felt the gentle click of release and then pushed against Hedda's door with my shoulder, stepping into total darkness. My eyes adjusted in a few seconds, helped by the skyscraper lights outside and a huge neon sign, its red light straining through the closed shades. A mechanical whir, the sound of something starting up, caused me to freeze. An alarm? Had I triggered something? Footsteps passed in front of the door, and I heard paper shuffling. A printer.

I waited for silence, forcing myself to count to one hundred and eighty as my eyes skirted around the office. The red light gave the room an Amsterdam feel, until I saw the panda bears. Hedda Brynn was a fan, apparently; they were everywhere— smiling from framed pictures on her wall and playfully posing on her calendar.

The file cabinet against her wall, dotted with panda magnets, was locked, as was the top desk drawer. The bottom drawers were open but useless: multicolored files, blank employment forms, rubber bands in a ball, staplers.

I sank down in Hedda's chair, my lower back supported by a chair pad with a panda bear patch sewn onto it. Hedda obviously had not seen the nature documentary Dave and I had watched that spring: pandas looked cute, we learned, but they were capable of murder. Or maybe she knew that. Maybe Hedda selected panda collectibles instead of, say, bunnies, as a threat to those rule breakers nervously bouncing their legs in her guest chairs.

My momentum for the mission was obviously fading. I rested my hands on Hedda's desk, and my left one landed on something soft—a file folder that I'd mistaken for part of the blotter.

I skimmed the handwritten notes inside—they were barely legible, all written in a bubbly script in some sort of shorthand. About halfway through I saw it: one sheet. *June 30, DT/AP Annie P. DT. NS? Hour meeting, 3 x. notified corp. dept. (phone), Stuben (phone). Implement handbook policy.*

DT—Dave's initials—and the date was one day before his breakdown, so I copied it into the little notepad I had brought.

What else, what else? My eyes darted around for a minute. All I saw was an army of thug pandas, eyes narrowed and claws bared at me.

I opened the door, peeked out and bolted toward the elevator bank, riding it down to the lobby. When the doors opened, I was still charged with adrenaline, so I didn't get out. I pressed the button for twenty, and as I did, Dave called my cell phone. I hit the IGNORE button and pressed twenty again.

I walked there quickly, just as he had twelve days before. I half expected yellow police tape around his door, but his office looked like all the others, just a shade neater. He had a magnifying glass on the desk (really, Dave?), clean legal pads stacked on top and two photos, one of us from our wedding—our walk back down the aisle, fingers entwined—and his favorite of me, the one from our Bermuda trip, where my sunglasses sat atop my head and my hair had streaks of bright blond from the sun.

I opened the desk drawers. Blank notepads, everything neat in its place. In the top desk drawer, there was a notepad, dated from last week, with Dave's squared-off handwriting.

I was about to leave when I decided, for good measure, to go through the Redweld folders leaned against his windowsill. They were labeled, typed italicized titles declaring the matter on the back tab. *Messinger Co. Frederick Trust.* And then, three in a row: *Mission Bank. Mission Bank. Mission Bank.*

It took a moment to sink in.

And then, in a relentless *whoosh*, it did. My legs buckled at the knees and I flopped down to the floor, my legs splayed in front of me like those of some six-year-old's Barbie Doll. I sat for a moment staring at the frayed beige carpet before forcing myself into frantic action. I opened the folders, flipping past e-mail and binders and organizational flow charts and Dave's handwritten notes. I couldn't have understood them if I'd had limitless time, and I finally bolted, bumping into one person on the way back to the elevator bank, a guy so riveted by something on his phone that he didn't even look up.

I felt safe only when I was out on the plaza. I sat at one of the white metal tables for a beat, looking for Sloane, who was supposed to meet me there. I checked my phone. There was a text from an unknown number—*hi cab we taincjek?* For a moment I tried to find some meaning: did I know anyone who spoke Serbian? Was it a botched autocorrection? Clients sometimes sent late-night flares, but I had my limits—tonight, if they couldn't bother to self-identify, I wasn't about to reply. *No*, I decided, *no "hi cab we taincjek."* At least not right now.

I texted Sloane and waited for a moment, but she didn't write back, which miffed me a little, given how involved she'd made herself. Whatever. This was probably how Sloane operated, either coming on strong or disappearing completely.

I called back Dave.

"How were the needles?" His voice was far away.

"The needles?"

"Isn't that what they use in acupuncture?"

"Sorry. Little light-headed. I'll be coming home soon."

"Where are you guys?"

"Midtown."

He chuckled. "No, I mean—where."

"On Fifth Avenue. I got sidetracked a bit. Window-shopping."

"Ahhh."

"I didn't buy anything. Do you need something?"

"Are you okay? You sound a little cranky."

"No, I'm fine."

"Okay. I was about to order food. Are you guys eating?"

I was hungry. But the last thing I could imagine was sitting at our dining table, forking dumplings into my mouth and pretending I'd been anywhere else. "No, thanks."

"When will you be back?"

"In a little bit." I hung up the phone abruptly. There was a restaurant across the street with warm yellow lighting, tables on the sidewalk and people spilling out. I had never been inside.

The lively scat and roar of the diners' conversations swept me up as soon as I opened the door. It was an Italian place, big jars of olives and curly dried pasta lining shelves against the wall, the enveloping smell of garlic. I wanted—needed—something warm to eat, so I found a seat at the bar and ordered some penne and a glass of wine.

I took out my steno pad and stared at Hedda's notes. Now, in the bright glow of the restaurant, I saw them for what they were: a collection of meaningless letters. My eyes blurred until everything was fuzzy, as if I were straining to see the tiniest line of the eye chart.

The real news was Mission Bank.

chapter twenty-seven

I HAD SLIPPED out of bed early and was pulling on a sports bra when Dave started to stir.

"You are the earliest freaking early bird of all the early birds." Dave grabbed one of the pillows from my side of the bed and plopped it down on his head as if suffocating himself. "Why are you out of bed at"—he reemerged and looked at the clock—"six forty-five?"

"Beat the heat."

"Great idea." He jumped out of bed and stretched his arms over his head.

"Wait. You're coming?" We hadn't been running together in almost a year. "Will you be able to keep up?"

He threw the pillow at me. "Will *you* be able to keep up?"

"Um, given that I exercise almost daily and your rate is about"—I squinted—"once a month, I think I can match any sputtering pace you manage."

"I accept."

"You accept what?"

"I accept the gauntlet that you just threw down."

I hadn't been trash-talking, but it was easier to pretend that I had, so I briefly shadowboxed and left to brush my teeth. He walked into the bathroom a minute later, his shoes tied. "Whenever you're ready." He leaned against the wall, watching me pull on my socks. "If I didn't know better, I'd think you were trying to avoid me. You come in late; you get up early."

"Are you kidding me? You've been holed up in your office for the past week and a half. No, for the past four months. What am I supposed to do? Wait around?"

"Paige, calm down." He put both his hands on my shoulders. "I was just joking."

"Oh. Right." We walked down the hall to the elevator, where we stood silently, watching the LED panel broadcasting the floors we passed.

It was not a good day for a run; the humidity was so strong that I could feel my hair bunch and curl immediately. I clipped off at a pace faster than usual, though, as soon as my feet touched the sidewalk. Dave matched my stride, but I could tell from his breathing and the way he grimaced that it was a struggle. "You okay?"

"Great." He pushed out the word like a grunt.

We got into the park, our feet clopping in unison. I was annoyed not to have my solitude; the plan for this run had been for me to think about the night before.

I barely registered that when we got to the hill at Ninety-sixth Street, Dave picked up the pace.

I turned toward him, eyebrows raised. "Really?"

"What's the matter?" he said. "Too fast?"

"Kamikaze mission." We ran in silence after that, working too hard for speech, accelerating through the hills of the upper loop even as the sogginess of the air made us work harder than normal. By the time we got to the reservoir, we were all-out sprinting. I wasn't about to quit, even though I wanted to, but when we traversed up to the reservoir gate, Dave stopped abruptly, pulling my shirt so I'd stop too.

"Holy shit," he said, gasping for breath and bending over his knees. "Holy shit. That was fast."

Even though my heart was racing and I wanted to collapse, I shrugged.

"Come on," he said. "You're kidding."

I just smiled. "I usually do five miles. That was only three."

"Just give me a moment."

I laughed, patting Dave's back when I saw it from the other direction: a flash of familiar blond hair, a slice of cheekbones. Percy. Swear to god, the man was shimmering, the sunlight tripping all over itself to illuminate him. Perhaps it was my lost footing with Dave, perhaps it was my light-headedness because my lungs were still recovering from our mad sprint, but I couldn't turn my gaze away.

Something made Percy recognize me, slow down and glance past me to Dave, who was standing upright, pressing his index finger deep into his side cramp.

I blushed beneath my already reddened cheeks, but managed to meet Percy's eye and shake my head subtly. *No.*

"What?" Dave looked around and caught Percy, who sped up and was about ten feet away, watching us. "Who's that guy?"

"I don't know."

He draped an arm, warm with sweat, around my shoulder. "He was totally checking you out."

"I don't think so." I didn't correct him and point out that I'd been the one doing the ogling. "I think he was wondering if you were okay, or if you needed medical attention from running too fast for your own good."

"No, he was admiring my form and how in shape I am." He removed his arm, and then it was safe to turn around, so we both did, watching Percy's retreating back.

Dave wasn't acting like someone with a secret. Maybe there was nothing untoward about his workload. Maybe he hadn't lied to me at all. Maybe my gut sense was broken.

Regardless, I was now lying to him.

chapter twenty-eight

AT SEVEN THIRTY in the morning of the first day he was due back in the office, Dave was conked out on our living room couch, binder-clipped documents littering the floor around him. His arms were folded on his chest; his head was tilted to the right; the front shock of his dark hair was even more vertical than it usually was.

I tiptoed closer, hoping for a message from his inner consciousness, a fleeting expression or a muttered word. He was expressionless in sleep, though, as if anticipation of the day ahead had him too exhausted to dream. I sat down next to him, resting on the sliver of a couch in the margin next to his torso. When that didn't wake him, I stretched out, easing my body on top of his, our faces aligned so that my toes stretched down to his calves.

His hip bones pressed into the fronts of my thighs, and his heartbeat pounded through my abdomen, warming it. I counted the pulses. One. Two. Three. I noticed for the first time that summer how pale he was, paler than I'd ever seen him.

Are you that desperate, Dave? Hungry enough to break the law?

When I pressed my forehead right up against his, as if I could access his thoughts through osmosis, the magnetic pull of my brain to his, his eyes flew open.

Dave's eyes are brown, but they are so warm, so lit within, that when I picture him, I inevitably imagine his eyes lighter than they are. Liquid chocolate, I've described them. Molten amber. Weapons of charm.

Lying there, our faces so close—eyelash to eyelash—all I saw

was the blurriness and light. One thousand little dots of beautifully illuminated pigment.

*I could understand if you did it, Dave. I could forgive you. You
can tell me. Blink if you did it. One little blink and I'll know.*

I tried to push the thought from my mind to his. For a second
I thought I had. He stared back at me and moved his hands down
my back until they were resting in the waistband of my pajamas.
He didn't blink.

We lay there for minutes, transferring body warmth to each
other, wordless. When my cell phone rang, we both shifted by
pulling back our heads—only a little, but enough to ruin the
moment. I climbed off Dave in a scramble and he got up off the
couch. "Shit," he said with a casual yawn. "It's late."

I picked up my phone.

"Paige?" I recognized Percy's voice immediately. "Is it too
early? You sound like you just woke up."

"No, I'm up." I checked the clock. "It is early, though."

"I know, sorry. But I won't be able to call later. I referred you
to some people and just wanted to leave word."

"For what?"

He paused. "For marriage counseling. Are you interested in
referrals for something else?"

"Um, no. Marriage counseling is what I do."

"Great. She'll probably call you today—Selena. I gave this
number, okay?"

"Yep. Thanks."

"Okay, see you tomorrow."

Twenty minutes later, Dave came out to the living room, showered and in a suit. "Who was on the phone?"

"Potential client." I followed him down the hall, where he picked up his messenger bag and slung it over his shoulder.

"Any golden therapist advice for me going back?"

"You'll be fine. Just act normal." *Act like it's no big deal.*

"You mean if I act normal, I'll fool them all into thinking I feel normal?"

"Something like that."

He gave me a peck on the lips, opened the door and closed it behind him. I opened it and ran down the hall after him. "Dave?"

"Mmm?" He was already gone, concerned with the day ahead.

"What were you thinking?" I hated that question; it was impossible to ask without sounding desperate. I'd always told clients if you sprang that question on someone, hoping to receive reassurance, you should expect either lies or disappointment in return. "On the couch?"

"I wasn't thinking. It was just nice."

"Yeah." I waited for him to ask me too, but he was apparently confident enough to not need to know. He gave me another peck, then continued down the hall to the elevators.

"Good luck," I called after him. Without turning around or stopping, he raised his arm in victory and punched the air.

I was in the drugstore, buying more candy for the jar, when my dad called my cell phone.

"What a treat." My tone was a little too bright and phony from the surprise; he never called.

"How's, um, work?"

"Fine. You?"

"Good."

"So, what's up?"

"Have you heard from Sloane?"

"No." I had called her and left a message to debrief her on my break-in mission, but she hadn't called back. Or checked in. "Where is she?"

"I was hoping you knew."

"I don't. Sorry."

"Have you spoken to her recently?"

"Saturday, I think."

"So not since acupuncture."

"Mmm." I scratched my collarbone as if I could brush away the lie. "She's probably seeing the *Eyes* or taking the ferry to Staten Island or something."

"Did she tell you that?"

"No—I'm just saying. They're ingesting a steady dose of tourism while she's here. What are you guys up to?"

"Paige," he said, lowering his voice, "are you in the middle of something? I was going to go home for lunch and was wondering if you could come. I think it would mean a lot to your mom."

◆

She was hunched over the counter when I walked into the kitchen. Seeing me, she brightened with the meager energy of a fritzy lightbulb. "Have you eaten?"

"No," I lied. "I'm starving. Feed me."

The three of us sat down at the set table—place mats, candles, flowers—in silence, picking at our food with all the gusto of actors on their thirty-seventh take of a waffle commercial.

"What are you doing after this?" my mom said.

"Just some administrative catch-up."

"No clients?"

"Not today, although I got a call from someone new. Summer's always slow."

"Any news with the redecorating?" I realized that we hadn't talked about any of this stuff—the updates that usually flowed so easily between us—since Sloane's arrival.

"Nah. Taking a break."

Mom stirred her iced tea with a tiny spoon, her fingers crooked delicately. "Why?"

"It just got lost in the shuffle."

"The shuffle of?"

"I don't know." She accepted this without comment, stirring her tea. Stirring and stirring and stirring.

"Are you guys really worried about her?"

"No." My dad didn't look up from the paper. "We're not." My mom was silent. "She's different now," he said.

"How?" I asked. They looked at each other across the table. "All I remember is one horrible night. Do you remember it, with the bloody nose and that guy passed out? Poor Mrs. Chanokowski was there?"

"I remember," said my dad.

At the same time my mom said, "Why would you even bring up that night?"

"Because it happened." No response. "Does she really seem different this time?"

"Yes." My dad didn't look up.

"How?"

My mom stirred her tea. My dad sounded defensive. "She's centered this time. She's doing acupuncture for chrissakes."

"Let's talk about something else," said my mom.

"Why do you look like you didn't really sleep last night?" I said, and my mom absently patted down her hair at this. "And why are things so weird between you guys and Sloane? What's the tension?"

"Did she say there was tension?" My mom shifted her eyes from left to right.

"No. But it's pretty palpable. Even Dave commented."

"She's had big problems, Paige. It's normal that things are strained."

"Plenty of people are addicted and recover and manage to do it without completely ditching their family." Dave had said the same thing to me when we were dating. At the time, I had asked him if substance abuse ran in his family, and when he'd said no, I'd countered—as sweetly as I could—that some things you just have to live through before you can truly understand them. "Is there more to the story? Or is Sloane really just that touchy?"

My mom got up and left the table, walking over to the iced tea pitcher and the pile of mint next to it. She tore off a handful, rinsed the mint, chopped it into little pieces and sprinkled it into the pitcher, even though no one had asked for it. "I'm thinking of starting needlepoint."

My dad nodded as though needlepoint were a logical segue.

"There was a story about it on the radio." She brought the pitcher to the table. "A club of women who meet in a library, somewhere in the Midwest. They knit and tell their stories. It sounded like something I'd like to do."

"Since when do you tell your stories?" At first I worried it was a little too harsh, but when no one even reacted, I got up and left the table.

chapter twenty-nine

Vanessa

WHEN PAIGE WAS four, we went strawberry picking at Mack-ahack Fields with Cherie and her kids. We were walking around, plopping the berries in our buckets, nibbling on them as we skipped along, when boom—Paige's eyes got red and teary. She kept rubbing them with her little fists, and Cherie and I tried to figure out what the problem was. "Maybe she's allergic to straw-berries," Cherie suggested. The pediatrician on call, a huge mus-tached man with pockmarked cheeks, insisted I bring her in. I never liked his bedside manner, but he looked like the boogey-man, so I usually did what he said.

During this visit, Dr. Boogeyman was glowering at me over Paige's chart because he thought that I was not concerned enough. (As it turned out, Paige was not allergic to strawberries, and the redness was most likely due to some irritation, like dust or an eyelash. Take *that*, Dr. Boogeyman, and add to it a little respect for Mother's Intuition.)

"Mommy," Dr. Boogeyman tsked, "food allergies are cumu-lative." It was disturbing how he did this, called us all Mommy and Daddy. The sign of some major issues, Cherie and I agreed.

"What? Like she could become allergic to other things?"

"Of course she could," he said. "But it's not just that. Even if you start with a mild reaction, if you test your body by eating just a little bit more, you can overstress it. Your system will react by going haywire."

"So you're saying that the later reaction would be worse because of the earlier reaction?"

"I'm saying, Mommy, that she could die."

♦

Worry is fuel for parents. It enables us to do the job: we listen to our nagging sense to gauge whether the child's being overdramatic or the teacher is that bad, whether the stomachaches are from a bug or being left off some little brat's birthday party list, whether the rash is something a doctor should observe firsthand. *You trust your gut.*

There's a physical element to the worry, of course: the pounding heart, the sour, churning stomach, the hummingbird mind, unable to settle too long on any other topic. If you didn't have these indicators, you'd be as adrift as those poor kids born without nerves—the ones who burn through layers of skin and smell it before feeling a thing.

Sloane didn't answer my call on Saturday night. She had said she would be available to discuss exchanging the VIP exhibit tickets I'd gotten her for Sunday, but she wasn't. Then I couldn't reach her on Sunday, and I started to feel the first twinges.

I wasn't overreacting; I'd dialed her twelve times. I went to the MoMA myself to see if she'd somehow gotten other tickets for the exhibit, unlikely as that seemed. (I'd had to pull quite a few strings for the exhibit, the *Room Full of Rainbows* apparently being the trend of the summer.) I waited outside the damn rainbow room for an hour. I finally went in and saw it. It was actually kind of neat. They'd reflected light through prisms, and you felt like you were traveling somewhere—to Oz, I guessed— over the rainbows. Then I waited outside some more, and then I went home.

I'd braved far worse than a twenty-four-hour silence from

Sloane, but for some reason I was done and toasted on this one, too distracted to be comforted by any of my usual cheap thrills. All I felt like doing was walking up and down the grid blocks in Manhattan with Sloane's picture, asking strangers if they had seen her.

The flip side of parental worry is that it works best on the small stuff. When you actually have something to sink your teeth into, you can't turn off the indicators. Nobody can absorb that much frantic energy.

I thought Sloane's return was all I wanted, but the fact was, I'd functioned without her. I thought I needed her to enjoy my company, but I was able to handle being rebuffed. The worry, though—the ups and downs of fear—I couldn't exist while being whipped around on those. My body had hit its limit.

My system, as predicated by that awful Dr. Boogeyman, was finally going haywire from the cumulative effects. I hated that he was right.

chapter thirty

THIS TIME, I brought the coffee to Percy's office. He smiled in thanks, appearing genuinely touched, and as he got up from his desk, I noticed he was again wearing those jeans.

He wasn't the only guy I'd been attracted to since meeting Dave—it was a common enough thing for me to see, and appreciate, a cute bartender, a good-looking stranger on the corner next to me, waiting for the light to change or, once, horrifyingly, an especially charismatic client. My reaction to those men had been harmless, I now realized. I'd notice them with a little more intensity; perhaps I'd have a brief moment of self-consciousness if I thought they noticed me too, and then I'd forget all about it.

Intellectually, I knew the reason my attraction to Percy felt different was the crush of my current circumstances—it was less about how well his running shirt had outlined his abs (it had) than how confused I was about things at home. I thought this while watching his hand grip his coffee cup and wondering how it would feel on my skin.

"Have you heard from your sister lately?" he asked.

"No, not for a while actually."

"Me neither. I was supposed to see them last night."

My head felt light. "Is Giovanni . . . Does he . . . Are you worried about something?"

"Giovanni's never had a substance abuse problem"—he looked right at me—"if that's what you're asking. It's a little strange, because he's usually in pretty good touch, but I'm not worried."

"Okay."

"Really. Not worried," he said.

At the same time I said, "So! Let's get to work!"

Percy looked both startled and amused. "Alrighty."

"Full confession: I went into Dave's office—and to the HR rep's. On Saturday night."

He smiled slyly. "That's what you got from our call? You should break into his firm?"

"I know. But I found stuff."

"Is this standard for you to buck conventional wisdom? When you hear something is a bad idea, you interpret that as 'Go for it'?"

"Not at all. I'm usually very obedient."

"Right."

"I swear, Sloane will provide verification. I won't do it again. I trust your expertise, and I also especially appreciate that Annie isn't here today."

"I fired her. When you complained."

"You're kidding."

"Yes, I'm kidding. She has a thing."

"A fashion thing? Like a show?"

"I don't really know."

"What kind of friend are you, Percy?"

"Good enough to provide employment that fits her schedule, but apparently not good enough to care about the details of her time outside the office. Please. Continue rationalizing your break-in."

"I trust your expertise generally, but specifically, I was right to go. I found stuff."

188 L. ALISON HELLER

"Like what?"

I told him about the file folders and gave him the copy of Hedda's undecipherable notes, adding that I thought the presence of the Mission Fund files pretty much crossed everything else off the list.

"Not necessarily," Percy said.

"Really?"

"Aren't they one of the largest hedge funds? They probably do a lot of work with lawyers at big firms."

"I don't know. It's just sort of like . . ."

"A gut hunch?"

"I feel like that's the phrase of the summer, but yeah. A gut hunch."

He was about to say something, but his phone rang before he could, and he fumbled for it in those jeans pockets. "Sorry. It's Giovanni. Hey," he said into his phone. "I'm in the office. With Paige. Really? No, I had a meeting, but it's fine. Let me—I'll call you back in one second." He muttered, "Sorry," dialed one number and held the phone to his ear.

"Is everything okay?"

"Fine. They're fine." I could hear the phone ringing endlessly until a voice mail message picked up. Percy sighed and punched in another number. "Mrs. Fitz?" he shouted. "Yes, it's Percy. Percy Stahl, 3B. Yes, can you buzz in my friend and give him the key? The one on the green chain." He nodded. "That's right! The green one. His name is Giovanni. Yes, Gio-van-ni. Thank you!"

It sounded lovely and neighborly, having a Mrs. Fitz. She probably watched over her young neighbors' spare keys with bespectacled blue eyes and knit them afghan cozies. In return, they—what?—split her firewood? Unlikely, but possible, I supposed, in a prewar building.

Percy dialed Giovanni back. "Buzz 5C, Fitz. Go up there and ask for my key. It's the green one. I'll meet you there."

Percy stood up and then stopped, looked behind as if wondering why I was taking so long to get off the couch. "You coming?"

"Sure."

◆

I bit back a grin when Percy told the cabdriver to take us to the East Village. Of course he lived downtown. The model employee, the offbeat job, his styled-to-look-disheveled hair—he was one of those king-of-the-scene New Yorkers. My tone a tad challenging, I said, "Why do you run in the park if you live in the East Village?"

"It's not *that* far from the office," he said. "Plus, have you seen Central Park? It's a marvel."

I snapped into my seat belt. "Can't argue with that."

"Thank the lord for small miracles."

"I really am not the argumentative type, Percy, but the more you claim I am, the more I think *you* are. Classic projection."

"It must be nice to be a therapist and have such terms at your fingertips. When you're debating something and your argument veers toward the fantastical, as it tends to do, you can hide that behind terminology."

"It's handy. For instance, when someone is using misdirection in such a textbook fashion, I know to ask something like this." I cleared my throat and leaned in, in full eye-contact mode. "Percy, if *your* parents described you, would they perhaps say *you* buck conventional wisdom? That you do the opposite of what's expected?"

"Wow." He closed his eyes. "It's like my father is right here in this cab. Thank you for that. I feel . . . What's the technical term for the opposite of affirmed?"

"Maligned?"

"Of course. I feel so maligned."

"What's the deal with your dad?"

"He thinks being a private detective is a duck and cover from real life."

"So, it's not a family business?"

"Partially. My aunt was a detective and I inherited her shop. It's all I've ever wanted to do, and he's only ever been disappointed."

"If you introduced him to Annie, he might change his mind. He might think you're an impressive little rapscallion."

"I assure you, he wouldn't."

"He's told you that he's disappointed?"

"No, but I know."

"How?"

"The sighs when I talk about my clients. The mailed clippings of articles about classmates who are doing well working for banks and ad agencies and law firms. It's all very subtle. Oh, up here on the right." We got out of the cab, and I followed him into the lobby of one of the new high-rises that filled an entire city block with its too-clean red brick and large windows reflecting light blue sky. Percy paused in the lobby before the unmanned front desk. "Thank you, Lou, for giving my friends the key."

"Yeah," I said, pretending to tip my hat. "Thanks a lot, Lou." I followed him onto the elevator. "Have you lived here long?"

"About four years," he said, pressing the button for the fifth floor. "Lou is the seventh concierge, but there's a rumor that he moved to Estonia last month."

The hallways were painted white, and each door was black, for a starkly disorienting effect. I followed Percy down the hall until we reached a studio apartment tucked next to the corner.

It wasn't decorated much differently than the hall: nearly empty except for a queen bed (with gray sheets), a small black architect's table with one chair and a small, gray, low couch on which Sloane and Giovanni now sat. There were no photos or art, except for an ancient-looking map hung in the corner. I knew if I opened the tall silver Sub-Zero, there'd be chilled water, a bottle or two of something expensive, but no food.

Who lived like this? It was good, though. It was a wake-up call. I had two solid reasons why Percy was not to be taken seriously: the jeans (which could, in all fairness, also be on the other, more dangerous list that I was not about to catalog) and his home environment. Hipster monochromatic minimalism.

Sloane and Giovanni had launched into a comedic retelling of how difficult it had been to get the spare key from poor Mrs. Fitz—who turned out to be a guy named Fipps. That I had misheard his name was also for the best. My Mrs. Fitz did not belong here, walking through those stark halls in her Christmas sweaters, asking sweetly for a hot cocoa at the wheatgrass-shot bar on the corner and being perpetually disappointed.

Sloane and Giovanni were utterly, breezily unaware that anyone might have worried about them, and when they stopped talking, I couldn't help but say, "You just disappeared." Embarrassingly, my voice wavered a little, which of course made everyone turn around.

"Sorry," Giovanni said. "Christophe came back. And he's in love. But they fight."

"Again?" Percy shook his head.

"We had to get out of there last night," said Sloane. "They were noisy."

"Who is Christophe?" I said.

"We scrambled a bit and wound up at the Lincoln," said Giovanni. "It's very affordable."

"You should've called," Percy said.

"Who is Christophe?"

"The friend they were staying with," said Percy. "You really should have called," he repeated to Giovanni.

"But you said we shouldn't bother you on Sunday or Monday, that you had big jobs all day. And I did call Paige."

"No, you didn't," I said.

"I meant I *texted* you."

"I never got a text."

"Yes, on Saturday, when Sloane was supposed to meet you. Her phone fell in the toilet." Giovanni started to laugh and then stopped. "It's not funny. Well, it was kind of funny. Have you guys ever done that? Apparently it's quite common, not that you would know that from how much of a pain in the ass it is to remedy the situation, but anyway. That's a whole other story. Luckily, she remembered most of your number, so we tried a few and—"

"Were *you* the one who texted *cab we taincjek*?"

"I don't know what that means." Giovanni smiled helpfully. "But I texted you that we needed to change our plans."

"Is this your number?" I pulled out my phone.

He peered close and slapped his forehead with his palm. "I'm so sorry. I meant that Sloane needed a rain check."

"Oh." I looked again. *Can we take a rain check?*

Giovanni flashed his teeth in a bashful grin. "Oops?"

Sloane gave him an incredulous look. "What is wrong with your brain?"

"I will say"—I slipped my phone back in my bag—"that as a heads-up it was kind of lacking."

Sloane slapped her palm against her forehead. "You work with computers, for crying out loud."

"Different skill set," Giovanni said, and to me, "Sorry."

"It's fine."

"When I said I was busy," Percy continued, "I meant that I wasn't free to eat dinner with you guys, not that you couldn't crash here in an emergency. The Lincoln? Seriously?"

"It's very affordable," Giovanni said.

"You have to relax your standard in New York," Percy said. "It's almost impossible to find a decent room on short notice under one hundred fifty bucks."

"We found two," Giovanni said with triumph. "The Staten Island Garden View and the Lincoln. They're all the same, you know—four walls, a bed. I refuse to pay—why should we have to pay—"

"I know," Percy said, and Sloane added tiredly, "It's the principle of the thing."

"Exactly." Giovanni looked very pleased.

"The Lincoln was still preferable to the sounds of Christophe's love gone wrong."

"Screechy," said Giovanni. "Love gone wrong is a very screechy sound."

"What's the Lincoln?" I said.

"It's near Hell's Kitchen. Between a hostel and a fleabag motel," said Sloane. "Way beneath your grade of luxury. Water bugs. Communal showers. Creepy pale men who sit in the lobby, drooling and watching the news really loud."

"The news?" I felt as lost as Mrs. Fitz. Who were these people? Where were the gingersnaps?

"The TV—there's only one in the place, in the lounge—is up high, like a hospital TV, without a remote, and set to the news. The residents seem more like the type who'd prefer porn or greyhound racing."

"Hence no remote," Giovanni pointed out.

"You guys are not staying at the Lincoln." Percy looked

around the room, trying to figure out how it could fit three people. "I have a job tonight and after that I'm away—"

"I don't know why you guys don't go to Mom and Dad's," I
said. "You'd have your own wing."

"No." You could have sharpened an entire block of knives on
Sloane's voice.

"Then ask them to get you a hotel room somewhere. They're
not tightwads anymore."

"No."

"Stay with me." It could work—Sloane and Giovanni off doing their art-tourism thing; Dave busy working. No one explicitly acknowledged my invitation, although Sloane oscillated her
head rather noncommittally when I added, "You'd have your
own room."

"Where are you going away to?" Giovanni asked Percy.

"The Hamptons," Percy said. "Short job. Last minute."

"I've always wanted to go there. It sounds so . . . sea grassy."

"It is," said Percy. "Come along. I'm taking the train out on
Thursday."

Giovanni looked at Sloane, eyebrows raised. *Why not?*

"I have a place out there. For the summer." I was happy to see
Sloane and Giovanni, I realized. I wanted to fill in Sloane on the
Duane Covington break-in. I wanted to spare them staying at the
Lincoln. In a way that was weirdly—I assumed—sisterish, I
wanted to protect her. I wanted her advice. "I mean it. A genuine
offer. You could stay here tonight, then come to the Upper East
Side with me for a night, and then go out to the Hamptons and
stay as long as you like. I'd be so happy if you guys used the house.
It's been sitting there empty. Just make sure you're back for boat
day." Sloane rolled her eyes at the mention of boat day, but she and
Giovanni stared at each other in silent, one-couple-brain telepathy.

After a second, she said, "Okay."

"Really?" I clapped my hands together.

"Yeah. Thanks," she said, and Giovanni gave me a sweet, if dorky, thumbs-up.

After a pause, I got the sense that I was an obstacle to a more natural conversation between the three of them. When I excused myself, Percy walked me the three feet to the door. "We never finished our meeting."

"Was there anything else?"

"Just"—he patted the doorframe near me—"keep an open mind."

"To?"

"Anything."

"My mind is open. I will be pleasantly surprised by anything that doesn't involve a felony charge."

"Do you have a firm directory? Something that lists all the people—not just lawyers but staff too? Those might be initials in the HR notes."

"Yeah. I'll get one to you when you stay at the Hamptons house."

"That invitation extends to me?"

I wondered if it'd been inappropriate to offer. I decided not, especially now that I'd seen his apartment and I felt less risk of temptation. "Sure. There's room if you want to."

"Maybe just Thursday night. That's really nice, thanks."

I pointed at Giovanni and Sloane. "So tomorrow?"

"Tomorrow," Sloane shouted from the couch.

"Yay." I shook my arms in a little cheer. "It'll be fun."

I didn't know why Sloane had one of those perpetually sullen faces—perhaps it was the underlying bone structure, what her body had been through or however our family had disappointed her. But when she allowed a smile to shine through—like she did right then—I believed she meant it.

I decided to walk to the subway and was mowing through the push of people on First Avenue when I realized I should call my mom. She picked up on the first ring. "I just saw Sloane."

"Is she okay?"

"Fine." I explained that they'd be staying with me, and my mom inhaled sharply.

"Paige," she said, "that's fantastic." She kept repeating it, "Fantastic, fantastic," until I finally cut her off.

"So," I said, "she'll stay with us for a while, but then maybe we can convince them to stay with you next."

There was a silence. "Sometimes," said my mom finally, "people need their space."

It was the type of platitude that in a prior universe I would've blown off as meaningless, but her tone made me flash to the journal entries I'd read and question what else might lie beneath her words.

chapter thirty-one

I've been thinking a lot about friendships.

Deep, right?

How each one has its limits, its perimeter. For example, as much as Cherie helps me—and she does—there's only so much she can really understand. I mean all her shit looks pretty minor when lined up next to an addict daughter who refuses to talk to me. So she can't complain to me about anything because if she does, she worries that I'll secretly be thinking, Big whoop, sweetie pie, you wanna hear a real problem? *(She's right. I would be thinking that.)*

And if I try to really open up to her, you know what happens: a) she cries; b) she nods her head like she's trying to understand; or c) she shakes her head like she just can't believe it.

Maybe we'll regain the normalcy; maybe we won't.

G., on the other hand, because he's been through it, might have the same reaction—shaking or nodding his head—but it just reads differently.

Like when I told him about the clusterfuck of Sloane's visiting-day weekend, I knew he got it. How she refused to even look at me. How I was putting on such a pathetically friendly face—doing the pottery, holding the truth stick, earnestly listening to her counselors. Even trying to be supportive when she ripped into me in that group therapy session, calling me a liar, telling me she hated me in front of everyone, when she said that seeing me made her want to use again. "Trigger point," they called it.

I couldn't tell Cherie that. Cherie might ask whether I knew why or how to fix it. What did Frankie think or do? Nothing. Just let me grip his hand, which felt as uncomforting as a dead flounder. And the whole time, Cherie would be thinking, Thank god it's not my kid.

But G. listened, shook his head and said, "Is that the Sloane you remember, or is she a stranger?"

An excellent question. It got me outside of myself, made me smile, because the reality is, Sloane has always been the one to full-on tantrum when not getting her way. Once, she told me she hated me over not getting a second ice cream. Granted, this felt different—after a three-month absence, in a room full of strangers whom she clearly preferred over me. This felt final.

She's never really been the sunny type, though. Brooding and artistic, I'd said. Moody. "Was your point that I have to separate myself from that? That she's responsible for her actions at some point?"

He stared at me. "No," he said. "Although there's probably a lesson, but I was just curious."

When we stopped laughing, he picked up the check, and I tried to fight him on it—he works in a party gift store, for crying out loud, and I know what Pressman charges. The guy can't have much spare change around.

"Stop," he said, "with your Guilty Feelings. I want to do this." Then of course we laughed harder because that's our oldest joke: my hundreds of thousands of brooms' worth of Guilty Feelings and how Pressman has granted them their own continent.

"Okay," I said. And I reasoned that it was only burgers. Plus, the whole lunch—all time with G.—is an elixir. Which probably means it's highly inappropriate. But you know what? I'm wise enough to grab the thrill and see where this goes. I let him pay.

chapter thirty-two

IT HAD OCCURRED to me—after I offered our place to Sloane—that I should have run the idea by Dave first. But he didn't have a problem with it or the fact that I hadn't consulted him; he didn't seem to have a problem with anything since returning to work.

"Really?" I said. He was lying on the bed watching the History Channel, his features relaxed. "And you're okay with her boyfriend, sorry—fiancé—here too?"

"Unless he's an asshole."

"He's really sweet."

"Maybe just keep an eye on the silver?"

I pointed to my eyes with my middle and pointer finger and then reversed the *V* in the direction of the dining room buffet—watching like a hawk. "On it."

"I'll come home early, so we can all go out tonight."

"Really?"

"Of course."

◆

Giovanni had a conference call early in the morning, so like a member of the advance team, Sloane had dropped off their bags first. She walked in and started turning in slow circles as if she were in a museum exhibit. "So. Much. Space," she said. "How much space does a person need?"

"Some, sometimes."

"O-kay, Yoda," Sloane said, and I didn't tell her it was wisdom from dear old Mom.

I showed her the guest room, which still looked to me small and cramped with piles of decorating detritus: stray sconces and carpet samples and wallpaper tears piled all together. "Thank you." She slung her arm around me. "This way beats the Lincoln."

She might have recanted if she knew that the first thing I did after hearing the elevator door's ding was to peek in her bags. I didn't find anything of note: a laptop, remarkably few clothing options, a notebook dedicated to listing the restaurants and exhibits and sketches of the *Eyes*. I zipped everything back up, feeling guilty.

After work, I got home early enough to put out fresh towels and flowers in the guest room before the buzzer sounded. I ran out to greet them in the hallway, and the first thing I noticed when they stepped out of the elevator was that something in Sloane's arms moved. A tiny little ratlike head. I jumped back.

Sloane hiked up her crooked arm. "Paige, meet Bandito."

"You have a dog?"

"Whoops." Sloane had turned to Giovanni. Giovanni slapped his forehead. "We thought you knew."

"It's fine," I said. "But where has . . . Bandito been?"

"We forgot you hadn't met him," said Giovanni. "He was probably napping in his soft crate." He pointed with the index finger of his right hand to the mesh black bag hanging over his shoulder. "It's his happy place."

"Bandito is the captain of our family." Sloane put it—him?—down on the floor, and he nervously tottered around, sniffing.

"Hi, Bandito."

"Not a dog person?"

"No, but I'm sure I'll love him."

"You will. He's a real champion. And he's pad-trained. Everybody loves Bandito."

"Cuz his feet, they smell like Fritos," said Giovanni.

"Excuse me?"

"He looks great in a Speedo," Sloane added.

"But he always forgets the Apostles' Credo," shouted Giovanni, and the two of them started laughing.

"Nice one," said Sloane, reaching up to high-five Giovanni.

The dog was still sniffing, oblivious to its owners' attempt at a late-night comedy shtick.

"Sorry," said Giovanni. "Bandito inspires the rhymes. You'll see. It's infectious."

◆

Giovanni wanted New York pizza for as many meals as possible, even though we tried to explain that the Upper East Side wasn't where you went for that kind of pizza.

"I don't care," he said. "It's the symbolism. I've eaten it almost every dinner so far."

We left Bandito on a blanket with some pads near him— when I saw him squat on one, I realized what pad-trained meant—and walked to a little Italian place on Sixty-eighth Street with red-checkered tablecloths and carafes of water on each table. A waiter sliced off hunks of nutty Parmesan cheese for each of us as soon as we sat down.

I nibbled on mine, realizing how tense I was about all the subtext in this group: what Dave knew about Sloane; what Sloane was trying to find out about Dave; me, the connecting joint of it all; and Giovanni, sunnily clueless. I watched Sloane. She didn't look stressed at all. She looked like she'd captured the sun.

"Welcome! To the family," Dave said.

"Thank you," said Giovanni, and when I met Sloane's eye, she mouthed, "Mafia?"

The waiter approached, and Dave jumped to it. "No wine for the table." He covered his glass with his hand and handed it back. I had desperately wanted wine, and I really didn't think Sloane would care, given how much secondhand smoke I'd inhaled this week.

I was sure he was only trying to be a gracious host, but there was something odd about how Dave was acting, as if he was assuming the role of grown-up for the group. Based on the way his curly hairline receded a bit and the laugh lines around his eyes, Giovanni was probably older than all of us, but he didn't appear offended. He suffered politely through Dave's questions about his job, which had something to do with corporate computer systems.

"He's a genius," Sloane said. "Just know he's a genius."

"Who can't send a text message," I said, and Giovanni gave me one of his thumbs-ups.

At the first lull in Dave's questions, Giovanni put his hands on the table. "Is anyone else ready to ditch the work talk?"

"Please," I said. "Enough. Enough with the work talk."

"Yes," said Sloane.

I popped an olive in my mouth, biting down on its oily flesh with my molars.

"Do you guys like games?" Giovanni leaned forward.

Dave and I exchanged a wary glance. "Games?"

"He's just like this." Sloane shook her head. "Too much time at summer camp. You'll get used to it."

"What kinds of games are you talking about?" Dave looked seriously concerned.

"Don't do it. No, not Bananagrams." Sloane swiveled her head toward Giovanni and patted his hand.

"Is that the one with the tiles?"

"In the banana-shaped—"

Giovanni thrust his torso back while reaching into his shorts pocket and pulled out the banana-shaped bag, bright yellow.

"You carry that with you?"

"Always. Bananagrams and a wallet."

"Seriously?"

"Seriously."

"Are you going to make us do them?"

"I never force Bananagrams, right, Sloane?"

"Right," said Sloane. "He never forces Bananagrams."

"Which is not to say," he said, "that one day in the not-so-distant future you won't be begging me to play. But I'll heed the advice of my lovely lady."

"Thank god," I breathed. I was certain I was not up to Bananagrams.

"Here's what we're going to do. Each couple is going to tell two stories of how we met, and the other couple has to guess which is the true one and which is the false one. I'll start." Before Dave and I could respond, he nudged Sloane. "You want to tell one and I'll tell one?"

"I want no part of this cheese-fest. You tell both."

He sighed and addressed me. "Story one: This is about a lonely young man. Everything was going well in his life— swimmingly—except for one thing. All the women he met were—" He gestured, searching for the right word.

"Horrible nut jobs," said Sloane.

He laughed. "Let's say—"

"Psychos," said Sloane.

"Not right for him. But he had heard wonderful things about the caliber of people on the illustrious Web site iheartdating .com." Sloane, in midsip of water, started choking. Giovanni whapped her on the back a few times and then started laughing, and the two of them dissolved as Dave and I sat, hands folded, like prim Christians at a rave. "So he signed up for a profile on this site. *What do I write?* he asked himself. *How do I summarize myself so perfectly that I'll attract the perfect partner?* So he pondered and pondered and scratched out drafts and, finally, he wrote about his love of Morrissey."

"The musician?" Dave's nose was wrinkled.

"The musician. And he also wrote of his love of hiking and travel. He posted it and looked around at some of the viable candidates. And what do you know—a lovely lady had also written about her love of Morrissey and hiking in the Cascades. They met and the rest is history. True love and all that. Any gut reactions to the veracity of this?"

"Let's hear story two first."

"Wait." Sloane sat forward. "I want to tell it." Giovanni swept his hand in a yielding-the-floor gesture. "Story two. We rented apartments in the same building but three floors apart. One night, I got locked out—without my phone—so I banged on the door of all my neighbors. Giovanni was the first one home, and he helped me call the locksmith. We didn't see each other for three weeks, but then bumped into each other at the grocery store, and I offered to buy him dinner as thanks."

"That one," said Dave. "Definitely that one."

"Paige?"

"Yep. Story two. The locksmith one."

"Nope." Giovanni and Sloane high-fived each other. I wondered how many times a day they'd be doing that.

"You met online?"

"Don't knock it," said Sloane. "It cuts out all the bullshit."

"Ideally," said Giovanni.

"It did for us."

"We got lucky, but some people don't."

"True." She leaned into him.

"Your turn," said Giovanni.

"You start," I said to Dave.

"I don't know."

"Start." I tried to wait him out. I wanted to see which he'd choose—the lie or the truth, but he shrugged and shook his head, as if still trying to figure out how he had gotten to this table.

The four of us just sat there awkwardly until Giovanni finally said, "It's just a game. For fun."

I bit another olive. Giovanni pointed at me. "Story one. Go."

"Okay. It was summer, and I was going through a serious cooking phase. You guys know about that, right? I was really into smoothies, so I went to Gracious Homes to buy a blender for strawberry puree." I glanced at Dave to see if he was smiling. He was, and even if we didn't dissolve into giggles like Sloane and Giovanni had, I felt satisfied. We were connected. It had worked out for us too. "And, of course, Dave worked there all through law school. I saw him, he saw me. And the rest is history."

"Okay." Giovanni peered at me through narrow eyes. "What were you wearing?"

"Um, red shirt and jeans."

"Story two." Giovanni pointed at Dave the same way.

"My turn," said Dave. "I was walking through Central Park with some friends—Binnie and Michael—on a gorgeous sunny day. And one of these friends, Binnie, pointed at this beauty who was walking, a bit in her own world. If I'm totally honest, maybe she was even talking to herself. And she said, 'I know her. Paige!'

She shouted, 'Paige!' As I said, this girl was a little in her own world, so it took a couple times for her to respond, but she did, and I basically went all out with my moves until I got her number, and the rest . . ."

"Is history," we all said together.

Sloane and Giovanni turned toward each other. "Hmm," Giovanni said, stroking his chin dramatically.

"Story one," said Sloane, looking straight at me. "I vote for Paige. Plus, there's no way Binnie Rabinowitz introduced you."

"I don't understand that name," Giovanni said. "Binnie Rabinowitz? Who would do that to a kid?"

"It's from camp," I said. "She was a great softball player and that was her nickname. The Binnie is *from* her last name."

"Ah," said Giovanni. "Like saying A-Rod Rodriguez. I say story two. I felt the love in story two. Didn't you feel the love? Sparkling, sunny day, beautiful stranger . . . And she"—Giovanni pointed at me and smiled—"is beautiful. It's a good narrative."

"Story two," said Dave. "It was story two." Sloane snapped her fingers exaggeratedly, all mock disappointment.

I looked at Sloane. "What did you mean about Binnie?"

"I just don't like that girl. Never have."

"Me neither. It's always been so uncomfortable to be around her. When I was little, I always just thought the problem was me."

"Not liking her?"

"I didn't even realize I didn't like her. I would just get a stomachache around her."

Sloane lowered her eyebrows sternly. "How can you not realize that? Especially with someone like Binnie?"

"I don't know." I swallowed. "I guess I figured I was supposed to like her because our families were friends, so I held out as long as I could. Haven't you ever gotten a feeling that lingers for a while before your brain can assimilate it?"

"No, but clearly that's how you operate." I could've killed her for sliding her eyes, lashes lowered, in Dave's direction and punctuating the gesture with a sly wink at me.

"Really? Why?" Dave hadn't noticed the wink; he turned toward me, surprised.

"She's so judgey," I said.

"Affected," said Sloane.

"And smug, but honestly, I could deal with all of that if it weren't for the judgment."

"Well," said Giovanni, "she introduced you two, so that's a good contribution to the world."

The pizza came and we were all silent, watching the waiter roll the slicer through the steaming cheese.

"That was a good icebreaker," Dave said when he left, although his saying it made things stale again.

"Yeah," said Giovanni. "I love it. It just goes to show you can think you have someone's story figured out, but you never really know."

Sloane snaked her arm around his shoulder, dangling her fingers down his chest. "Except unless you do."

"Except unless you do," Giovanni repeated.

chapter thirty-three

I WOKE TO the sound of a dog yapping. *That's not right,* I thought before recalling Bandito's tiny rat nose and quivery body, as well as the miniature puddle of urine we'd found in the entry hall when we returned from dinner. Sloane was awake already and was in the kitchen pouring Bandito some food, which made his little feet skate with excitement on the tiles.

I looked at the clock on my phone. "It's nine already? Jesus."

"I know. Giovanni's still sleeping. I didn't even hear Dave leave."

"Me neither, and I was a lot closer than you."

Bandito rushed to the bowl, munching on his bits of kibble, and Sloane pressed together the yellow and blue seams of the plastic dog food bag until it snapped. "Where's your coffee?"

I pointed to a cabinet and was watching her scoop it out with a spoon into the filter when the buzzer rang. We looked at each other. I shook my head and picked up the phone. "Ian's on his way up," Bert announced.

"Crapcrapcrap." I hopped in place. "I forgot I had a meeting with my anal decorator."

"Your what?"

"My anal decorator."

"Your *what*?" she repeated, and we heard Ian's key in the lock and the front door creak open. "He's coming in?"

I positioned myself in front of the door as Ian came in. "Hi, Ian!"

He blinked behind his perfect-circle tortoiseshell glasses

frames. "You're in pink pajamas. With bed head." He reached out his fingers as if tempted—but too grossed out—to touch my hair.

"I am. Yes, I am. I—"

"Who's this?"

"My sister, Sloane. She's staying with me."

He nodded, looked around the apartment quickly, scanning. "Where's the Cocoracci piece?"

"The blue vase? In the guest room." I had been charged with displaying the glass sculpture in the living room, but since its arrival the Monday before the Patty Melt, I hadn't even removed it from its box. "You want some coffee, Ian?"

"Coffee? No. I had mine"—he looked at his watch—"three hours ago." With a delicate twist of the wrist he whipped out a tape measure from somewhere in his pants pocket and strode toward the guest room.

"Wait—," I said, but not before Ian opened the door. He stood in the doorway, staring at the room filled wall-to-wall with boxes and clothes and the pulled-out couch where Giovanni lay sleeping.

"What am I supposed to do with this?"

"I'm sorry. I forgot you were coming, and we have guests."

"What am I supposed to do with this?" He said this louder and shrill enough that Giovanni sat straight up under the sheet like a shirtless haunted-house Dracula.

Ian apparently hadn't seen him sleeping there, because he jumped backward and screamed, high enough to threaten Bandito, who yapped, jabbed and weaved at Ian's wrinkle-free seersuckers. Giovanni got out of bed, confusedly scratching his curly hair.

"What am I supposed to do with this?" screamed Ian.

"I don't know," said Sloane. "What *are* you supposed to do with this?" She said it in a genuine tone—emphasis on the second word, like she honestly had no idea why he, a stranger, would've barged into our apartment with a tape measure.

I caught Giovanni's eye while trying not to laugh and he was trying not to laugh and it was like being nine and in synagogue, where the prohibition against giggles makes stifling them impossible. I snickered into my hand, my mouth twitching, and Giovanni's snorts were escaping out of his nose and Bandito was tap-dancing like he was auditioning for the canine version of *White Nights*. Every time we looked at each other, we lost a little more control. Sloane and Ian stared at each other, trapped in the crossfire of their gazes. Keeping one eye on the dog, Ian finally backed toward the door. Before leaving, he stared at me and said, "I cannot do the job you hired me to do if *this* is the canvas. Think about it."

Giovanni and I collapsed on the floor as soon as he left, clutching our stomachs, and Sloane shook her head with a slight, still-bewildered, smile. "What the fuck was that?"

I wiped my eyes. "My anal interior decorator."

"Oh—*that's* what you were saying." She poured a cup of coffee and handed it to Giovanni, who had collected himself sufficiently to find a chair. He sat, blinking in his boxer shorts, and accepted the cup with a nod. "Yes. That description fits."

"He's one of those fragile geniuses."

"Yeah. Genius. That's exactly what I'd call him," Giovanni said, and we started laughing again. When we stopped, he swallowed a few times. "Do you pay him?"

"Yep."

"I want that gig." He stood up, flounced into the kitchen, opened up the cereal cabinet and screamed, *"What am I supposed to do with this?"* Then he did it with the TV cabinet and in the bathroom and into the coffeemaker. *"What am I supposed to do with this?"* By the time he said it to an unimpressed Bandito, I was collapsed on the floor again.

"Hate to break up the party," Sloane said, "but we should get moving."

I patted my stomach, which was cramped from laughter. "What are you guys doing today?"

"Gelato and *Eyes.*"

"Sounds like a Dali painting." We started laughing again.

"What time are you meeting with clients?"

I checked my calendar. "I'm not. No appointments today. Oh. But I have a meeting with my decorator at nine."

"I think you can assume that's canceled." Giovanni raised one eyebrow, and he and I broke down in giggles again.

We showered and got dressed and put Bandito in a tote bag, which Sloane slung over her shoulder. The four of us subwayed down to Houston Street and walked south for a bit until Sloane pointed to a blue door. "There." She snapped a picture.

"We're doing gelato first?"

"I'm hungry," said Giovanni.

"But it's"—I checked my watch—"ten forty-eight."

"If you break it down," Giovanni said, "sugar, milk, eggs. Perfect breakfast food."

"Like sweet coffee. And eggs," said Sloane.

"Without the coffee," said Giovanni. "Or pancakes."

"Without the flour."

"Enough," I said, pretending to be annoyed when I was really thinking how well Giovanni lightened up Sloane, while our family seemed to do the opposite.

We all ordered the lemon—Sloane said it was their signature

flavor—and watched the guy scoop the gelato, soft and pliable as taffy, into small paper cups before pushing them over the counter. Mine came to a mountainous point, and I stuck my tongue out to lick the peak, which was creamy with a hint of tartness. I ate another bite, spoonless, before bringing it to a small table.

"This is amazing," Giovanni said in an Italian accent.

"That sounded legit."

"It is. He's bona fide Italy-born." Sloane sucked on a lump of gelato in her spoon, eroding it but keeping its humpback whale shape.

"I moved here when I was four—young enough to soak up the surfer dialect from California, but my parents have thick accents, so I just imitate them when the situation requires it."

"Have you been back?"

"A lot. All our family is still there. We've been"—he squinted at Sloane—"four times together?"

"Five," said Sloane. "Three with your parents and at the end of the France trip and then the time we just went to the Mediterranean."

"Right."

"Wow," I spoke through a mouthful of gelato. "You travel a lot."

"We love to travel," he said.

"I can tell by your blog. It makes me want to go places and eat things." The day after we'd eaten at the noodle place, I'd read Sloane's post on it. The photos had that professional look—the glossy wash that magazines had—and what she'd written had renewed my excitement at having eaten there.

"That's the goal." Sloane finished the spoonful.

My phone rang. "It's Mom." Sloane's eyes were flat as I picked up. "Hello?"

"Paige? How did it all go?"

"Fine." In the pause I heard her hunger for information. "We're downtown now."

"Would you guys want to come for lunch maybe today? Or I could meet you?"

I covered the phone and mouthed "Lunch?" Giovanni shifted his eyes to Sloane, who shook her head.

"The thing is, we just ate."

"Oh. That's okay. I get it. You probably want to do young-people things."

"Yeah." As far as I knew, the youth had not cornered the gelato and public art market, but if it made my mom feel less left out, I'd let her think we had staged a revolution to claim it. "I'll call you later, Mom. Okay?"

"Okay. Go . . . have fun."

"Are you okay?"

"Sure! Cherie had asked me to get together anyway, so . . ."

When I hung up, Sloane crumpled her empty plastic bowl and tossed it in the trash can. "Talk about being trapped in an unhealthy marriage."

"Unhealthy, really? They're a team."

"Trust me. It's all a farce."

"How so?"

She tossed the bowl into the garbage can. "It. Just. Is."

I looked at Giovanni. "You're going to like them." He smiled quickly and then focused on smoothing back Bandito's ears.

"You done, Paige?" Sloane's voice was a little icy.

"Just a minute." I concentrated on finishing my gelato, and for a minute, the only sound was my spoon scratching against the bottom of my paper cup.

When I looked up, Sloane was smiling; the ice had melted. "Let's keep moving." She took out her phone and started scrolling through it.

We stepped onto the street, and Giovanni removed Bandito from the bag with one hand. Immediately, he squatted from the effects of the gelato.

"Bandito thought the ice cream was yummy," sang Sloane distractedly, still absorbed by her phone.

"But it didn't sit right in his tummy," Giovanni added, also singing.

They both waited expectantly—for me, I guessed—until Sloane shrugged and grabbed the reins again. "And in the end, things got pretty runny."

"Ten points for the pun, babe—in the end. Nice one," said Giovanni. To me, he said, "Join in, please. Just so we feel less moronic."

I changed the subject as we started walking slowly east. "What time are you guys leaving tomorrow?"

"Whenever," said Sloane. "Are you working?"

"I have a long weekend. No clients." I felt a surprising but unmistakable sharp pang of emptiness in my chest.

"Come with us!" Giovanni bounced up and down right there on the sidewalk.

"Sure," I said.

While Sloane didn't jump for joy, neither did she shudder the way she had when my mom called.

I tried not to sound as enthusiastic as I felt. "I could give you guys a ride out there."

"Whatever you want." Giovanni, who had lapsed back into his accent, was hamming it up with expressive hands. "You drive us, you take the train, we walk. The transport is meaningless. It's being together, the journey, that's"—he kissed the tips of his fingers—"*bellissimo!*"

Sloane and I ignored his performance. I was picturing it: the three of us riding out to the beach in my car, chased by the golden light as we listened to road-trip music. I could finally swing in that hammock, nap in the shade. "I do want to see the house. Maybe just for an overnight, if Dave doesn't feel too abandoned."

Sloane's expression shifted from her default sneer to something more opaque, but I could still read her thought bubble: *Who gives a crap what Dave thinks?*

"Where are we going?" We'd been ambling east for several blocks, and Sloane, who had stopped and pulled out her phone, was looking at the map.

She pocketed her phone. "How about the one in Tompkins Square Park?"

"Fine with me," said Giovanni. "Has Paige seen that one?"

"I haven't seen any of them."

"It's a good starter for you," said Sloane. "It's called *Lentoptical*. It's not supposed to be disturbing at all."

◆

Lentoptical was pleasing: a large, round blue eye with pretty eyelashes and a wide-open lid that made me wonder why the project had gotten such a bad rap.

"I think," said Giovanni, walking around it, "that the name is a play on lenticular printing."

"Which is . . . ?" Sloane said that to him, but to me she said, "It's hard to be a genius. Always having to stop and explain things to the little people."

"It's the technology behind this kind of image. Many different pictures beneath and a layer of grooved layers above it. The image changes depending on where you are."

"Like those stickers we had when we were young. Do you remember those?"

"Those, I remember. There was that one of the guy punching another that said—"

"Kablam," said Sloane, and I stepped to the side. The eye shifted—blue open iris to green narrowed one, then a few more shuffles and it was closed, swollen and puffy and discolored.

I stepped back. "Creepy."

"I love it," said Sloane, snapping pictures with a camera she'd pulled out of the bag. "The power of perspective." When she rested the camera by her side, Giovanni took it from her hands.

"Let me take one," he said, motioning his hands together. "Memorialize the day, which has been as fun as promised, right, Paige?"

"It has. Stand there." I pointed to the right. "So the blue one is our backdrop."

Sloane and I stood, smiling in front of the eye, arms around each other. When Giovanni showed us the digital image, the only thing that stood out was how normal we looked. Just one sister in town to visit another, catching an art exhibit.

chapter thirty-four

WE'D PACKED FOR Quogue the disorganized, drawn-out way. By midafternoon the hallway was lined with the canvas bags of food for our trip, which would be two days max, we'd decided. The plan had been to leave an hour earlier to avoid rush-hour traffic, but Sloane was taking forever to buy cigarettes and Giovanni was having trouble focusing. He was right then using his foot to kick Bandito's mesh carrier soccer-ball style.

"Hey," he said when it landed askew, partially on one of the bags. "Should we summon Percy here, or is it easy to pick him up at his apartment?"

"Oh." I'd forgotten how Percy had initiated the trip. Or maybe I hadn't. Maybe my subconscious had tricked me into *pretending* to forget that I'd be in a car with Percy for a couple of hours so that I'd invite myself along with impunity. But it didn't matter anymore, I reminded myself. Percy had lost his magic as soon as I'd set foot in his apartment. It was all no big deal. No. Big. Deal.

"He's downtown," Giovanni said, trying to be helpful. "Wrong way, right? Past the Long Island Expressway?"

In fact, it would easily add an hour to the trip to schlep downtown and back again, but so what? This trip was obviously not about scheduling. "We can get him." I straightened Bandito's carrier against the wall. "Where's he staying in the Hamptons? With friends?"

"Paige." Giovanni arranged his features in the sternest look

I'd ever seen him command. "You offered your place. Is that a problem?"

"Oh, right. No, of course not. We have three bedrooms. And a pull-out."

Giovanni texted Percy the news that we were almost en route, and I rushed into the bedroom, shutting first that door behind me and then the one to the master bathroom where I sat on the toilet lid, dialing Dave's cell. He didn't pick up, so I called his direct line and asked his secretary to page him in the office.

After about four minutes of silence, he picked up the phone. "Are you okay?" Paging was understood between us to be strictly in case of emergency.

"Fine. So—we're about to leave for the Hamptons."

"Right." When I had broached it with him, Dave had not had a problem with the Hamptons trip. Of course he wished he could go, he'd said. He didn't feel abandoned, he'd said, unless I was planning to stay there forever. Was I? Ha, ha, ha, ha. It was a couple of days; he was pretty sure he could handle it.

I had lost my ability to take anything at face value. Was Dave really okay with the plan or putting on a brave face? Had I cleared the coast so he could have secret meetings with members of the criminal underworld in our living room? The biggest question, though, the hardest to answer, was whether I was tagging along on someone else's vacation because I wanted a beach getaway or just to avoid being home with Dave.

It was crazy to start second-guessing a summer trip to the Hamptons. I was slowly, smoothly, surely going mad, picking at the corners of the yellow wallpaper of my life and peeling it all away.

"And we're going to be driving up with someone."

"Okay."

"Giovanni's childhood friend."

"All right." I hadn't wanted to say his name, and Dave didn't ask it.

"I've met him before—he's nice and kind of young, I guess, but he didn't have a place to stay, so I offered him one of the bedrooms at our house."

"Sounds good."

"You don't care."

"I mean, is he an axe murderer?"

"I don't *think* so."

"So reassuring." He laughed. "Guess we'll find out!"

Driving downtown to Percy's building took about forty minutes. In the garage, I had insisted that Sloane sit up front next to me. She'd mumbled, "Whatever," and looked longingly at Giovanni, but I held firm. We would not be coupling off, with Percy riding shotgun while she and Giovanni drooled all over each other in the backseat. We would not.

Because it took us forty minutes to reach him, Percy was waiting for us outside, leaning against his building, a knapsack slung over one shoulder. Giovanni got out and held open the door rather than sliding behind me in the driver's seat—god forbid he and Sloane couldn't hold hands through the seat gaps, which they had been doing since the garage.

While Percy loaded his bags and settled in, I texted Lucy that I might be coming out that weekend. I had visions of her meeting Sloane and Giovanni, even Percy, but I thought I'd leave things deliberately vague until I knew everyone's plans. When I looked up from my phone, they were all buckled in, watching me.

"Let's go!" Percy was right behind me, which was probably worse than shotgun; I was hyperaware of him, and every time I glanced in the rearview mirror, his piercing blue eyes met mine.

I put the music on shuffle, and when a song from *Graceland* came on—the guitar strumming out the melody of "Under African Skies"—Sloane sat up straight in her seat. "I love this," she breathed.

"You remember it?" I said. "From growing up?"

"Same as you. The backseat of Franklin's Toyota Camry." She started singing along with Linda Ronstadt's harmony. On the second verse, I joined in too.

This is the story of how we begin to remember,
This is the powerful pulsing of love in the vein

The harmonizing had such sheer beauty that accompanying it was enough to make us feel like we could sing. Still, we had more feeling than tone, warbling and wavering loudly on the high notes. When the song ended, I waited for a smartass comment from someone, but none came.

"This," said Giovanni, "is a great album."

"Every song is a masterpiece," Sloane agreed. "Except 'Homeless.'"

"But every album needs a 'Homeless,'" said Percy. "A decent B-side song to let shine the genius of the 'Myth of Fingerprints.'"

"Do you have the whole thing on here?" Sloane scrolled through my music. "Yesss!" She pressed the screen and leaned back in her seat.

Three songs in, we were all four shouting the whoops of "I Know What I Know" when Sloane stopped abruptly. "Can I smoke in here?"

"No," I said. "Do you need to because of the music?" It might bother her, I realized, given that I remembered it as the sound track of our childhood.

"Paul Simon?" she said. "No, it just seems like from someone else's life."

It didn't to me. I could visualize it: sitting in the backseat of my dad's sedan, right in the spot where Percy was now, Paul Simon singing about poor boys and pilgrims going to Graceland, my head leaned as far back as it could go so I could stare straight up and out the rear window. Above me would be the thicket of bare tree branches reaching across the yellowing evening sky. To my right would be Sloane, zipped into a brown-and-orange puffy coat, her knees pressing through holes in her jeans, her Keds inked with graffiti and pressed flat against the back of my mom's seat.

A whoosh of air drowned out "Gumboots." Next to me, Sloane had opened the window on the highway, forcing her lit cigarette out into the gusts.

"Sloane!"

"I *need* to because I'm addicted. Don't mess with addiction, Paige. Seriously." But after three drags, she let the cigarette slip out of her fingers. It flew away and upward as if yanked by a string. Sloane rolled up the window, sealing us back in. Then she turned to me and sang, "Don't want to end up a cartoon in a cartoon graveyard." Still to the melody, she pointed to the dash-board and sang, "Mr. Bonedigger, bonedigger—you're almost out of gas, you are."

When we pulled up to the gas station, Giovanni announced he had to pee.

"Traveling with you is like traveling with a toddler," said Percy.

Giovanni didn't argue. Instead, he rubbed his stomach in a circular motion and announced, "It needs food."

✦

"Fat Charlie, the Archangel, files for divorce," Giovanni mused while we sat at our table in McDonald's, yellow wrappers crumbled in front of us.

"You're still on the Paul Simon?" I said.

"It sticks in your head. Who is this Fat Charlie, the archangel? Paul Simon always makes me want to ask, *What do the words mean?* What does it mean? What does it mean?" He pointed at me.

"I don't know."

"Obviously not. If Fat Charlie, the archangel, had had as good a marriage counselor as our own Paige Reinhardt, he wouldn't be filing for divorce, right?"

"Obviously."

"We didn't listen to this Paul Simon in high school," Giovanni said. "We listened to Slayer, right, Perce?"

Percy, expressionless, lifted his hand in the death-metal devil horns gesture, index and pinky finger up.

Giovanni devil-horned him back. "We just sat in the basement blaring loud music, smoking pot, talking about how we were going to get out of Ohio, and look at us, we did it."

"Please," Sloane said. "You were all Four-H club and yearbook and stuff."

"He was," said Percy, "all of those things, although there was a brief period with heavy metal music and a rattail."

"That wasn't a rattail," said Giovanni. "That was a Mohawk."

"Whatever," said Percy. "It was an embarrassment."

"What about his girlfriends?" Sloane asked.

"I didn't have any girlfriends," Giovanni said. "I never met a woman until I met you."

Percy smirked. "There was the crush on Mrs. Stetler. Remember, Giovanni? She was the Four-H adviser and she smelled, as Giovanni said, like lilacs in bloom."

"She was a goddess," Giovanni said, "and her husband did not appreciate her. At all."

"Then there was Miriam. He used to watch her at cheerleading practice."

"A lovely person," said Giovanni. "Although she really, as it turns out, was only interested in what I could do for her as the yearbook editor." We looked at him curiously. "She wanted the immortality only I could promise. Pictures in the yearbook. A lot of them."

"And then Valerie, your prom date."

"Right. Valerie. Enough said." They exchanged a loaded look, and Sloane and I glanced at each other wide-eyed.

"You're like brothers."

"We are."

I tried to soak it up, the bond between them, and respect it, rather than allow it to be a referendum on Sloane and me. Maybe we could build up to this; I was starting to think it was possible.

Giovanni pointed to me. "Paige. Share one of yours."

"My what?"

"Childhood stories."

I intercepted Giovanni's glance at Percy because Percy was staring down at his soda lid. "Well," I said, pointing my chin at Sloane, "apparently this one used to dress me up like Nana the sheepdog."

"From *Peter Pan*?" Percy asked.

"Yep," I said. "Word on the street is that young Sloane had her own fringe festival."

"We did. Together." Sloane looked at me. "You don't remember that either?"

"Wasn't I, like, three?"

"That's the whole point of *Peter Pan* anyway, right?" Percy said. "The Lost Boys and the haze of forgotten childhood."

"I like that." Sloane brightened as she slurped her soda. "Paige, you'd make a perfect Lost Boy, given your lack of recall."

"Are you kidding me?" My voice had come out heated, so I lowered it. "First of all, the Lost Boys fell out of their prams and went missing from their families. If anyone's a Lost Boy, you, Sloane, are the Lost Boy. I'm the perfect Nana, when you think about it, stuck at home with Mr. and Mrs. Darling, barking to herself."

"I don't remember the falling-out-of-their-prams part," Percy said.

"It's in the book. But they all grew up eventually. One became a judge."

"Oh," Percy said. "I didn't read the book. My analysis was based on the movie *Hook*, and I got the distinct impression that there was some forgotten, hazy childhood stuff going on with Peter Pan and the woman from *Downton Abbey*. You know, like she remembered him, but she didn't."

"Right," I said. "You're absolutely right. We should be looking to *Hook* for themes and deeper meaning rather than the book."

"I didn't know you did that." Giovanni smiled at Sloane. "Were you Peter Pan?"

"I wasn't really anyone, but I tended to tell stories in defense of Captain Hook."

"Of course you did," I said.

Sloane pulled her straw in and out of the plastic top and then sipped. "I can tell how much this means to you, Paige, so I'm promising you right here and now—when we do the fringe festival this year, you can be Nana."

"Well, thank god." I laughed. I hadn't even known she could be funny like that.

"It must be pointed out, Paige," Giovanni said, "that if you don't remember the *Peter Pan* plays, that doesn't technically count as a story from your childhood. You still have to tell us one."

"Okay." I pointed at him. "Special for you, a real unknown story from my childhood: our grandfather."

"What about him?" Sloane said.

"Mom's dad. He's like He Who Must Not Be Named."

"That's technically not a story," Sloane said. "You really do need to work on your narrative form."

"Okay, fine. Once upon a time when I was growing up, my parents never mentioned or divulged the name of my maternal grandfather. It remains a mystery to this day. The end."

"Maybe," Giovanni said, lowering his voice, and we all ducked our heads in, "you're direct descendants of Voldemort."

"I would almost believe it at this point."

"Russell Cohen." Sloane chewed the end of her straw as she spoke.

"I guess that's as likely as anything else."

"No, that was his name. Russell Cohen."

"How do you know?"

"Basic research. It wasn't that hard."

"Are you kidding me?"

She held up her hand, palm up, fingers spread like she couldn't believe I was asking. "Obviously you've never really tried to find out."

"I have. I've asked several times. I kept getting stonewalled."

"Relying on someone else to hand you the information is the same as giving up." She stared me down so intensely that Giovanni and Percy swiveled their heads away from us in reaction, each in the opposite direction. "That's not the way to learn anything. You always have to get it yourself."

◆

When we got back into the car, the summer sun was low and burning, its light so strong as to appear almost solid across the road and treetops. In the front seat, Sloane put "Crazy Love, Vol. II" on repeat, and Giovanni made up silly words about poor Fat Charlie coming to counsel with me, and opting against filing for divorce.

We listened to *Graceland* the whole way up, on a loop, the sun setting golden all around us, the energy infused with nostalgia and excitement. It doesn't happen a lot—an anticipated memory playing out just as beautifully as you've visualized it, but when it does, you just have to soak it up.

chapter thirty-five

WE PULLED UP to the house at dusk. Above the sound of the tires crunching over the gravel driveway, Giovanni read loudly from his phone, in the Italian accent that I was realizing he did whenever he felt like a tourist. "Quogue is one of the western-most beach towns in the Hamptons, known for being family oriented and on the sleepy side of things." He looked up and, still in accent, asked, "Where is the disco mirror, Paige? Where are the T-shirt guns? I was promised T-shirt guns!"

We got out of the car and stood on the front lawn for a moment, stretching our legs before grabbing the bags out of the trunk. It felt cooler out there in all the leafiness, and the house did appear, as I'd hoped, like a small fairy-tale cottage: sloped triangular roof, strong trees in the front and that hammock between them.

Giovanni spun around in circles, his arm outstretched. "The beach is that way?" He pointed away from the house and sniffed the air.

"I don't know," I said. "It's about a mile. There's a small pool in back, though."

"Let's go now," he said. "We missed sunset, but we can walk in the water."

"Oooh." Sloane sounded freakishly girlish. She walked up behind him and wrapped her arms around his waist, pushing her face into his back. "Let's."

"The walk will be really dark," I said.

"How much trouble can we get into?" Giovanni said. "It's a sleepy family town."

The two of them set off with Bandito's bag slung over their shoulders, amid Giovanni's warnings that the surf made him "romantic" and we shouldn't wait up.

Percy and I looked at each other. "I know beggars can't be choosers," he said, "but I'm really, really hopeful that I can sleep in the room right next door to theirs."

"I might make them sleep outside next to a cold-water hose."

We walked up the flat stone path to enter the house and went about turning on the lights inside, checking it out. Percy's voice came from the kitchen. "Uh-oh."

"What?" I poked my head in.

He pointed to a straw gift basket on the kitchen counter. There was a paper card folded in front of it: *Welcome from Bob and Michael McCan, owners of Blossom Cottage.* Pressed into the gift straw were decayed bananas, now completely black, and an oozing pear. Stacked next to them were wrapped crackers that were probably fine, cheese wrapped in red wax that probably wasn't and, in the middle, a bottle of wine.

"When did Bob and Michael McCan leave this, you think?"

"Memorial Day, probably."

We found a plastic bag under the sink and emptied everything except for the wine and crackers into it, after which we double-tied the handles. Percy volunteered to take it to the outside trash can while I searched the house for anything else that might have spoiled.

The upstairs really should have been two rooms—a master and a spare—but the McCans had divided the spare into two mirror-image cubbies with just enough room for a full bed crammed against the wall and a dresser each. They had painted one room sea green and the other light blue. Across the hall were a tiny beige bathroom and the master suite.

I went back downstairs to find Percy at the kitchen sink, pumping hand soap into his palm. "Slugs," he said.

"Thanks and sorry. I checked out the bedroom situation."

"Oh?"

"A master for the lovebirds and then two identical rooms—one green and one blue. Which do you want?"

"The better one."

"They're identical."

"I don't care. You assign them—it's your house."

"I'm trying to be a good host. You choose."

"What shade of green?"

"Like the first grass of spring."

He whistled. "Nice. What color blue?"

"Palest wash of robin's egg."

"You speak some real Pantone poetry."

"Why don't you take green? It's slightly closer to the bathroom." I sat on one of the kitchen stools and regarded the bottle of wine standing forthright on the kitchen counter. I wanted to sit out on that hammock and drink wine until I was as mellow and relaxed as someone should be in a beach town in summer. I held up the bottle to Percy. "I should throw this out, shouldn't I? Because of Sloane."

"I'm sure it's okay. She works around wine."

"Yeah, but here, in New York, with all the reminders of her childhood . . . might be too much."

Percy smiled—*I see where this is going.* "We could hide it in the trunk of your car."

"Right."

"Or we could bury it in the yard. Pour it into the sink?"

"Or we could drink it."

"Drink it?" He mimed surprise. "We'd have to do it quickly, though."

"So that there'd be no trace of it when they get back."

We pulled open the kitchen drawers in a rush, looking for a corkscrew, but came up empty. "Come on," I said. "They have *this*"—I held up what looked to be a rubber diaphragm with perforated holes—"but not anything for wine. I mean, what is this for anyway?"

Percy regarded it. "Maybe it's an oven mitt?"

"An oven mitt?" I pulled out an actual cloth oversized hand with a rooster print. "This is what an oven mitt looks like, Percy." He held up a corncob holder with a tiny fake ear of corn on it. "And *that's* a corncob holder. You, sir, are no help. No help at all."

I continued to open and shut drawers. I glanced up, about to make a caustic comment about his lack of assistance, when I saw him sticking the corncob holder into the top of the wine bottle. "It's all right." He braced the bottle against his thigh—those jeans again—and after a few twists, his biceps moving under his T-shirt, pulled out the cork. "No apology necessary."

We decided against glasses and walked out shoeless to the hammock. The sky was completely dark when we eased into the rope seat, swinging gently, our heads at opposite ends of the hammock.

"So that was Dave running in the park that day, right?" Percy handed me the bottle, and I took the first swig.

"Yep."

"Is that your thing? Running together?" I handed the bottle back to him.

"Not at all. I was freaking out, couldn't you tell?"

"You have a bit of a poker face." He swigged from the bottle and then passed it back. "But speaking of Dave, I have some updates on your case."

He had figured out, he said, a possible meaning for the notes from Hedda's office. Stuben was the head of the corporate department—something I should have remembered—and if the random letters were initials, which Percy thought they were, this could be a possible translation:

June 30, (met with) AP (Annie Poleci) about DT (Dave Turner) and NS? (three possible combinations—Noah Styles/ Nathan Shreeky/Nick Sebly) *Hour meeting, 3 x. notified corp. dept. (phone), Stuben (phone). Implement handbook policy.* I took a sip, holding the wine in my mouth and letting it sit for a while as I listened.

"Get it?" Percy said. "She's memorializing a meeting. Someone named Annie Poleci was saying that Dave and this other guy did something, so she took the steps in the handbook and notified his department heads, et cetera."

I swallowed. "How do you know Annie Poleci is AP?"

"Believe it or not, she's the only person at the firm with those initials. She's a junior associate in the corporate group, just started last fall."

"That's Dave's department."

"I know. She and I are now Facebook friends. And in the same singles book club."

I tilted the wine bottle to my lips for a long swallow and wiped my mouth with the back of my wrist. "That's a weird coincidence."

"Not a coincidence. I friended her as part of this. Everything's sort of falling into place. The book club meets every two months. You know when the next meeting is?"

I shook my head. "Two months from now."

"Next Monday. Near Washington Square Park."

"How—"

"Once I got the name of the host, it was easy to get her address through the DMV. It never works out this easily, Paige—everything rolling along without need for a plan B."

I should've asked some questions then, but the wine was starting to blur the edges of our conversation. "Let's talk about something hammock-y."

"What are some hammock-y topics?"

Percy's feet were sprawled by my elbows. "Like your crooked toenails."

He glanced at them. "What?"

"You should file them. It's sandal season."

"I don't wear sandals."

"Why do you always wear jeans in summer? Isn't it too hot?"

"Um."

"How many pairs of jeans do you have?"

He flared his nostrils. "Three? This is hammock-y conversation? My wardrobe?"

"Yes." I passed him the wine and watched him tilt it back. "And another bit of hammock-y conversation. How come you live like a Calvin Klein ad from the nineties?"

He cough-choked, tipped the bottle back over. "Uh." He pressed his temple.

"You have no furniture. Everything's black and white and downtown and cool. Doesn't it turn off the ladies?"

"The ladies, they seem okay with it."

"Do you play the field, Percy?"

"Do I—what—I'm sorry?"

"That's a yes."

He smiled, shook his head.

"And you're like a German design student with no furniture." He started to laugh, and I laughed too. "Minimalism everywhere except in romantic partners. What's with the no furniture?"

"I'm sure I'm supposed to be insulted, but I'm a little too confused."

"I just think people who live in a place for four years should have acquired some stuff."

"I don't blame you for my confusion. You're being very clear, and I'm sure there's an excellent reason why my lack of furniture is a personal affront. Are you maybe a hoarder?" He placed an index finger on his chin. "Or part of the carpenter's lobby? Business has been troublingly slow lately?"

"I just think it's weird."

"Jeez. Hammock-y talk is brutal."

"I should use it at work. How funny would that be? If I cut through the bull, just told people what I was thinking." I used my soothing nonjudgmental therapist voice. *"Mr. Jennings, it's clear to everyone here that the problem with the marriage is that* you're *an* asshole." I laughed. "I don't think I'd have many clients left."

"You'd probably wind up with a syndicated radio show."

"Maybe. So seriously, though, why have you collected so few grown-up things? Are you, like, twelve?"

"Yes, Paige. I'm twelve. I'm glad it's out, actually. It's less awkward to ask you for a field trip permission slip, which obviously I'll need."

"I knew it." I swigged. "All the good ones are underage."

Percy didn't respond, and maybe I should have felt more embarrassed, but I was emboldened by the wine and the darkness, which played with Percy's features so they morphed and faded into an unfamiliar, nighttime version of his face. What didn't shift with the moment was the sensory data—his warm leg against mine, the sound of the dry tone of his voice, the featherlight touch of his fingers brushing against mine as he reached for the wine.

"So how old are you?" I said.

"Thirty-one. To answer your question about why I live like a loser, I guess I have odd hours. I spend a lot of time at the office."

"That's like saying you don't wash your clothes because you go to church."

"I don't think it is, actually." Percy reclined his head against the back of the hammock, and his legs pushed a little into mine.

"No! No sleep!"

"All right, all right." He sat back up. "I'm awake, see? Are you keeping me off balance on purpose? Mrs. Paige Turner." He emphasized the "Mrs." in a way that sobered me somewhat.

"I don't go by that name. That's Dave's." I leaned back and closed my eyes. "Let's not talk about *that* whole drama."

He pushed me with his foot. "No sleeping."

"Okay." I sat back up.

"So no hammock-y talk. No talking about that whole drama. What's left?"

"Hmm," I said. "I'll tell you something that no one knows, because you opened up to me about your age and your clothes and all."

He laughed in a one-syllable punch: "Ha."

"I'm reading my mother's journals."

"And no one knows that, including your mother?"

"It's awful, right?"

Percy sprang off the hammock quickly, wine bottle in hand. "Where are you going? Have I ruined the hammock moment?"

"Not at all." He walked deliberately toward the tree, heel-toe, heel-toe. "Foot cramp." Then he sat back down in the middle, arms outstretched on the sides, so our bodies made a T, his body the base and mine the top. "Tell me."

I told him—how I'd found the notebooks. How she seemed like a different person in writing and how I felt annoyed and fascinated to learn how much was going on under the surface that she hadn't shared with me.

"Yeah," he said. "But isn't she entitled to not share that with anyone?"

I thought for a second. "In theory. But I did so much based on how I thought she felt. That's why I think it bothers me."

"Like what did you do?"

I shrugged. "We didn't discuss Sloane—ever—so I trained myself not to think about her. I didn't let myself because I thought it would be too painful for everyone. Meanwhile, my mom was already tortured by the whole thing, which makes a lot more sense when I think about it. Pass the bottle, please." He handed me the bottle, and I drank a little more. "Be straight with me, Percy, as I have been with you about your issues."

"I'm sorry. How have you been straight with—"

"The toenails and the—"

"Oh, right. The whole German design student thing, yes. Okay. I wear jeans because I used to wear shorts in the summer, but a client told me I looked like a British schoolboy."

"Really?"

"Really. She called them short pants, which sort of undermined my professionalism. I seem to be able to get away with jeans. At least I could until now."

"No, you do fine by those jeans." We swung in silence for a bit. "I'm a horrible, disloyal person, right?"

"I'd say more full of zesty opinions. But, ah, you mean about the journals. There's something very funny about asking for a blessing from a private investigator. I'm professionally obligated to tell you to go after the knowledge."

"I didn't know that."

"Hell, yeah. Run toward the ignorance rather than run from it. Attack the facts. I think Sloane has this one right—both for the stuff with Dave and your mom's journals."

"You know, what we do is not so different."

"Who said it was?"

"I thought it was. Because we have different endgames."

"What's your endgame?"

"Resolution and harmony, while yours is confirmation of wrongdoing. But it's not. We're really both trying to help people find what's true."

"What's true," said Percy.

"Right," I said, hoping I wasn't slurring. "That's exactly right."

"No, I meant what is true? As in—how do you even know what true is? I mean there are facts, and then there's perception."

"Whoa." His words swam before me, dipped around my brain, wiggled away. "By that logic, you might be totally incorrect about what your father thinks of you."

"I'm not, though."

"No, you have perception, not truth. You can't separate how much of his sending you newspaper clippings is disappointment and how much is, say, trying to connect by keeping tabs on your old friends."

"Please."

"Unless you've asked him outright."

"I haven't. And as logical as your point is, I know you're wrong. There's a beef."

"A beef."

"A long line of conflict between my father and my aunt. According to my father, I chose her when I chose being a detective. It wasn't personal to me, but it was to him. I wasn't trying to choose her; I was trying to do what he'd always told me to do—make a living doing something interesting. See? There's a price. There's always a price to doing something you want to do. Even if you don't realize it, anytime you go after something you want, you end up at least hurting someone else's feelings. It's a given."

"What was the beef about?"

"Don't know. Don't want to know." We swung in the hammock, watching our feet. "So, yes, read the journals. No judgment here. Still, I acknowledge the weirdness of accessing your mother's innermost thoughts when you were—how old?"

"Twelve, just like you are now."

I had shifted at some point in the conversation, I wasn't sure when, and we sat next to each other in the middle of the hammock like it was a big giant swing, our feet on the ground, pushing us off, our shoulders almost touching. He pressed his feet to the ground before pushing us off again. "What were you like as a twelve-year-old?"

"Nerdy and oblivious. What were you like?"

"Really into baseball. Nerdy and oblivious, huh? Is that what the journals say?"

"About me?" I considered. "She doesn't say anything."

"Oh. Maybe *that's* why you're annoyed." His voice shifted, so I turned to the left to look. He'd leaned his head back, his eyes closed.

"I think it's better your way, Percy."

"Which way?"

"To know what messed you up, like you and your dad's disapproval."

"Yeah. It's a real luxury."

"It must have been so jarring to me as a kid, how Sloane just disappeared. I don't remember it that way at all, though. I remember it like a peace."

"Maybe it was a bit of a peace." His voice was sleepy.

"All my friends have kids. I haven't wanted them, and not that there's anything wrong with not wanting kids, but I think my whole personality—my whole life as I know it—has been formed by things I've never questioned."

"How old are you?"

"Thirty-two."

"You have a bright future ahead of you, Paige. Plenty of time to identify what's messing you up."

"Let's hope."

After a moment of silence, his eyes flew open. "No sleeping, sorry. Forgot the rules."

"It's okay." His eyes closed again, and I leaned back too and closed mine.

"That was a cool trick," I said. "With the corncob holder."

"Mmm," he said, and mumbled something that sounded like *I've got moves*.

"I'll go get the rooms ready," I said. "I should."

"Who needs rooms?" he responded. "Give the lovebirds the whole house."

"What do you think *they're* doing?"

"Heh, heh, heh," he said, with more space between each syllable.

I was drifting off to sleep with predream thoughts, when I heard thunder crack and felt the hammock buckle under me and arms around my shoulders.

Percy had pushed me over to the side; his face was inches away from mine. "A branch fell." His eyes were a little wild, and indeed, there was a large jagged tree branch piercing through one of the holes in the hammock, right where we had been sitting.

It felt inevitable to have no space between us. Little shivers of recognition prickled up from my toes at the atmospheric pull, crackling and alive. It was the moment right before a first kiss, when someone new, a former stranger, turns into someone known. We'd been building to this, probably for weeks, and he must have thought the same, because we both jumped back and stood up.

"You can have any room you want," I said. "The blue, the green or even the master," and then before he could respond, I blindly ran into the house and up to the first room. Only after I'd shut and locked the door did I realize I was in the green one I'd promised to him and my bag was still downstairs. I lay on the bed with all my clothes on, my heart pounding hard enough that I could see my chest jump with every beat.

I heard the back door close, the clank of the trash lid and then, about ten minutes later, the creaks of the stairs and Percy's footsteps pause at the top. When he entered the blue room, the walls were thin enough that I heard the groan of his mattress as he reclined on it.

I pictured him in there, staring up at the ceiling fan just as I was, hands folded across his chest. I imagined, as if in a movie, donning a gauzy white nightgown, knocking on the door softly, turning the knob and slipping inside. But it wasn't a movie, so I lay there in my shorts and T-shirt and, instead of counting sheep, enumerated the reasons why my temptation had nothing to do with Percy Stahl:

I was confused. About Dave's secrets and my family's secrets.

I was, to be honest, a little tipsy.

I was far from home.

Percy wasn't the main event; he was a mirage, a classic textbook distraction from the tumult of the summer. I was just grateful that nothing more had happened.

chapter thirty-six

NO ONE HAD thought to turn on the air-conditioning, and the green bedroom was hot, stuffy and bright when I woke up on top of the covers, in my clothes. First thing, I called Dave and got his voice mail. "The house is great." I tried to sound casual. "But it's weird without you. See you tonight."

I opened the door to the hall slowly just in case Percy was lying in wait, curled up on the floor outside my room. He wasn't. The doors to all the bedrooms were swung open and filled with sunshine, the beds made as if no one had slept there.

Under the hot spray of the shower, my brain lingered on the glow of that instant immediately after the cracked tree branch. I cooled the spray, dousing the thoughts in ice-cold water until they calcified into guilt. I'd been about to kiss someone not my husband, and now I was replaying it for kicks? I barely recognized myself. I stood under the cold water long after the shampoo was out of my hair and its sharp grapefruit scent was gone.

Downstairs, the kitchen was neat as a pin. Barefoot, I walked outside, hopping down the warmed stone path until I saw Sloane and Giovanni in the hammock, cuddled up against each other. I turned around to go back in the house just as Giovanni yelled, "Sleeping Beauty!"

"Hi."

"It's eleven thirty!" Sloane sat up on her elbows. "People in offices across the land are about to break for lunch."

"Some people somewhere are already on their commute home," Giovanni added.

I walked closer. Their feet were intertwined, making a V formation with Bandito sleeping between them. I was surprised he was big enough to not fall through the hammock gaps. "Are you hungry?"

"I'm all right. Be careful." I pointed up. "A branch broke off last night." Their eyes lifted up lazily, in unison, but they didn't move.

"The beach is wonderful," said Giovanni. "We were there until midnight and were the only ones. Quogue is . . . We need something to rhyme with Quogue. Quogue is grand."

"We're going back there today," Sloane said.

"Seriously, you guys. Move. A branch broke off when Percy and I were out here."

"I'll take my chances," Sloane said.

"Have you guys seen Percy?"

"Selena called. She beckoned and he left to go meet her."

"Who's Selena?"

"One of his . . . people," Giovanni said. "Percy always has a lot of people. And they're always female people. And they're always, like—what's the word?"

"Needy?" I said.

"No, no." Giovanni scratched his head. "When you're a model, but more. Not just a mere model, a . . . ."

"Supermodel!" said Sloane.

"Yes! Supermodel," said Giovanni. "They're all supermodels." My throat closed up a little at that. "Is he coming back?"

"No. He's out for the weekend."

They were annoying me, both of them. "I need to go," I said. Sloane sat up, perturbed. "Back to the city. Today. You can stay here."

"No." Giovanni smiled his sunny smile. "The city is grand as well. We'll go back with you."

I was walking through the kitchen when I saw the note folded on the toaster.

Paige,

Thanks for letting me stay. Someone from my office will be in touch next week with work updates.

P

Someone will be in touch? It was a good-bye note, and I read it with relief and crumpled it, tossing it in the trash. Home. I just wanted to be home. I wanted to bury my head in Dave's shoulder and smell the fresh laundered smell of his shirts and forget that I'd ever met any other human being.

"We've spent more time cleaning and neatening than being here." I wasn't sure how long Sloane had been in the doorway.

"Like I said, you can stay."

"I didn't mean that, but—why the sudden move to leave? Is it coming from Dave?" Her tone was accusatory.

"No, me. I'm not some rag doll. I miss him. And some clients really need to meet tomorrow." Actually, I had been the one to e-mail the Jacobys, but Sloane didn't need that information.

"Oh my god. You are too much."

"What's that mean?"

"Nothing." Sloane met my eyes. "I promise not to say I told you so whenever we find out about the bad shit he's involved in."

"You sound like you *want* him to be involved in bad shit."

"It's not about what *I* want."

"Exactly. And if I think about what *I* really want"—I stabbed my finger against my chest so hard, the knuckle buckled—"maybe I shouldn't be looking so hard for something that will wreck my marriage."

"That sentence," she said, "had too many words. Like you're trying to convince yourself of something."

Glib. It irritated me that she could be that way about my marriage. I turned away and picked up the tote bag that was on the counter. *Glib, glib, glib.* I didn't say it, though. What was the point of fighting with Sloane?

She stood there for a second. "We're ready to leave whenever you are."

◆

On the drive home, Giovanni sat in front, which the two of them had probably orchestrated. He tried to keep up a friendly banter about various things none of us cared about—surfing, the Mets, which he insisted on calling the New York Mets—but eventually he gave up, turned on the radio and for the rest of the trip sang the wrong words to pop songs under his breath.

As soon as we parked, Sloane mumbled something about going to a Szechuan restaurant in Flushing and did I want to come. They looked relieved when I demurred, and vanished almost immediately after leaving me with Bandito.

I turned my key in the lock at five o'clock, assuming I'd have the place to myself for several hours. But Dave was already home, sitting on the couch, legs up and crossed at the ankle. I immediately wondered what had happened this time.

"You're back!" He uncrossed his ankles and bounded up.

"What is this?" I asked.

At the same time he said, "You have the dog?"

My voice had more edge, so he yielded to me. "Why are you home?" I tried not to sound as accusatory.

"I missed you." He gently eased Bandito's carrier off my shoulder and unzipped it. The dog hopped out and promptly curled up on the rug. "You don't look happy about that."

It was a wonderful thought—that for the past two hours he and I had been making our way back home toward each other with the exact same purpose and now, after weeks of disruption and guests, we were finally alone together. This was the moment when we could put an end to the madness. We could erase all the confusion of the past few weeks.

I probably should have swallowed that flash of anger I felt—a snap so crisp I could almost hear it, like that branch breaking off the tree. "Am I supposed to infer that all these days when you've been working so hard, you haven't missed me?"

He got that expression on his face indicating he was riding out a tidal wave in an inner tube. "No, you're supposed to infer that on those days I had a mountain of work that I couldn't put down."

"That's so helpful, Dave. Telling me what I'm supposed to infer. How on earth would I use my brain if I didn't have you to direct me?"

"You want me to go back to work right now?"

"Of course not."

"You want me to stop meeting my obligations so I can come home at four every day?"

"No. I'm not usually even home at four."

"I don't get why you're mad."

"I want you to stop lying." I was sure my face appeared as startled as his did because I couldn't believe it was out there—not a question, an accusation.

"Paige." He stepped closer, hands up in surrender mode. "Still?" I nodded. "I've told you everything I know. What's the problem here?"

"I don't know."

"Why are you so stuck on thinking that—out of nowhere—I'd start lying to you?"

"Not out of nowhere."

"I told you I'd never do it again and I haven't. The worst thing about this hasn't even been the suspension. It's been finding out what you think I'm capable of, like I'm this amoral hulk of ambition. Or, maybe worse, this pathetic little lamb."

"Maybe we should go talk to someone."

"What, like a therapist?" I was offended by his incredulity. "We don't need that, Paige. You need to open your eyes."

"I'm trying."

"Think about the past few weeks. Sloane appearing, staying with us. Meeting this Giovanni. Your parents acting insane. Your having more free time than usual. I shouldn't have to tell you this: you always get a little whacked-out when you don't work enough."

That list doesn't even count my mother's journals, I thought. *That's not even factoring in Percy. And Selena the beckoning supermodel.*

"You look like you're about to cry." Dave spoke in a kinder tone. "Do you have any cash?" Jarred, I rolled my eyes and reached for my wallet. "I'm running down to the newsstand to buy you your magazines—you know, *Oh My God That Happened!* and *Buy This Dress Now* and *Famous People Looking Like Crap?*"

"That's not what they're called."

"They might as well be." He touched the sides of my weak smile with his thumb and forefinger and made his voice campy, dramatic with schmaltz. "Love means sometimes I know what you need better than you know yourself."

♦

I read about a Disney star's rehab stint for "exhaustion," a movie star's inability to lose the baby weight and a married singer's rumored affair with a stripper. I had all but forgotten about the tension between us when Dave got into bed. "Do you feel better?"

"Much." I switched off the light, reached out and circled my hand around Dave's bicep. I didn't imagine Dave was Percy or anything, but I could still hear his voice golden in the darkness and feel the sway of the hammock. I drove him from my mind as I responded to Dave's kiss, my mouth opening to the warmth of his like we were both reclaiming our apartment, each other, our lives.

chapter thirty-seven

WHEN I WOKE up, Dave was standing over me. I nudged my-self upright, and he ran a finger along the length of my hair, tugging at the ends. "I think your clique is waiting for you."

"My clique?"

"You know, those strange bloggers overtaking our apart-ment?"

"Gawd. They're overtaking things."

"You know what they say about fish and houseguests smell-ing after three days."

"Tell them I'm still sleeping. I need a break from hearing about which corner of the city they're going to tramp around. Find the spiciest little corner of dirty food and—" I mimed tak-ing a snapshot.

Dave laughed, even though we both knew I was being unfair. The one thing about this summer that had been beyond re-proach was the gusto with which I'd eaten: noodles, breakfast gelato, more Hershey's Kisses than I could count. The snugness of my clothes seemed inevitable. One of those five-day juice cleanses my mom did—that's what I needed. I would start the second we were able to ditch our houseguests. Family boat day—bigger than Christmas, the way my mom had been yammering on about it—was in two days. I could get through that and then show them the door, gulp the juice, emerge from it all detoxified.

"Don't you need to get ready?"

I lay back down. "First clients aren't until ten."

"Nice work if you can get it. I'll go be your hatchet man." He leaned down to kiss me—a real kiss, not a peck—and closed the door behind him. I heard low voices, and then the front door shut.

I lay immobilized until I heard the door close a second time. I forced myself to stay in bed for another twenty minutes just to be safe, keeping silent even when my mom called. I hadn't talked to her in a few days, but I would see her tomorrow, I reasoned, and I wouldn't know what to say if I picked up anyway.

◆

When I opened the door to my bedroom, it was after nine. There was a note in the front hallway and next to it, Bandito was curled up on his dog bed. He lifted his head and stared at me mournfully.

"Are you really that sad, or is it just your face?" I asked this out loud and promptly felt crazy. Bandito didn't answer, but he did follow me and cocked his head when I read the note to him.

Hey,

Went to the Cloisters as planned. Call if you can come—it's actually pretty easy to get there. After that, off to Flushing.

—S and G
P.S. Don't worry about Bandito the Burrito. He can take care of himself. We'll clean the pads when we get back.

It was friendly, sure, but come on. *I have a job, people.*

"Bandito?" He looked up. "Can you take care of yourself as promised?"

He wagged his tail, and together we went to the laundry room where Bandito had already left a little lump of a present. I flushed it down the toilet with him at my heels.

"I think they oversold your self-sufficiency, Bandito." He looked at me. "But talking to you does feel normal."

Bandito licked his leg, no argument. He followed me around the apartment, sitting on the bath mat and licking the floor when I showered, waiting patiently by my closet as I got dressed and coming expectantly with me to the door.

"You're a fair-weather friend, Bandito. I don't recall getting this much attention when anyone else is home."

He stared at me, did a little tap-dance.

"Okay, fine." I snapped on his harness and leash, but once we got outside into the sun, Bandito stopped cold. He wasn't such a good walker, it turned out, so I carried him most of the way to my office.

"Oh." Helene Jacoby stopped halfway through the door. "A dog."

Bandito had curled up under the desk, asleep.

"Who's this?" Scott approached him and, crouching, leaned forward with his hand out. He made a gentle tsking noise, and when Bandito raised his head and licked Scott's hand, Scott scratched between his ears. "I love dogs."

Bandito followed Scott over to his chair and curled up underneath it. Helene gave a tiny, uncomfortable smile. Of course she was uncomfortable. After my impulse that weekend to mash my face against Percy Stahl's, I'd had a taste of what it felt like to fail your own standards, to know that deep down you were as weak as the next fool. I pushed this out of my mind. "Who wants to start telling me about the journals?"

"I will," said Scott.

"Okay." I braced myself for an explanation of how the idea wouldn't work and the trust between them was too damaged for him to follow the journaling exercise through.

"The thing is," said Scott, "we didn't read them to each other."

"But you wrote them?"

"Three."

"I wrote four," said Helene.

"We thought we could each pick one and read it to each other in here," said Scott, "as long as we don't have to reflect afterward." Was that a shadow of a grin?

"I promise, no reflection. Go ahead."

With one hand stretched under the chair on Bandito, Scott began to read: *"Delmarva Peninsula."*

Before he could get any further, Helene started to laugh, a real throw-her-head-back, belly kind of laugh, and Scott chuckled with her. "I still think they should have gone with WareLandIa."

"What's Delmarva?" I said.

"It's where Delaware, Maryland and Virginia come together. We went there once on a road trip to see the"—Helene started laughing again—"feral ponies."

"They populate an island out there," said Scott.

"Was it a good trip?"

"No." Scott shook his head and started chuckling again. "It was not. Well, it was—"

"We had fun," said Helene, "but we went down on sort of a whim, thinking we were so spontaneous."

"We couldn't get a reservation," Scott said, "because it was spring break."

"People see the ponies on spring break?"

"No." They were both laughing. "But we stopped at Ocean City on the way because"—Scott was laughing harder—"it sounded nice."

"It sounded nice," repeated Helene. "But have you ever been to Ocean City?" I shook my head. "Of course you haven't, because it's a pit. Is that what your journal entry's about, Scott?" She cracked a smile. "Is that your way of telling me we're doomed?"

His smile froze right there on his face. "Let me keep reading."

"Okay," said Helene, immediately sober. "Sorry."

"*It wasn't just that the weather was sunny and beautiful or that we were on vacation and I hated my job.* Remember that?"

"Those assholes at System Optics." Helene nodded. To me, "Sociopaths."

"*I'm supposed to write about trust and what it means to me, but when I sat down to write this, it's what came out.*" Scott took a shaky breath, removed his hand from Bandito. "*If I think about that trip, I can conjure it, just how I felt with you, standing in the lobby of the Safari Hotel with those drunken high schoolers doing headstands, thinking about the ponies, cursing System Optics.*"

He paused and looked up at Helene's shiny eyes. "I remember it, but not like a memory. I remember the feelings too. I just couldn't figure out how to put it into words."

"It's okay," Helene said. "You said it perfectly."

I lived for these moments, when I could see a couple's unearthed connection, palpable as a cord from one to the other. After a few moments, Scott passed the journal to Helene so she could read aloud too.

Sloane and Giovanni were curled up on the couch watching a movie when Bandito and I got home. "There he is!" Giovanni scooped up the dog, held him above his face.

"He was a therapy dog today," I said.

"Ah, we're glad he made you feel happy." Giovanni paused the television. "That's what he does best."

"Not me," I said. "I took him to work saving marriages."

"How did he do?"

"Quite nicely. How was the Cloisters?"

They smirked at each other. "Amazing." Giovanni paused the TV. "We're watching *The Devil's Own*." In response to my raised eyebrow, he said, "Because it was filmed there!"

"Enjoy." I walked past them into my room. I was in my bathroom washing my makeup off in rough, broad strokes when Sloane came in a few minutes later.

"Hi."

"Hi."

"Thanks for taking Bandito."

"My pleasure."

"Thanks for letting us stay here."

"Of course." It wasn't her fault. It really wasn't, and she certainly wasn't the monster I remembered, but since the trip, every time I saw Sloane, I wanted to run away. She had a roughness around the edges, a misplaced intensity, that made me anxious. "How long do you think you'll be staying?"

"Are you mad about something?"

"No."

"Really?"

"Well, I feel like—" I put down the cotton ball. "I feel like you're not totally with me on the Dave thing."

"Actually, I'm all for you getting to the bottom of it."

"Exactly. You're a little *too* with me that way."

"Don't fall into the trap, Paige."

"The trap?"

"The sweep-everything-under-the-rug trap." Her eyes got a little crazy. "The accept-what-you're-given trap. The don't-ask-questions trap."

"See, I feel like those are all concerns that might apply to you and your"—I wiggled my fingers, grasping for the right word—"dynamic. But they aren't necessarily helpful here. You're projecting." That was it. That was the right word: "projecting."

She gaped.

"It's very common."

"You're in denial. Also very common."

"I'm not. I'm not saying things in my life are perfect, Sloane. Or that I wasn't trying to find out what really happened, but you have to agree—it's between me and Dave, right?"

"Yep."

"I only just met you, and Dave has been my family for years." I could tell I had hurt her. "I'm not trying to make you feel bad, Sloane. I'm trying to explain. I have to go about this in a way that makes sense to me, okay?"

She raised one shoulder and set her jaw.

"Let's change the subject. Are you and Giovanni bringing a change of clothes to boat day? I don't know if I should, but it's not like we're going swimming, right?"

"Boat day sounds like hell."

"You're going, though, right? You and Giovanni?"

She didn't respond.

"You're going to boat day, Sloane." I kept my voice even. "What were you just saying about sweeping things under the rug?"

My phone started to ring and shake on the bathroom counter. Lucy. "I've got to take this."

Sloane gave another half shrug and stalked out, pissed. "I'm not trying to be mean, just honest," I called after her.

"Hey, Luce." With my free hand, I saturated a cotton ball in toner and dabbed at my face. "What's happening?"

"Where are you? This week is almost over!"

It was easier to not get into it. "I'm going to have to push things back."

"Why? Come out! It's getting boring."

"Really?"

"No, not really."

"Maybe in a couple of weeks when my sister leaves. There's some weird stuff going on here."

"With her?"

"Yeah." I tossed the cotton ball in the trash and tried to sound casual. "And with Dave."

"Such as?"

"He's got work stress, I guess."

She sighed. "They're always stressed."

"I guess. He won't talk about it. It kind of . . . worries me a little. I want him to open up."

"They don't have it easy. . . ."

"Who?"

"You know, the Daves of the world, spending all their time in pressure-cooker office cubbies."

"Yeah."

"Poor guy. Cut him some slack."

Once I hung up, I popped my head outside, hoping to smooth things over with dinner choices, but the TV was off and the door to the office was closed. The only one out there was Bandito, curled up on the couch asleep with his head tucked into his crotch, little breaths inflating his body. I patted his head, but disappointingly, he didn't look up at me, even though I desperately wanted the same liquid-eyed approval he'd granted to everything else I'd thrown at him that day.

chapter thirty-eight

ON BOAT DAY, I woke up with seventeen minutes to spare before the car was due to arrive and whisk us to New York Harbor.
I rushed through getting dressed to find that everyone was ready
and waiting for me in the living room. Dave stood right outside
the kitchen, inexplicably holding a coffeepot upside down.

"Bummer," he said, filling me in. "We forgot to get more beans."

"We," I knew, meant "me." "Sorry," I said. "I meant to. It
just got—"

"That's okay. It's been a weird week."

Sloane and Giovanni were silent, and a stranger might have
blamed this on the early hour and the lack of beans, but the way
Sloane was avoiding my eyes, I knew those weren't her reasons.

"So we were thinking," continued Dave, "we should go to the
coffee shop first."

"No time. I still have to pack sunscreen and stuff."

"We'll run out." Sloane seemed eager to leave. "Just have the
car stop to pick us up." And they were gone.

Dave handed me his sunglasses and a book to put in the bag.
My stomach did a little twist; the book was about the Mike
Milken insider trading scandal.

"Are you okay?" Dave put the back of his hand on my forehead.

"Fine." I slipped them both in my tote. *Fine. Fine. Fine.*

Once again, Dave cast himself in the role of group elder. He
insisted on getting in the front seat of the town car so the three

of us had enough room in the back. Giovanni was squashed in the middle between Sloane and me, but he wasn't enough of a barrier for our wordless cool. It felt familiar, the sulky brooding, and I wondered if this was how we had fought growing up—surely we fought growing up?—more cold war than skirmish. It might have been, or it could have been a side effect of my not knowing why I was mad, just that I was. I had no words.

"Do you guys know about this boat?" Dave leaned his head to direct his voice to the backseat. His attempts at conversation, his sunny good nature, only inflated my anger at being the bad guy. Why was I the bad guy? It was so unfair.

"No," Giovanni said. "Tell us about the boat."

"It belongs to some sultan."

"Of what?"

"Something in the Middle East. We should expect gold toilets."

"Cool."

Awkward silence. Dave tried again. "Giovanni, your first time meeting Vanessa and Frank?"

"Yep."

"Oh boy."

"Any tips?"

"No, I'm just teasing. They're great. You'll love them."

"I'm sure."

"And the Rabinowitzes too. They're great. Like family."

I tried not to snort. Like family. What did that mean anyway? Because I'd been avoiding my mother's calls, Dave had passed along the news to me that the Rabinowitz clan was included on our family boat trip. "She says she's been having trouble reaching you, but she wanted to make sure you were prepared."

Prepared for what? I was finally seeing her passive-aggressive pattern: information disguised as a lure for more facts. It'd been a few days since she'd seen Sloane, and she was starving for contact; right now she was probably riffling through prepared note cards on Giovanni, like a talk show host before a big interview, poring over the small details I'd told her days ago—his curly hair, his Italian heritage, his aptitude with computers, the existence of Bandito. I would not have been surprised if she'd decorated the sultan's boat in red, white and green and posted *"Benvenuto!"*

She hadn't. As we pulled up to the harbor and got out of the car, it was clear that decorating the whole yacht would've been impossible without a staff and the contents of at least two Party City stores. The vessel was huge, bright white with darkened sleek windows. The four of us stood on the concrete borders of the harbor, straining our necks to take in the whole thing, which bobbed along, dwarfing the smaller yachts like they were matchbox boats.

My mom waved down at us from somewhere above. "Hello, landlubbers!"

"Hello." Dave was the only one who waved back. We stepped down into the living area single file and were immediately handed freshly squeezed orange juice by a white-gloved expressionless gentleman who ushered us up the left side of a double-curved staircase.

My mom was waiting at the top. Her pupils moved back and forth between us as if following a speeding train until they settled on Giovanni.

"Mrs. Reinhardt—"

"Vanessa, please."

"Vanessa, thank you so much for including me."

"We're just so happy to—who's this?"

Giovanni gestured to the rat-sized head poking out of his tote bag. "This is Bandito. Hope you don't mind we brought him along."

"Not at all. I love dogs." She stroked under his chin. "His eyes are so intelligent. So soulful."

I did snort then, pulling Dave's arm over to where Binnie propped herself up on a lounge chair, little bare lump of stomach sticking out of her bikini. She removed her earbuds.

"Where's Mike?" Dave asked.

"Home with the kids. Our sitter's sick, and he has golf tomorrow, so I came alone."

"Why didn't you bring them?"

She gave me a skeptical look. "You don't bring little kids on a boat, Paige. Safety."

"Isn't that what life preservers are for?"

"Oh, Paige." She laughed as though I'd suggested we hook 'em to a pole and make shark bait. With her index fingers she pushed her earbuds back in her ears.

"So, that's the fiancé?" Cherie had bustled over and pointed toward my mom, Sloane and Giovanni, who were all clustered around Bandito. My dad had joined them, having materialized from somewhere, and Giovanni was shaking his hand, as Sloane pinned herself against his left arm, her body twisted away from them.

"That's him."

"Give me the dirt."

"He's been staying with us." Dave offered this up. "He likes games."

"Games? What does that mean? Like manipulations?"

"No, literally games," I said. "Like Bananagrams."

"What's Bananagrams?" Darren asked.

"Something with letters on squares like Scrabble, I think. We haven't played it yet."

"What does that mean, 'He likes games'?" Cherie was talking to herself. "Is he simple?"

"He's not simple. You'll like him," I said. "He's polite, sickeningly into Sloane and very easy to get along with."

"Oh. Good," Cherie said. "So, you think she's doing okay?"

"I guess."

"What's with the sulky tone?" She regarded me sharply. Cherie had never been one of those grown-ups who felt uncomfortable disciplining another's kid. I'd been staying with them the time I got in trouble for talking back to a teacher in health class—see Percy, *that* was my minor rebellion stage, lasting all of thirty minutes—and she'd grounded me for three days. "I thought you all were on a bonding spree."

"No sulky tone." There was, I realized, no way to claim your tone wasn't sulky without sounding defensive or sulky, and Cherie looked unconvinced, so I excused myself, bag still over my shoulder, to find the gold toilet.

Downstairs there was a living area with couches and an open kitchen where three people in chef jackets were preparing food. One of them looked up as I walked downstairs. "Can I help you with anything, miss?"

"Ladies' room?"

He pointed me down the hall. The bathroom was large with small appliances—metal, not gold, and a weird flusher. No matter how much money you had, I guessed, a boat loo was a boat loo. I wandered into the living area and ran my finger over the book spines on the shelf. I opened the cabinet and stood back, counting the board games (twenty). They had everything— Pictionary, Scattergories, Trivial Pursuit—heaven for Giovanni.

My phone rang and, surprised at getting reception, I picked it up.

"I would like to speak to Paige Reinhardt, relationship counselor." The voice was girlish.

"This is she."

"I, well, we—my girlfriend and I—would like to make an appointment. We're not married. But there are just some issues." She giggled, nervously. "Rather big issues."

"That's okay. You don't have to be married to work on the relationship."

She gave a pleased little tinkle of a laugh. "I guess not."

"Who is this, by the way?"

"Oh, sorry. My name is Selena Richards."

The Selena? "How did you get my name?"

"Percy Stahl."

The sprig of inappropriate hope that I'd felt hearing her name bloomed into elation. "Great!" And then, because that sounded a little too enthusiastic, "It's always nice to get a referral."

My cheeks flushed while we made arrangements for the next day and when I hung up, I realized Dave had come into the room at some point and was watching me carefully.

"How's it going upstairs?" I said.

"Fine."

"Is there any cross-pollination?"

"Between factions? Everyone's pretty much doing their own thing. Although your mom keeps trying to talk to Sloane and Giovanni."

"How's that going?"

"Kind of sad. I actually have to make some calls." He grimaced. "You think I can get reception in here?"

"I did. The room is yours."

When I walked back upstairs, no one acknowledged my return to the group. I sat down on a chaise lounge that allowed me to turn away from my mother's pathetic attempts to bond with Sloane and started flipping through one of the fashion magazines I'd brought. Other than Dave's popping up now and again before returning downstairs for calls, I could have been at a luxury hotel, on a beach full of strangers. I kept reading, until at some point one of the kind uniformed men bent low enough to block my sun and informed me that it was lunchtime.

Most of the group was already at the table, so I pulled out the chair next to Dave. Poor Giovanni—Darren was grilling him about his job, which seemed to be all anyone ever wanted to talk to him about. No wonder the guy found refuge in games.

Dave swung his head toward me and winked. I winked back.

It was good we were going out tonight. It was just what we needed, to rekindle. That's what I was thinking, so I didn't even hear Binnie's entire question, just Giovanni's response, my attention lured by the mention of my name.

"The best host. Paige has been so generous even though we must be wreaking havoc with her schedule."

"Her schedule?" Binnie laughed. "I'm sure it's no problem. Where are you staying? In the never-quite-renovated guest room? If you want a real room, you're welcome to stay with us."

It wasn't the worst thing she'd ever said by far. Had it come from Lucy, I would have laughed. But contents under pressure don't take much to explode, and Sloane, whose face I couldn't have seen unless we both leaned forward at the same time, said, "God, Binnie." She spat the word "Binnie" as if it were a type of disease. "Were you always this fucking rude?"

Binnie's face colored, and my mom jumped in, her voice soothing. "It's okay, Sloane. Paige is fine with it, right, Paige?"

"God. You are the worst. Just look at her." At Sloane's direction, all faces turned toward me and, although shocked, I gave a feeble smile. "Is that the expression of someone who's fine with it? I've only been back for a little bit, but to me it's clear as a bell. Paige is not fucking fine. But whatever, Vanessa. We know you only acknowledge the facts that fit into your little narrative."

Dave's mouth made an O, and he quickly covered it with his

hand, presumably to stop himself from humming "Sunday Bloody Sunday."

"Enough." Cherie put her silverware down. "Enough. It's not okay to talk to your mother that way."

"And it's not too late to teach your perfect daughter some basic manners," Sloane parried. Giovanni put a hand on her arm—I wasn't sure whether it was to calm her or support her. "And either you don't really know my mother, or you don't care that she's a fraud. I don't know which is worse. But we're not talking about that now. We're talking about Paige, and she is not fine."

"Paige," said Cherie, "tell her you're fine."

"Paige." Dave nudged me.

"Paige is just fine." My mom said this so definitively that it pissed me off.

"How would you even know?" I didn't think before I said it, and her head snapped back as if from a slap. She didn't look at me, though. She looked, worriedly, at Sloane for a long time. I watched her for a few moments, my anger ticking down until I shouted it again. "How would you even know? Why ask me when you could tell me? When you can just decide yourself?"

They all had the same expression—dumb and confused, and it whipped my anger into peaks. I could have cannonballed off that over-the-top boat right into the Long Island Sound. I could have climbed the mast and rained lightning down on them like Zeus for the rest of the trip. Instead, I retreated to the lower level. Midway down the stairs, Sloane caught up to me and grabbed the sleeve of my cover-up. "That was fantastic. Did you see her face?"

I didn't say anything, just kept walking downstairs. "Hey," she said. "Stop."

I turned around, level with her elbow. "What?"

"I'm so proud of you. For finally standing up to them."

"Why are you even here, Sloane? I'm maddest at myself for letting a stranger shake up my life."

I didn't wait to hear her response.

I spent about ten minutes in the bathroom trying to calm down before bracing myself to go back upstairs. I didn't feel normal when I reached the deck, though. I shook with that impulse I trained my clients to fight against—the itch to be heard and speak my mind. To wound because I was hurting.

I wasn't even sure who was my prime target—although it seemed in that instant like it had all started with Sloane. It almost didn't matter. I hated the world.

But the lunch table was empty, and the little groups had dispersed into protective little huddles. My mom and Cherie were on the other side of the boat, and I couldn't even see where Sloane and Giovanni were hiding. I felt it drain, the anger that had been boiling one second earlier, that had seemed uncontainable. Where, I wondered, does all that anger go?

"Are you okay?" Dave was in my recliner lounge, going over a document with a red pen. He glanced up and exaggerated his voice. "What was *that*?"

"I'm fine." I felt a rote muscle memory as I said it. "I'm fine. I'm fine. How many times this summer have you heard me say I'm fine?"

"Not that many."

"So then this is it?" I gestured around the top deck. "We all pretend that never happened and go back to avoiding one another?"

"I had a little talk with Giovanni while you were downstairs. He and Sloane are going to hang back for a bit after we dock. They'll come fetch their things while we're at dinner."

"Thank you for that. So Sloane will be at our apartment unsupervised?"

"Yeah. I mean they have to get their stuff."

"Lock up the silver." It hadn't been fair to say, nor had I meant it, but it was what emerged.

"Really? I don't think they'd steal at this point." But he looked worried. "You think we need to monitor them?"

"No."

"This is just eerie. Family boat day, silent picture version." He ruffled my hair. "You're not done, huh? You want to go a few more rounds?"

"That's not it; it's just . . ."

He cocked his head. *What?*

My mother—what was that? All huddled up with Cherie, not even coming over, barely meeting my eye. Was that shame? Did she know I was onto her—the secrets and the mysteries and the unknowns that I couldn't be privy to but that affected me all the same?

I could start with her, march over there and insist that we continue the conversation, but there was a great allure to staying put, sitting quietly with Dave, feeling the sun on my face, slipping my own earbuds in and pretending to read my book. I wanted to forget about all the questions. I wanted my regular life to resume.

"It's just eerie." I kept looking at Dave. Was it evident to him how unsettled I felt? Did he suspect, as I did, that just over our shoulders was a long train of all the unfinished conversations from this summer? That we were starting to drag them around like chains?

If so, he didn't press me on it. He returned to his papers, raising his uncapped red pen over them like a dart, and I settled back down in my chair, earbuds in, book open, until we docked.

◆

Dave and I were the first off the boat—an easy win because everyone else was moving like molasses to avoid us. Still, we sprinted to a cab as though someone were chasing us.

At home, I threw on white pants and a passably clean top under which I stabbed some deodorant. "Okay," I shouted to wherever Dave was, "let's go. Let's get out of here!"

He was still in his boat clothes, typing on his work phone. "Can I shower? I was sweating in the sun all day."

"Hurry!"

I sat on the couch, tapping my foot for a while, and then wandered into the bathroom. "Do you think I was unfair?"

Dave, lathered with soap, opened the glass shower door a crack. "What?"

"Today? To my mom and Sloane."

"Oh." He shut the door and stepped back into the shower. "Jesus."

"What?" I perched on the toilet lid across from him. He shut off the spray and stepped out of the shower, pressing his towel into his face before tying it around his waist and combing his hair while looking in the mirror. He left the bathroom, and I heard him pulling and closing his dresser drawers.

"Okay." He appeared in the doorway, smoothing out a crease in his shirt. "I'm ready."

I decided to ignore the "Jesus," which for all I knew had been in response to a shaving nick. "Where are you taking me?"

"It's a surprise," he said. "You won't be disappointed."

"Not as long as they have wine."

"They do."

"Let's get a whole bottle and talk about anything else other than this day."

"That's the goal," he said.

Dave had ordered a car, and as we eased into the backseat, his work phone rang.

"Take it," I said.

"Okay, but only to tell them I can't talk tonight."

"It's fine." We'd caught the stretch of perfectly timed green lights down Fifth Avenue, and I looked out the window as I listened to Dave's conversation. It felt so normal—no whispering, no straining to hear, just a slightly impatient voice. He said nothing about financial tips or shady insider advice. There was no whispered *Talk to me before you buy*.

"Sorry," he said when he hung up. "New associate on the team. He doesn't really have a handle."

"Oh." I grabbed Dave's hand as our car pulled in front of the Yarn. "Here?"

He smiled.

"So romantic. How'd you do it so last minute?"

He raised one eyebrow. "Secret sources."

Dave and I hadn't been to the Yarn since getting engaged. Securing a table required waking up at five in the morning exactly one hundred twenty days before your desired dining date and pressing REDIAL until you developed carpal tunnel. It wasn't just the food; it was the service, as though each couple were royalty. Last time, I—and every other female diner—left with a box of homemade bonbons, a bouquet and an ivy wreath. An ivy wreath! As if we were all mini twenty-first-century Caesars.

Thousands of New Yorkers had knelt on those wooden floors, shakily holding out oversized rock-candy rings to their shiny-haired beloveds. The first time we were there, I'd drunkenly asked the waiter what was up with the name, whether it was supposed to make us all want to sit by the fire and knit sweaters and tell stories.

He had leaned forward with the manner of someone sharing an oral tradition round a campsite. The owners had named it, he said, after the expression that getting married was like throwing a ball of yarn into the woods and following it past the stumps and brambles to its conclusion: a commitment to stay true to the path regardless of where it leads. I'd leaned forward, the new diamond heavy and glinting as my left hand flourished my champagne flute, my legs snaked around Dave's. It was so very romantic, that thought of the two of us, following the yarn, braving together whatever life might bring us.

"Good?" Dave smiled at me as we waited for the maître d' to place us.

"It's perfect." And really, it should have been.

chapter thirty-nine

WE WERE SITTING almost where we had sat three years before, at the end of a row of five tables in front of the fireplace. The time before, we'd been at the middle table, a spot occupied now by a couple whom I immediately labeled the young Turks for the way they were holding each other's hands across the table while leaning into each other with complete focus. I could've dashed, naked and madly, back and forth through the dining room, screaming about fish crackers, and neither would have looked up.

Dave flipped through the oversized blue leather menu. "You want to do the tasting menu?"

"How many courses?"

"We could do three, five or eight. I'm up for anything."

"Three."

"Really?"

"I'm a little beat."

"Whatever you want."

As he ordered, the young Turks were ignoring the plates in front of them, still not talking, just staring into each other's eyes, entranced. After the waiter left, I poked a finger in their direction. "Check out the frozen people."

Dave watched them for a second. "They look stoned."

"Maybe they're on ecstasy."

"Maybe they speak different languages and can't understand each other, and finally they just gave up."

"Maybe someone superglued their hands together, and

because they speak different languages, they can't figure out how to get unstuck."

We laughed even though it didn't really make sense.

The waiter brought over the amuse-bouche—a tiny little puff of foam in a votive-sized glass that was explained as cauliflower carpaccio with a cappuccino reduction.

"Thank god," I said, downing it like a twenty-one-year-old with her first legal shot of tequila. "Not much of a lunch from the sultan's crew."

He swallowed the cauliflower. "Surprisingly good. I was nervous about the cappuccino part."

The waiter brought our wine and after a rather long-winded congratulatory explanation about something we'd ordered or should order—I wasn't paying attention—I downed my glass. "Fruity." In a flash, another tuxedoed gentleman refilled my glass.

"You think?" Dave cocked his head. "I taste oak."

"I was kind of joking." I drank half of my second glass; two big gulps.

Dave looked surprised. "You came to play."

"I did." By the time the cauliflower cappuccinos were cleared, I felt the looseness of my tongue like a release. "Were you surprised by me? Today?"

"Jesus."

"Don't Jesus me again."

"I don't know what that means."

"You did it in the shower when I asked you about today. You said, 'Jesus.' And then didn't answer."

"I thought we weren't going to talk about it."

"Maybe I want to."

"I just don't want to bicker."

"Then answer and we won't."

He looked at me head-on. "I guess so. I've never heard you talk like that to your mother. But maybe it was good."

"You think?"

"Yeah. Maybe a little independence for you is necessary." He rested his shoulders flat against his chair back as if bracing for my reaction, but I wasn't mad.

"Have you thought that always?"

"She's always been so front and center in your life."

"I know." I leaned toward him. "I feel like . . . I feel like I'm the one who didn't disappoint her, I'm the one who does whatever she wants and I'm still sloppy seconds."

"That's not true."

"Prove it." I finished my second glass, and the tuxedo guy poured a third.

He shrugged. "Your mom really loves you. You know that." I did. "Did you ever find out what the deal is with her and Sloane?"

"No, but I'm learning. I'm reading her journals from twenty years ago."

"She gave them to you?"

"Not on purpose. She doesn't know."

"That's . . . disrespectful, I guess."

"Yes, but informative. They're from the year Sloane left." I finished the third glass, and the guy refilled it.

"Wow. Well." He shrugged and moved back in his chair to cross one leg over the other. "I mean what could be in there that's really incriminating, right?"

"Dave!" I waved my glass at him, and the liquid sloshed up to the rim. "It's someone's innermost thoughts. It's not okay to read someone else's journal."

"Yeah, but it's like all about your family and her feelings, right? It's not like there were state secrets in there."

"You think it's okay?"

He uncrossed his leg and stared to the left for a second. "I'm trying not to bicker with you, so even though this is the last thing I want to talk about, I am."

"What do you want to talk about, Dave? Interest rates?"

"How about our next vacation? Finally making it out to Quogue? How about anything that's not what we've done all summer, which is devolve into fighting."

He was right. "Mother of Mercy," I said, and something about the way I said it made him flush and point to the wine.

"Slow it down, babe." He patted the middle of the table, right next to the lit candle.

"Why?"

"You're acting off."

To our right, we heard the squeak of a chair pushing out, and the man of the intertwined couple—the international ones high on ecstasy but no longer superglued together—was kneeling on the floor, blue velvet box in front of him. We stopped and watched as his fiancée, hands pressed to her cheeks, mouth in a perfect bud, delicately extended her hand for the ring. Eyes glistening, she nodded quickly. "Yes!"

"Guess they understand each other after all," I said.

"I'm not perfect," he said. "I don't always do the right thing. And you're right. It was shitty to read the journals."

"Okay."

"I don't like seeing you like this—all twisted up because of some ridiculous family drama. You want to know what I think about the little scene today?"

"Yes."

"You'll apologize to Binnie—"

"I'm not going to apologize to her—"

"Just my opinion on what you should do tomorrow morning. Apologize to your mother too, and they'll both forgive you; Sloane will clear out of our apartment and our lives, and we'll take August and go out to the Quogue house and then we can get back to normal. This summer has been a disaster, but we can still fix it, okay?"

"Sloane's not a druggie loser," I said.

He sighed, as though saying, *That's what you got from what I said?*

"Ugh." I pressed my palm heels into my temples. He was right. *Just tell him.* "Dave?"

"What?"

"I've been worried you got suspended for insider trading."

"Yes," he said drily. "I believe you've mentioned that."

"The big investigation that's been in the news, specifically." I saw, I was sure, a jolt of connection in his eyes. "With Mission Bank. So this whole time, I've been trying to learn about it."

"How?" His voice sounded a little strangled, and when I didn't answer quickly, he said again, louder and clearer, "How?"

"Nothing drastic. Just by reading the papers, talking to someone."

"Someone?"

"An investigator." I swallowed.

"You had me followed?"

"No, no. Nothing like that. I've just asked him to help me find out more about it."

"Has he?" He lifted his hand and motioned for the check, causing a flurry of concern from the waitstaff.

"He's found squat. Zilch. I know you're probably mad, but the reason I'm telling you is not only to clear the air. It's also because

I realized that if you did something like that? If you ever did, I could understand why you did it. I would hate it more if you lied to me than if you did it and told me. You understand?"

"I understand the content of what you're saying, yes."

"And I don't want to lie to you anymore. It's getting in the way of everything."

"Whoa." He held up his hands. "Whoa." The waiter appeared, swooshing down the quilted envelope, and Dave scribbled with the pen and got up to go. He didn't speak to me on the way out of the restaurant. He didn't say anything at all, and if I hadn't jumped—fast—into the cab that he hailed, he most definitely would have left without me.

"I'm sorry," I said in the backseat, a couple of blocks from home, but Dave didn't respond. We stood silently in the empty elevator, walked single file down the hall. As soon as he unlocked the door to our apartment, he went into the linen closet, getting extra sheets to put on the bed that Sloane and Giovanni had carefully folded up.

I sat on our bed, too confused to do anything else. What if I'd been the one to get suspended without knowing why? What if I'd come home to tell him and, instead of offering blanket support, Dave had turned on me, picking fights and hiring a private investigator and then announcing his mistrust at a romantic dinner I'd planned?

At this point, I was the only obstacle to going back to normal. And what did I want, if not for things to go back to normal? The normal had been lovely. My lovely, lovely life.

But even more than I wanted normalcy, I wanted to know the truth. Not just about Dave, but the rest of it: the thirty-two years' worth of secret facts that I'd been trapped up against without knowing it.

I went into the closet and found my pink notebook.

Dear Me,

Hi, Rock Star! How was school today? What? It was fine.
Yeah, I know that because I was there too. Did you see me?
Following you around all day? You know what? It wasn't
that great—you had apple skin in your teeth and it
probably got in there during lunch, but you didn't notice
until after you got home, but better luck next time.

Love, hugs and kisses,
Paige

All the entries were like that.

Reading them felt like watching the early scenes of one of Dave's horror movies, when you know before the doomed character does that her murderer is right there inside the house. Your instinct is to scream out to stop her from going into that room. Or shake her—how is she missing the obvious? It's dark; there's creepy music; everyone else has left.

Until you realize the character's stupidity is the whole point of her existence—she wouldn't be in the movie otherwise. You resign yourself to her demise and wonder how she's lasted so long, given her industrial-strength sense of denial.

I don't know anyone who identifies with those head-in-the-sand characters. Everybody is so sure they'd see the writing on the wall, that they'd go into that room, aware and fighting just like the heroine. No matter how much I wanted to be that person—sentient and wise—I had to admit to myself that for a while now I'd been utterly clueless, bumbling in the dark.

chapter forty

DAVE HAD LEFT an apology note on the floor outside the closed bedroom door. I was sure he'd never done that before— left an apology note after a fight—but it felt like the fiftieth time. Like we had this dynamic down pat.

I'm so sorry, it said. *I wanted things to be different. Fire drill at work but home by dinner.* I was pretty sure that by "things" he meant "last night," but perhaps he'd meant more. It could easily mean between us—we were fighting, we were apologizing, we were veering off track.

Bandito was probably the only living creature I hadn't alienated. Maybe my dad too, which was more a sign of apathy than anything else.

My phone buzzed for the sixth time that morning. My mom had apparently found her voice. As soon as I picked up, she launched in, her tone rat-a-tat and accusatory: "We need to talk about yesterday."

"Listen," I said.

She kept going. I held the receiver away from my head. A bit louder, I said, "Listen."

She stopped.

"I'm sorry I exploded at you and Binnie and for—" She waited. "I read your journals. From twenty years ago—"

"I know which ones." Her voice was neutral.

"It was a violation and I'm sorry. But I don't want to—I can't—talk now. After I cool down, okay?" Silence. "Okay?"

I heard her suck in her breath. "Okay," she responded. And I turned off my phone and went to the office.

♦

Selena Richards might have been the tallest person I'd ever seen, except for her girlfriend, Bianca, who was even taller. I welcomed their kneecaps and pointed them to their seats, feeling like the lollipop guild greeters for Dorothy. I tried not to be intimidated as they folded themselves into chairs.

"Candy?" I pushed the jar closer to them.

"No, thanks," Bianca said in a crisp British accent, and Selena shook her white-blond hair and laughed that tinkly giggle she'd used on the phone. Of course they didn't eat candy. They were shiny gazelle creatures who subsisted on wheatgrass and egg whites. Their hands cradled, Bianca's café au lait skin entwined with Selena's peach, draped together like some expensive fabric.

This was when I should ask what they wanted.

They would be amenable. They had the ideal body language for clients—focused and open, both encouraged and encouraging.

"How did you guys meet?" I popped a Hershey's Kiss in my mouth. It was a punt of a question, small talk.

Selena looked surprised and relieved. "At a friend's party. About two years ago." They smiled with the memory and narrated it together, interrupting each other and telling their own versions in a way I knew they'd done before. I could picture it: two sequoias seeing clear to each other above a bumpy terrain of indistinguishable scrub brush. *Your hair was spun from fairy dust and the finest Chinese silk! Oh my gosh, oh my gosh, mine too!*

I half listened, but I had skipped forward in my head to that question, my cornerstone: *What do you want?*

It was a bid for an impossible conclusion. If someone had

asked me the same question in that moment, I would have stalled for a bit and tried to come up with something more graceful than the truth:

I wanted to eat that entire jar of candy and not get a cavity. I wanted the summer to be over and for Lucy to come back to Manhattan. I sort of wanted a dog like Bandito, for goddamn scientists to find a cure for addiction—what was taking them so long if it was all just an issue of chemistry?—and the ability to communicate with my mother as badly as I wanted a fifty-year break from her. I wanted Bianca and Selena to be happy, and I wanted to want to gaze at Dave the way they did at each other. I wanted to be an only child again. I wanted back my childhood with Sloane.

It wasn't simple, what I wanted. My answer wouldn't have been anything as concrete as what I demanded from the couples in my office.

About twenty minutes after Selena and Bianca glided out the door, my buzzer sounded. I assumed they'd forgotten something and didn't even look at the monitor before pressing the button to let them back in. Giovanni opened the door instead.

"I tried to call." He was slightly out of breath. "But you didn't pick up."

"My phone's off. Why aren't you flying home?"

"Nice office." He glanced around. "Hey! You made a rainbow out of your bookcase. Love it."

"Thanks."

"I told Sloane that I was going out to get Ziploc bags for the flight—which was an excuse—but I really do need some. Is there a place around here I can get them?" He exhaled and said in a rush, "I'm so glad I caught you."

"She doesn't know you're here?"

"I know. I feel awful. She's so sad, though. And you are too, right? I had to do something."

"Sad? The vibe I got was mad."

"No. Sad." He collapsed on the couple's couch, fanning himself. "Sorry. Hot. I assume she never told you the real reason why she came to New York this summer?"

"No." I sat down right next to him, across from my usual space.

"From the beginning, I asked her about you guys—her family. She always said the same thing, that there wasn't a relationship, there would never be one. She claimed to have a very strict belief that people should be able to choose their family, the same way they could their friends."

"Makes sense." It did, right about now, although I couldn't think of any friends close enough to be my family either, not even Lucy. The fact was, I'd confided in Sloane more than almost anyone.

"It's a bullshit theory."

"Oh."

"I said I understood, but come on, if she really believed it, would she be here? I humored her at the time, because I liked her. A lot. I mean how could I not?"

I nodded as though anyone in his right mind would be defenseless in the face of Sloane's overwhelming charisma.

"But I secretly thought she was exaggerating and eventually I'd meet you guys and you wouldn't be as . . . alien as she made you all sound. Which, as it turns out, you aren't."

"Thanks."

"When I hadn't met anyone from her family after we'd been together for a year, I started to believe her. My family's very embracing, a little too much, actually. She's had no choice but to get trapped in its fold, and I assumed my family would be *our* family and that would be enough. But then, when we got engaged, I threw her a surprise party after, with some of her close friends and my family waiting for us at our apartment, and everyone was so happy. And it was a perfect night. The most beautiful night until——"

"Until what?"

"When I woke up in the middle of the night and found her crying in the living room because she didn't have anyone to call about the engagement. I mean, she did——she has friends, and some of the folks from her recovery support have been in her life forever, but not having any family to call apparently meant something to her. I was so surprised. I realized you weren't out of her life; you were worse than that. You were one big pile of unresolved. All the time she was pretending not to care, she was feeling awful about it. And she kept talking about *you*. You were the one she wanted to see. You were the one she'd thrown away."

"Her whole life, she's basically acted like I don't exist. Why did she vanish?"

"She was sixteen, Paige. Sixteen and messed up. I don't think she ever meant to vanish from your life. She says she tried to reach out to you a few times, right after she left. When she was at that Gentle Breezes place and then, later, after she moved to California. And you know Sloane——she's too shy to keep trying if she feels rejected. I'm not saying it's a strength of hers, but . . ."

"She's not shy. She's mortar-tough."

"Tough and shy aren't opposites."

Had there been something? I felt a fuzzy recollection of her reaching out——a postcard maybe, or voice mail, hardly a deluge——and ignoring it, chalking it up to a therapy assignment.

It was possible; I'd certainly clung to my narrative of Sloane as a dark, shadowy figure whom we were all better off without. I'd given myself permission to clear her from my memory.

And you know Sloane. My immediate reaction had been to shake my head. I did not know Sloane. All I knew was that she ruined whatever she touched, and she was the one who'd been pushing me forward down this horrible path with Dave.

But . . .

I played the last two weeks in my mind like a fast-forwarded tape—her stringy appearance at the first breakfast; her general availability; taking me to the restaurants she wanted to try; generally having my back; right up to my harsh words on the boat.

I *had* gotten to know her this summer: she was rough around the edges and vulnerable and messed up, but she wasn't intent on destruction. She was trying to be involved in my life. If I had opened up to her about an interest in skeet shooting, rather than my suspicions about Dave, perhaps we'd be happily pummeling shots into clay pigeons right now.

"I'm not trying to force things with you two," Giovanni continued, "but our flight is later on today, and I was wondering if you had any interest in just saying . . . good-bye. Leaving on a better note."

I had already grabbed my bag. "Where is she?"

♦

"Crapola," he said as our cab pulled up to the Lincoln, which looked run-down even in the early evening's golden light. "After all that, I forgot the Ziploc bags." He checked his watch. "You go in. She should be in the lobby with the bags."

As soon as I recovered from the lobby's overwhelming smell of stale hot dogs, I saw Sloane gesturing to someone behind a double-glass booth. Eventually the concierge nodded and slid something through the partition. Sloane took it and shoved it in the back pocket of her jeans. Her relief was evident when she turned around and saw me, and then she gave me a look that asked, *How?*

"Giovanni," I said. "He's out getting the right size Ziplocs."

She sighed. "The man is obsessed with those." She swept her arm toward the other side of the room where two men in plaid shirts sat on a row of mismatched chairs. Their heads were frozen in an upward tilt, watching NY1 News. "I invite you into our sitting area. Lovely, right?"

We both perched on the edge of our chairs. "This place," I said. "I feel so bad you came here."

"It was fine."

"Where's Bandito?"

She put her hand to her lips, but it was too late. At the sound of his name, one of the bags—the black one on top with mesh sides—moved. "No dogs allowed," Sloane mouthed.

"Sorry," I mouthed back. "You don't have to go back, you know."

"It's time," she said. "But it's not good-bye. I'll come and visit you if you want."

"Or I could visit you."

"That'd be great. We'd love to have you guys."

"Both of us?"

"I really wasn't trying to break you up or anything."

"I know."

"I thought I was being helpful. I was maybe a little too enthusiastic, trying to force things. Sorry. It's awkward."

"You really have nothing to apologize for. You've been great. You're great."

"I think you're great." She said this quietly. "I wish I'd tried harder to reach out. Before now."

"Why didn't you?"

"I guess I thought you'd reach out too. I didn't realize what a number they were doing on you back here, that if you brought up my name, you'd get reprogrammed." She moved her arms like a robot. When I made a noise of objection, she moved her robot arms in surrender. "Let's agree to disagree. I'm just glad for this summer."

"Me too. On the whole," I said, "it's amazing how *not* awkward it's been. With us. If not with Mom and Dad." She was silent, studied. "But maybe that will just take more time."

She made a face. "I'd much rather keep this about us. I'm sure you don't want me to go there."

"Go where?"

"I saw them only because I figured that was the easiest path to you. I don't understand how you're all so much in each other's business. But"—she held her hands up—"to each his own. I don't particularly need to pretend to be close to them and their motley band of shopping buddies."

"What is the deal with you guys?"

"I can't stand the hypocrisy."

"Okay."

"I don't really hate them. I mean, Franklin is harmless, if a complete nonentity, but what I can't stand is everyone's sheepdog devotion to her. You know how growing up, she was all—family this and family that. Family's the most important thing?"

"Yeah."

"She talks such a big game about loyalty, but then she goes and does whatever she wants."

"Like?"

"Like enrolling me in that school."

"I don't think she really *wanted* to. And isn't that how you got sober?"

"Yes, I lucked out. But it was halfway across the country."

"I read her journals. I think the decision killed her. But she thought it was best for you."

She shrugged.

"Is that really it? You're mad she sent you away? You were self-destructing, from what I understand."

She set her jaw. "I really didn't want to tell you this. You're so blindly obedient when it comes to her. No offense."

"Tell me."

"So when you were reading her journals, you never came across anything about another guy?"

"I did. Nothing tawdry. She talks a lot about one friend. Someone called G."

"Maybe. I don't know his name."

"What about him?"

"One night, this was just before I left, I was out late. I was with a group of friends, and we were walking by the Friendly's on Sycamore. And I saw her car. It was about ten o'clock at night, so I walked closer and knocked on the window. She was in there with a guy. A much younger guy. And I know she saw me because she got all shocked, her eyes were like"—Sloane stopped and arranged her features in a catatonic look—"and she pulled away from him, but he didn't get the memo, so he kept trying to continue whatever disgusting things they were doing—the windows were all fogged—and she kept pulling back and finally I just left.

"The next morning, she's sitting at the breakfast table with Dad. He's reading his paper, clueless as ever, and she looks me square in the eye, asks me where I was last night and how was it and that was it. She's a total fraud."

I imagined my teenaged self upon seeing that car just as Sloane had. I would've crumbled.

"You're disgusted too." Sloane sounded triumphant.

"Not really."

"You're not?"

"I'm sure I would have been disturbed to see it, but . . . a fraud? Isn't that harsh?" G. had offered Vanessa something to get her through that year, and she'd grabbed onto it. I couldn't have understood that at sixteen, but now I could imagine: G. with Percy's face, in jeans.

"The definition of a fraud is someone who pretends to be what she's not. I'd say it fits perfectly."

"It's not that black and white."

"She lied. To my face. Not just about how important family is, but about what she was doing that night. You thought I asked good questions about you and Dave?"

"All your therapy-inspired questions? Yeah."

"Trust me. I've spent a lot of time on this exact issue, going over and over it with various experts. What I can't get over is how she expected to know everything about me—where I was going, what I was doing, the mileage on my car—and the whole time she was lying."

It was funny; I'd thought the very same thing a few weeks ago when I first saw the journals. "Not lying. Just not telling you about one part of her life."

She snorted. "What's the difference?"

"This is what I've learned this summer: There are going to be hidden facts, right? You can't know everything about a person, so you base the relationship on what you *do* know."

"So what do I know?"

"She was trying to act in your best interest. She was having a confusing, horrible year. How about me? It's a fact that I was awful to you on the boat, but you know that I care about you and you're able to get over it."

"That's, like, the worst example ever. You weren't lying to me. You were being honest, if a little cranky. Look at the Dave stuff. It's not like you felt good about the possibility of his lying to you."

"But he's my *husband*."

"And she's my *mother*. We're very different in what we expect of people."

"How?"

"You're willing to twist things around. You accept whatever anyone tells you is true—Dave, Mom, Dad, to the extent he says anything. You just kind of go into your little box and stay. Your own little doghouse."

"Doghouse?"

"That wasn't the best image. I just meant—you're obedient. You stay in a little sectioned-off portion on the edge of someone else's property. I haven't even been back that long, but already I can tell that your whole life is Vanessa-sanctioned. She practically picked your husband and your apartment and that horrible decorator."

"She didn't, Sloane. I respect her opinion, sure, but I made those choices."

Her dark eyes were skeptical. "After all my years of therapy, I know exactly what I need from the people close to me. I need to be able to trust them. If they screw up, that's it. Game over."

"But don't you miss—"

"What? No, I miss nothing. It's called self-preservation."

Giovanni came back into the lobby, waving his Ziploc bags, and sat on the arm of Sloane's chair. "We should leave at seven thirty." He looked between us. "Which is in twenty more minutes. What am I interrupting?"

"She's just telling me I live in a doghouse," I said.

"And she's telling me I'm unforgiving."

"Oh." Giovanni appeared concerned until we both started to laugh, and Sloane stopped short.

"You're going to make it work with Dave, I assume."

"I think the whole thing might have been more about me than him."

"How?" Sloane shook her head. "He got suspended from work and lied about it."

"We don't know that."

"Shut up," said Sloane.

"I know you don't like that answer, but it is my life—"

"No," said Sloane. "I mean, shut up and watch. What's the name of the firm, Dave's firm?"

"Duane Covington." As I said it, the anchor said it too, and I stared at the screen's red banner: *Breaking News: Agents Raid Duane Covington, elite Midtown firm. Sources link these arrests to the government's investigation into Mission Fund. Details to follow.*

"Holy shit," I said as Sloane and I grabbed each other's arms. "Holy shit."

chapter forty-one

"I SHOULD CALL him, right? I should call him?"

Sloane and Giovanni nodded dumbly, and Giovanni said, "Maybe try?"

I dialed, my hands shaking. It went straight to voice mail. "No answer."

They didn't look surprised.

"Should I call Dad? No, Dave would hate that. Should I call a lawyer? What should I do?" I texted him: *R u ok?*

"He would be able to call you, right?" Giovanni frowned. "I mean, he'd get a phone call if . . . They always say you get a phone call."

"Let's change our flight," said Sloane. She nudged Giovanni. "We'll stay."

"Of course." He stood up, pulled out his phone.

"Stop. I'll be okay."

"Don't be a martyr."

"Really. I'll be fine. I'm fine. It would just make things weirder if you're here when this all . . . falls out."

They looked at each other, and I could tell they were imagining the awkwardness of staying at the Lincoln as their almost-stranger brother-in-law was run through an indictment process. Sloane nodded slightly.

"I'll be fine. This is—it's not totally unexpected." My head felt like it could float away. "Maybe I'll just—maybe I'll figure out—"

"Call Percy," said Sloane.

Giovanni was nodding. "Percy. He'll know what to do."

"So would Dad. Or one of Dave's friends from law school."

"But maybe, for Dave's sake," Sloane said, "you want to keep it as quiet as possible until we know something concrete."

I scraped my teeth over my lower lip. She was right. I would start with an apology for that night in the hammock, but when I dialed Percy's number, the phone went to voice mail on the first ring and I hung up. "He didn't pick up," I explained to Sloane and Giovanni, who were looking at me expectantly.

"Call him again," said Giovanni. "Leave a message."

I left things vague and polite, telling Percy that I was sorry to bother him and that I had some questions on some new developments. As soon as I hung up, my phone made the breaking-glass noise that meant I'd received a text. We crowded around; it was from Dave.

Fine. Things crazy here tho. So much work! Will be home v. late, not for dinner.

"What the hell? What. The. Hell?"

Sloane covered her mouth.

"He's probably just trying to protect you," said Giovanni.

"He thinks I'm an idiot. He thinks I can't handle this news." Sloane bit her nails, as though she had to shove something— *anything*—in her mouth so as not to scream about what an asshole he was. "That's ridiculous. I can totally handle this."

They nodded vigorously: *Yes, you can!*

"Okay," I said. "We're going to share a cab. First stop, Duane Covington. Then on to JFK for you guys."

"Really? You're going there?" Sloane looked like she thought this was not such a good idea.

"Not to do anything stupid. I just want to observe. To see for myself what's going on."

◆

The sky was peach colored when they dropped me off across the street from the GM Building. The cab couldn't get closer because of the glut of white vans around the plaza. Past the vans was a layer of reporters—their makeup so heavy I could see blush streaks from fifty feet away—and inside their circle of cameras was the story: a steady stream of agents trailing in and out of the building, those on return trips carrying hard drives and files.

I sat on the fountain and watched the action from across the street, counting the exterior windows up to the twentieth floor. Was Dave there, watching the carnage? I worried about the things to come: having to convince him to testify against whoever had dragged him into the scandal; the length of his sentence; what it would be like to see him in that orange jumpsuit and, oh god, would he be shackled? I scanned the crowds for signs of anything familiar. I visualized going to court and sitting in the front row. I could—I would—do it, just like Mrs. DeFranza had.

Because underneath it all ran my love for Dave, powerful enough to flood out any disappointment. I hated how he lied to me, but it was the flip side of the man I married—ambitious to a fault and with something to prove. What had caused the downfall was also what I loved about him, and why he complemented me. We could get past it.

This was what had been on the tip of my tongue while talking to Sloane, that forgiving someone—mining the hurt and pain to find the underlying love—is not a sign of weakness. It's a north star. When my phone rang again, I picked up, feeling calmer than I had in weeks because in some ways, it was a relief to finally know.

"Paige? It's Percy."

"I'm so glad you called. I need advice. I'm at Dave's firm right now. It's a total shit show."

"I was hoping we could meet in person."

"Okay. Where are you?"

"In my office."

Perfect. I hoped the location would help clarify that our relationship was professional only. "Fine. Do you have some lawyers on speed dial?"

"What?"

"Defense lawyers. Watch the news and you'll understand. I'll see you in twenty." I sent supportive thoughts to the twentieth floor and then to some of the vans in case he was already there and then, as the sun set to the west of Duane Covington, I left.

Percy suggested, in a solicitous manner that I might have mocked under different circumstances, that I sit down for our chat. I got the feeling that he was trying to break something to me.

"It's okay," I said. "Whatever you want to talk about, can I go first?"

"Sure."

"Did you look at the news? The feds are crawling all over Duane Covington, taking equipment, raiding it, presumably arresting people. Presumably my husband."

"No." He typed on his computer and shook his head. "I didn't know."

"Does it give any details?"

"No, just that there's a raid."

"The freaking news cycle moves so slow."

"That's nuts," he said, glancing at the screen again. "But that's not what I need to tell you."

"What could you possibly need to tell me that's more impor-tant than this?"

He looked down for a split second, and my heart fell. Was it about that moment we'd had? I wondered how I could best trans-mit that that was now the farthest thing from my mind. But then he said, "About what I learned at the book club party."

"The what party?"

"Annie Poleci's book club party."

"It was tonight. I totally forgot." Percy's expression said, *Yeah, well, I didn't.* "You went?"

"Of course."

"Was Annie Poleci there?"

"She was."

"God, she's so lucky she wasn't in the office tonight."

"Sounds like it."

"What happened?"

"We chatted, Annie and I. And I learned about her meeting with the human resources representative. The one who took the notes? You with me, Paige?"

"I'm with you."

"You want to know what she said? It's . . . relevant."

I could hardly see how anything other than the raid was rele-vant now, but he looked convinced. "Tell me."

It was basically a college party. They never even discussed the book—at least not in the first hour—even though Percy had bought it and actually read it. They drank beer; they gossiped. It was easy to get to Annie. She was standing in a group of people, looking bored while listening to a guy going on and on about getting into a little cage and being lowered into the water to swim with the sharks as if he were on some National

Geographic special. He was getting way too detailed—about the kind of Plexiglas, et cetera. And Annie just had that look on her face, like *Why am I wasting my night here?*

Percy started joking with her and then making small talk. He learned Annie was from Chicago, that—surprise, surprise—she worked at one of those gargantuan law firms that eats its young.

He told her that he had a sister who worked at one of those places and hated it—could never take a vacation, felt like a warm body—and Annie seemed to perk up. He made up some story about his sister not being allowed to go on her honeymoon at the last minute. And then Annie said, "At least that was about the work," in a really cynical tone.

"Your partners are worse?" Percy said.

"Not always." Annie had twisted her lips. "But a few weeks ago—I walked in on this young partner completely glomming on one of his associates."

"Glomming?" Percy asked, and Annie explained. They were in a stairwell, and the partner was totally blocking the associate's path, hovering over her, way too close. He was saying something— she didn't hear what—in a really low, menacing voice. And Annie distinctly saw this guy's hands on the associate's ass.

"Harassment?" Percy said.

"Exactly," said Annie. "It was like walking into a sexual harassment video. I mean, it was the type of shit I didn't think would go on anymore. What is this—*Mad Men*?"

I looked at Percy. "Can you check on your computer whether there have been any arrests?"

He looked at me like I was crazy but leaned over and clicked a key, shook his head. "Nothing."

"I heard you, yes. You're trying to tell me that the partner was Dave and that he sexually harassed someone?"

"Well," he said, "I think that's why he was suspended. Think about it, if you fill in the notes." He read aloud: *"June 30, Dave Turner/ (complaint by) Annie Poleci. Annie P. saw Dave Turner with NS? We met for an hour meeting and I immediately notified the corporate dept. (by phone), Stuben (by phone). We will implement handbook policy."*

"So, maybe. This woman, Annie, she sounds like one of those types, you know—overzealous college feminists that get a rude awakening when they're out in the real world."

"You think?" said Percy.

"Oh, I've seen it happen, for sure. But even if something like that happened, it would never be with Dave."

"It kind of sounded like Dave."

"Why?"

"She was clear on who he was. She said she'd talked to the partner before at some sort of dinner, and that part of what made it so crazy was that he seemed like such a nice guy. And he's young and married. I went online—he looks like the youngest partner by far in his group."

"He is. Except for William, who's single."

"I'm pretty sure she saw Dave."

"But growling and grabbing someone's ass? Please. And what am I supposed to believe—Dave's an inside trader and a sexual harasser? Come on."

"Even if he didn't do it," said Percy, "I'm pretty sure he was on the hook for it. Annie said she didn't say anything or do anything in the stairwell, but she ran right to HR, and the guy was suspended the next day. But I didn't get how far away she was in the stairwell, and I couldn't really press her without ruining my street cred as just some random disinterested member of the book club."

"And she didn't say anything about a financial scandal?"

"Nope."

"Okay, well, so this is a nonissue. He didn't do it. They figured it out, and he's back at work. Back to reality, please—check whether there have been any arrests?"

Percy clicked Reload on his computer and then shook his head. "There's one more thing about this."

"Okay."

"So, Annie didn't tell me the name of the associate in the stairwell, just that she was a midlevel associate and kind of quiet and in their group. I assume her initials are NS—as in 'saw Dave Turner with NS.'"

"Okay."

"So I checked, and there's no associate in the New York office that fits that description with those initials."

"Okay."

"Except, there's a Penelope Standish who does, and in her bio, she's referred to as Nell."

"Nell Standish?"

He nodded.

"Dave does work with a Nell. I've seen that name on e-mail."

"Yeah. She's in his practice group." He typed in his computer and pulled up her profile on the firm. "Just to check—does she look familiar?"

She had curly hair. She looked wholesome, young and innocent, trying so hard to be professional under that sharply pointed collar doubled over her lapel.

"She looks so sweet," I said, reading her bio, "and she went to Dave's college. God, you'd think she'd have helped out a little, cleared things up for a fellow alum." I looked at her again. There was something about her face that was familiar. The point of her jaw. With her hair pulled back . . .

I heard myself gasp.

"You okay?" Percy's hand clapped my back.

How did I not see it? How did I see anything but this?

"Now you know what I know." His voice was apologetic, but not surprised. Of course he knew. He'd probably known since we first met.

It was the most standard reason in the world why a husband would lie to his wife. It was something I saw the ramifications of nearly every day. A garden-variety affair. In this case, Dave and Nell, the deceptively prim-looking college girlfriend who, perhaps not so long ago, had thanked him for loving her like that.

chapter forty-two

THERE IS NOTHING slower than the speed of a news story in which you are personally invested. There had been three arrests at Duane Covington, and the first was Herb. When I saw his headshot flashed on-screen, I held my breath because this was how it was all supposed to play out—Dave riding his mentor's coattails straight into the sewers. But instead of Dave's, the next names were two partners from the real estate group, men I didn't even know.

They were, all three of them, accused of providing illegal tips on their corporate clients—which company was taking over another, which company was receiving a serious cash infusion—in exchange for cash from a more senior member of Rocher's team at Mission Fund. It wasn't the Jellyfish himself, a local reporter told us when she came on at four a.m., but it was the closest the feds had gotten. To me, of course, the Jellyfish arrest was not the headline.

I had time to picture it unfurling like the plot of a bodice ripper: Dave and Nell furtively glancing at each other across a conference table. Their initial, hesitant kiss. The murmurs of *We shouldn't*, the responding sighs, the being so overtaken by passion they were unable to help themselves. The serious discussions about how to end it, the exclamations of how this was all so wrong, so very wrong and yet felt so right. Then, two weeks ago, little Annie Poleci, horrified at the spread starting to collect on her backside because she sat in front of a computer for thirteen hours each day, resolved to take the stairs more and misinterpreted their tryst.

Of course he knew the whole time why he was suspended. *Of course* the firm had figured out—probably rather quickly—that it wasn't sexual harassment. I was sure Nell had come forward about the affair like the Good Samaritan that she was, but I was also sure there had been some minor smoothing over to be done—you know, *technically*, partners weren't supposed to sleep with associates, especially ones on their team—the whole botched power dynamic had probably garnered Dave a slap on the wrist—but everything was eventually cleared up. *Of course* Dave hadn't wanted me to tell anyone. One phone call from my dad—one of the firm's big clients—and everything could go up in smoke.

I hadn't yet cried, partially out of shame—every accusation I could throw at Dave he'd be justified in echoing to me: living in secrecy, selfishness, thoughts of infidelity—but mostly out of shock. All summer, I'd been trying to seize the information first, to guard against this very feeling of stupor.

I considered all sorts of grand gestures: stapling the picture of Nell to his pillow; copying it and using it to line our entry hall; throwing all of his clothes out the window. At four thirty in the morning, though, I realized how I was going to play it. I was going to attack the facts, these astonishing facts, before he could make it impossible. I changed into my running clothes, got my wallet and my phone and sat down on the couch to wait.

When the door finally creaked open at five in the morning, and he saw me sitting there, Dave, who looked as tired as I'd ever seen him, said, "Whoa. You're up early. Going for a run?"

"Yep. I want to beat the heat." It felt good to lie to him; I would have lied about anything at that point. "You sure did get stuck at work."

He exhaled, making his lips vibrate as he did. "You have no idea."

"What happened?" I walked out of the room and down the hall to the closet.

Dave followed me, leaning against the wall as I slid my toes into my running shoes and wiggle-stepped the heels. "The fucking FBI raided our firm. They were seizing computers and arresting people, and first we were all tied up in trying to do legal defense with the litigation team, and then there was an impromptu partner meeting about what we do—dissolve, rebrand. Jesus. It was the longest night." He pulled his work phone out of his pocket and tossed it on the small table in the hallway.

"Go change," I said, yanking up my laces. "Are you hungry?"

"Yes," he said, "starving."

"Eggs?"

"Oh, that sounds perfect. That way you do with the cream cheese?"

"You got it." I made a scurrying motion with my hand and as soon as he went into the bedroom, I picked up the work phone.

Password? it asked.

I typed in *N-E-L-L*, pressing each of the four letters down so hard that they made indents in the side of my thumb. And then I was in; I got what I needed and left out the front door, but not before grabbing the eggs from the refrigerator. The entire carton. *No fluffy eggs for you this morning, Dave.*

I tucked the plastic container under my arm and stepped in the elevator. And while I really wanted to egg something of Dave's—preferably Nell—what I did was give them, with a sweet smile, to the first breakfast-cart guy I saw on Lexington.

He was setting up, rubbing grease on his grill, when I rapped on the metal. "Could you use these?"

He held out his hand. "Sure could, miss. Thanks." He was as unsurprised as if I were his regular delivery guy.

And as soon as they were out of my hands and in his, I ran the thirty blocks downtown to the address I'd lifted from Dave's phone.

chapter forty-three

I DIDN'T STOP until I got to Nell's building. As soon as I saw its redbrick facade, my certainty faltered. I had no plan, just anger. I was so much madder than I'd been when Dave's crime had been bigger and more public.

I ordered an iced coffee at a café across the street, sat down on the bench outside it and stewed, watching Nell's front door as the city woke up.

Eight people exited her building between six and seven. Counting them, I tried to pinpoint what upset me the most. How could I handle Dave's transgressions when they were against the American people but not against me alone? It wasn't just the thought of the two of them together. Or even the lies. It was also the shock, like jumping into Antarctic bottom water. I'd never known that surprise could preserve someone in a moment, but look at Sloane. As far as she had come, a piece of her remained there on Sycamore Street, staring at my mom through the car's fogged-up windows.

But, to be fair, not so long after Dave had been with Nell, I'd been dreaming about Percy like a fool. If I worked with Percy during sixteen-hour days and through weekends instead of in little bits and pieces, would I have been unable to resist him? Maybe this was par for the course with marriage. You felt tempted; you acted or you didn't; you got over it. Had Dave gotten over it?

By eight thirty, First Avenue was crowded, people swarming to offices in suits that looked far too hot for late July; dog walkers staring at their phones, moving slowly as the dogs sniffed trash cans; parents pushing their children, all in solid color camp T-shirts, onto yellow buses.

At eight forty-five, I tossed my coffee in the trash and waited until the traffic ebbed enough for me to cross the street. Then, as Dave had probably done before, I pressed the buzzer for apartment 5J.

"Cameron?" a voice floated over the intercom. "I'll be right down." It was sweet, a little childish—not what I expected. Like Alpine Heidi inquiring whether Grandpapa would like more cake. I wanted to hear it again. I left quickly, almost bumping into a gray-haired man, and leaned against the doorway of the building next door, waiting for her to emerge.

A few beats later, Nell did, standing on the landing a bit lost, swiveling her head, wondering where Cameron was, but then she checked her watch and started walking south. So I did too.

I tracked that narrow little back like a homing missile: messy ponytail, gray hoodie, white Capri yoga pants through which I could see her (rather matronly) panty line. By the time Nell turned into the grocery store at the end of her block, I was close enough to catch her scent. I'd anticipated irresistibly floral. Instead, her bouquet was lemony sweet, like a cheap cleaning product.

I hung back in front of the misted broccoli as Nell accidentally toppled the pyramid of plums by reaching for one that was too deep in the bin. Two rolled down to the floor, and she bent to pick them up with one hand, first brushing them off on her pants and then, guiltily, putting both in her shopping basket. It was when she glanced around, to see if anyone had caught the moment, that our eyes connected. I walked toward her—got close enough to see her red-rimmed eyes. "Hi."

She paused. "Hello."

"I'm—"

"I know." She smoothed the halo of frizz on the top of her head. "I haven't talked to him. It's over."

"Oh."

"I'm not at the office. I mean, obviously. You should know that, actually." Her voice had an edge. "They found me a new job, and it starts on Monday."

"Well." I tucked a hair behind my ear. "That's probably for the best, considering . . . what's going on there now. You know, with the FBI." I stopped short of saying, *Who knew sleeping with your boss could be such a good business move?* Because the answer was *Plenty of people, since time immemorial, although usually it doesn't go down quite like this.* She gave me a funny look, so I just said, "Good luck."

"Thanks." Her eyes bulged—the whites prominent—making her look bovine and uneasy. She was, like me, trying to figure out what exactly I wanted. "I'm not some bunny boiler. I could've stayed at the firm and kept my mouth shut. I wouldn't have, like, chased him around the firm in my lingerie."

I nodded. Based on the practical shape of her underpants beneath those white yoga pants, I believed her. "Well . . ." I shrugged. "I'm sorry your affair with my husband disrupted your work situation."

"Oh my god." She covered her mouth. "You're right. Sorry. I'm in a bad place. I shouldn't even be . . . I'm sorry."

"Okay."

She wiped her eyes on her sleeve. "I know it was so wrong. Now that it's over, it's all so cheap." She opened her mouth to say something and then shut it. And then opened it again. She looked like a fish. Fish-mouthed Nell Standish. It should have been more satisfying than it was.

"What were you about to say?"

"Never mind. You don't need to hear this."

"Please."

"I thought it would be worth the obstacles. You know, like five years from now, no one would remember that he was even married when we got together. Because we'd have a whole life together. And when I did think of you, I thought that you'd be better off with someone else, your true someone, with whom you could have what he and I had. But I was wrong. It didn't mean that to him."

"It didn't?"

"It was just a . . . fling to him." She spat out the word, as though it still hurt.

"How long were you guys—"

"Three months. He wasn't counting, though. It meant nothing to him."

"He said that?"

"Oh, trust me. He's made it very clear that I'm never to contact him again. And I won't." She bit her lip. "For him, there was never even a second of deliberation. I, of course, idiot that I am, was all in. I never would've gotten involved if I understood what it meant to him. Not that it makes it right, what we did. Of course."

I wanted to know more. What had he been like in college? Why had they broken up? Had she followed him here? What did she love about the Dave she thought she knew? Who was the Dave she thought she knew?

I suppose it's how a parent might feel when her kid bites someone else at the playground; I didn't want to, but somehow, I'd assumed blame. I felt like showing Nell some kindness, offering her a tissue, touching her shoulder. Instead, I said good-bye.

"You got what you wanted?"

"Yeah."

"You needed to make sure that it's over?"

"Sort of."

"Well"—she pretended to examine a peach to hide the tears pooling in her eyes—"you have nothing to worry about."

chapter forty-four

"YES," I SAID when my mom opened the door, her eyes worried, "I've seen the news."

"Is the Boy okay?" She stepped aside, and I collapsed on the couch in the sitting room. She eased down next to me tentatively.

"Fine. He's at home."

"That poor kid," she said. "We just found out this morning, and your dad called some defense lawyers. He's planning to meet with some today."

"Why?"

"Just to get a handle on the situation. We don't think Dave did anything wrong, but, you know, in case he got caught up in something."

"Sloane left."

"Oh?" I could tell she was making a point not to react, as though she were fine either way.

"I found out what she's stuck on." She turned her head ever so slightly. "Your affair. She's pissed about your affair a billion years ago." I focused on one of their new art pieces—a big light box with neon script spelling out *Diner.* Why was I here? I hadn't even thought about how illogical it was, how I'd trudged straight over after seeing Nell like I was on some sort of zombie heartbreak scavenger hunt, but after I said it—"affair"—I understood.

I'd been reading the journals, identifying with her connection to another man, likening it to mine with Percy. But I'd been totally outclassed. "You probably knew that, though."

"What are you talking about?" She folded her lips together, rejecting that. "This is why you don't go reading people's private things, Paige. Because you get the wrong idea."

"Tell me, Mom. What's the right idea?"

"It's hard to explain."

"Try."

Her eyes sparked dark and flinty. "She needs her anger toward me. It keeps her going, so in a sense I welcome it."

"That's insane."

"Trust me, Paige. She and I are peas in a pod. You wouldn't understand. You're made of different stuff."

When I regained my breath, all I wanted was to shock her back. "You're wrong. She's nothing like you. She saw you guys in the car one night—you and this G. That's why she hates you, and you know it."

"In the car? I have no idea what that even means."

"Come on. You were having an affair."

"It wasn't an affair."

"Okay. Your *special friendship*. We can put it in the vault along with all the other things we don't need to talk about. Your father. Sloane—"

"It wasn't an affair. It could've been. But it wasn't."

"G."

"Yes. His name was Geoff, and we spent a lot of time together in a way that was perhaps"—her cheeks colored—"inappropriate. It's nothing I ever expected to have to rehash, but it was not an affair."

"Does it even matter?"

"Maybe not. Well, to me."

It was an escape, she explained. He had the appointment

after hers at Pressman's, and they started talking in the ten minutes between their sessions. One day, he told her to wait for him after. They went for coffee and from there, spent regular time together: dinners and walks. A movie or two.

"So what did Sloane see?"

"We were probably talking. We used to do that."

"Talk in cars?"

"Talk . . . anywhere. We'd go places—the strangest places, like a bank, the supermarket—and just talk about everything for hours. I don't remember seeing Sloane. Who knows what she thinks she saw? She was hardly a reliable observer."

"She's certain."

My mom sighed, dragged her left hand across her eyebrows. "If that's the excuse she needs to keep her distance, then what can I do? I know what I know."

My mom cheated or she didn't; her marriage to my dad worked or it didn't. Dave's lies were our sum total or just a tear that would heal. I thought of what Percy had said while we drifted in the hammock: truth is perception.

"Why did it stop?"

"I went to his house once. It was in the morning. As a surprise. I'd never been there before and I don't remember what I thought would happen, but when I got there, he was hanging out with his friends, people from his band. They clearly knew who I was, knew about Sloane. They were asking me questions about her, like—I can't describe it—like, they owned my problem."

"Like what?"

"Oh, this one woman—her name was Dolores—asked about her son's pot use. Minor pot use and did I think it was a big problem. As though I was an expert. And they wanted to know about Gentle Breezes, mostly how much we were spending, gawking at the expense. They were so casual about it all. I felt violated. Like this thing that was so special to me—this time that Geoff and I had—wasn't. And I realized that your father would never betray me that way. It was just this crystal clear moment that I knew your dad. I understood him and he understood me, and even though things weren't perfect, having that between us was pure gold. It was enough. I knew what I wanted."

"And if not for that?"

"Probably, yes. Probably something would've happened. Or not. I don't know."

"Does Dad know?"

She shrugged. "He might have suspected something. I wasn't around much that year, but we were both sort of muddling through for a while there. We've given each other latitude for that, Paige."

"Why didn't you tell me any of this?" I said. "Why have we never talked about it?"

"About Geoff?" She blinked at me incredulously. "I don't think children need to know about that much of their parents' marriage, Paige."

"Not Geoff. Sloane. Your dad. Russell Cohen. Why have we never talked about it?"

"I couldn't." She was silent for a long time. "The way I grew up, Paige. It was awful. And I felt so powerless as a kid. As I got older, though, I realized I could move past it. I could control what it meant to me, how often I thought about the past. When it started with Sloane, it felt like something was catching up, as though I'd escaped only because I'd unwittingly sacrificed my daughter, like in one of those fairy tales. I didn't want any of that to be your backdrop."

"Guess what? It was my backdrop."

"I know it doesn't make any sense, but sometimes if you give in to the weaknesses, if you acknowledge them aloud and build everything around them, you get trapped by them." She shrugged and her voice got a little harder. "You didn't need to know everything that was going on."

"Not everything. But maybe something."

"I would protect you from it all over again." Our gazes clashed like swords. I'd never know the half of it, I realized: her motivations or the past that had left her so broken and impressive.

You can go crazy watching other people's behavior, imbuing meaning and motive, trying to uncover the exact truth of their secrets without getting to the bottom of it. That little whiff of mystery remains, no matter how close you get. There is no turning of a person's hinges, no seeing inside to anyone else's motivations.

The intent of Dr. Pressman's artist was inconsequential. It was a bunny; it was a duck; it was both. It was whatever *I* saw; it was whatever *I* wanted it to be.

"I want you to be okay, Paige." My mom was asking, I knew, whether *we* would be okay. This was, I realized, the type of question—vague, unanswerable—that I usually deferred to her. I wasn't sure why I'd stayed tucked so far under her wing— perhaps Sloane's absence had scarred me more than I'd ever admitted; perhaps I was just born to be the type of person who bobbed in others' wakes rather than setting off a thousand expanding ripples. But in that moment, as she started to cry, I felt something between us unlink, and frankly, it made me a little lighter.

"I'm okay." I threaded my fingers through hers and gripped her hand. "And we'll be fine." It was the truth as I knew it then:

there might be new boundaries between us, but the love would always be there.

✦

I was dry-eyed until I walked out of their building, but there, on the same sidewalk where Sloane had first introduced me to Giovanni and Percy, it overtook me like a swoon: the lack of sleep and all the things I was now poised to lose. I leaned against a blue construction wall for a moment, too stunned to notice the man who approached from the direction of my parents' building.

He must have seen how stricken I was, because he put his arms around me before saying anything. We were both a little tentative and awkward—we hadn't hugged as grown-ups really, and he wasn't much taller than I was. I leaned my face down into my dad's shoulder, though, and let myself sob. I couldn't stop, and as I ruined the fabric of his suit with my tears, he stroked my hair and told me it all would be okay.

chapter forty-five

Vanessa

"FRANKIE, YOU'RE SURE you can take off today?" He hadn't changed and was still in his suit as we walked east to the promenade around Carl Schurz Park.

"I can," he said. "Are you okay?"

I nodded. Plenty of people were enjoying the break in the heat wave, walking their dogs and running and lazing on the benches as though they wanted to spend the whole day there. Frankie and I stopped at the railing and pushed our heads into the breeze to watch a tugboat usher a barge down the East River.

It was kind of a marvel. The tug was so small that at first I couldn't tell that it wasn't just a section of the bigger barge. It was a victory for tenacity, that little tug, the universe's way of letting me know that a strong latch could hold, if only in the world of maritime construction.

I didn't share these musings with Frankie. He didn't think the universe sent us such messages and would worry that I was obsessing. "You know," I said, "before we met, I used to walk in the city all the time."

"Where?"

"If the weather was okay, sometimes all the way downtown. Mostly to avoid the Lexington line. Do you remember how bad the trains were?"

"The murder express."

"Horrible. Although arguably safer than my apartment."

"You got mugged in your apartment?"

"Once, I came home from being out late with my friends. My dad was of course on the couch, empties all around him. We just grinned at each other. I'd just started with the drinking and the experimenting and staying out late, and he, prince that he was, had no problem with it. We were in it together. So we shared this father-daughter moment, and then I went into the bedroom and passed out, and when I woke up, the door was wide-open."

"To the bedroom?" Frankie's brow creased.

"The front door. He went out to do god knows what and left his fourteen-year-old daughter sleeping at home, alone, with the doors to the apartment unlocked and wide-open."

Frankie shook his head, met my eyes. "What about your mom?"

"She worked nights then, cleaning offices in Midtown. Which was actually a decent job, but she didn't get home until morning. Anyone could have come in. Anyone. And it's not like we lived in neighborhood-watch territory. No one was looking out for shady characters, because everyone was a shady character. I understood it all that morning when I woke up—I had no one to protect me, no one who'd stop me from self-destruction."

"Whether they're smart enough to appreciate it or not, your daughters are lucky girls, Vanessa."

"I'm starting to think that the stronger you grip something, the more you guarantee it slipping through your hand."

"I think there's a poem about that."

"This is why, Frankie. This is why—I can't keep telling stories like that. It takes me over. You know?"

"Sure."

"I have to move forward. I have to let it go."

"So let's let it go." We strolled south on the promenade until

Frankie stopped right there on the narrow steps down to the FDR Drive walkway. He put his left arm around my shoulders and rested it there.

Runners and dog walkers and commuters, they all streamed around us as we stood, holding each other in a firm grasp.

chapter forty-six

DAVE WAS SLEEPING on the couch, his upper body half propped on the arm, his mouth open and his head cast back. Yesterday I would have covered him with a throw blanket and tiptoed around him, but now I pulled up a chair from the kitchen and watched him sleep.

I kicked him in the knee. Nothing happened.

I pushed harder and his eyes flew open.

"You look awful," he said.

"Are my eyes red?"

He nodded, propped up on his elbows. "Did something happen on your run?"

"Yes, Dave. You know that ark scene in *Raiders of the Lost Ark*?"

"The face-melting one?"

"Yeah. I saw too much truth, and now my eyes are all red and puffy."

He couldn't tell if I was joking, so he frowned, then smiled, then asked, "What?"

"For starters, I just talked to Nell."

He swallowed, his thought process transparent for the first time this summer: *What does she know?*

"Don't," I said.

"Don't what?"

"Spin."

He swallowed again. An audible, dry-mouth click. "It really was nothing."

"What does that even mean?"

"It was, like, five times—that's it."

I didn't have a response to that.

"I'll tell you why too. If you want to know."

I nodded.

"We were working together all the time. I got caught up. I don't even know. It's the stupidest thing. She was just there." He watched me for a while, and I didn't respond, pressing into the chair. "We can get through it, though, right? People get through this."

"What's that? Marital advice from Herb?"

"What do you want me to do? Seriously. Anything."

"What do I want you to *do*? Doing something isn't going to change this." Although we would later, neither one of us was crying or screaming. It was flat and colorless, the moment right after impact, when the contusion-to-be is just a white trace on the skin.

"It wasn't about real emotion." He stared at me, his fingers distractedly playing with the fringe on the couch pillow. "She was what I thought I needed at a particular moment."

"You made her your password."

Dave regarded me with wary, disappointed eyes. Of the two of us, he'd assumed he was the real cheater and liar. "That was . . ." He was debating saying something. "That meant nothing."

Meaning he had changed his password for me, not Nell. It was a calculated move, done in order to keep me out. Something about that explanation made me feel like I was seeing him for the first time.

I tried to access the love that must be deep down beneath the hurt and muddle.

What do you want?

I willed myself to reclaim the certainty: We were a pair. We were a pair.

What do you want?

I waited for that crystal clear realization that I knew Dave. That I understood him and he understood me, and even though things weren't perfect, having that between us was pure gold. I waited to know that we were enough.

October

♦

chapter forty-seven

IT WAS MY first real run of fall and the air was chilled enough that my breath emerged in smoky puffs. I was happy for the change of season—not just because of the tumult of the summer, but because the first days of autumn for me always evoked thoughts of homemade applesauce and crisp blue skies instead of the bleak winter to come. I'd be disappointed in a matter of weeks—cursing needing a coat and the fact that the park would be dark right after lunch, but I was incapable of feeling that now. I decided to continue walking the loop, my steps padded by the yellowing leaves paving the path.

I fished my mobile out of my pocket and dialed Sloane. "I got the tickets," I said as soon as she picked up the phone.

"Excellent! We've been talking about all the places we're going to take you."

"Such as?"

"The shop. And there's this taco truck that we found . . . oh, and a Japanese teahouse, which is wonderful. And then the Halloween party on the beach that we go to every year."

"Maybe we can do one of those celebrity bus tours."

"Maybe not."

"You're still planning to come out here for Thanksgiving?"

"I'm not promising anything." She waited a beat. "*She* made another comment on my blog, you know."

"What did she say?"

"I'm surprised you don't know, seeing as you're the brilliant mastermind behind her finding the site in the first place."

The first time my mom had commented on Sloane's blog, Sloane had called me up, furious. "Sounds delicious?" Sloane had said without other greeting or explanation. "Sounds delicious? Can you believe that? Who *says* that?" Two months later, I believed that Sloane's complaints were getting less vocal, more begrudging. Or perhaps I had just built up a callus to them. Regardless, I was committed to slowly, subtly pushing Sloane toward our mom. Minds could be changed; ties that seemed broken could be healed. I had seen it.

"You'll promise to discuss Thanksgiving, though."

"Whatever." She shifted her tone back to friendly. "So, did you get the papers?"

I was about to answer when I sensed someone walking beside me. I glanced to my left. "It's Percy!" I told Sloane, the panic crisp in my voice. "Percy Stahl is here in the park."

"Tell him hi."

"Sloane says hi," I said to Percy.

"Hi," he said.

"Hi," I repeated into the phone. "I'll call you back, okay?" I hung up the phone and wiped my palms against the slickness of my running tights.

This was not the first time since July that I'd seen him around the loop—he'd taken to running counterclockwise, in the opposite direction from me, or maybe that had always been his routine. Once or twice I'd looked the other way and avoided his eyes, but on occasion mine would connect with his. I couldn't figure out his expression.

Over the past few months, I'd told myself that I'd conjured my feelings for him—that Percy Stahl was a nice-looking stranger in the wrong place at the wrong time. It was an argument that apparently required a distance of greater than ten feet between us to be convincing.

"How are you?" I could tell from his loaded tone that Percy was aware that Dave and I had split up.

After all of my weeks of searching and questioning, I had been surprised by the certainty and immediacy of my wanting out: I couldn't square the man I thought I'd known with what he'd done. I couldn't get a clear read on him—had I ever?—and within weeks of his moving out, I could barely remember believing that I had.

Percy's expression was so sympathetic that I suspected he had even heard the details from Sloane and Giovanni: How, when Dave moved out, I cried for a week. How, for about six weeks after that, I barely left the house, too embarrassed at others' disappointment at the failure of my young perfect marriage. And then, how one day in the not-too-distant past, I started to feel clearer and calmer.

With late August, my clients had returned, and Dave was distracted too—by his firm's implosion and the kaleidoscope of spin-off firms, which I was, frankly, glad to not have to track out of pretend spousal interest. Maybe that was how we'd managed to agree that we wouldn't fight or drag out the matter; we would put the apartment on the market, sell to the highest bidder, split the proceeds, cut the cord.

I'd moved out last week and had spent the days before filling up my own boxes, taping and stacking piles of things that I feared I'd always want to forget. I had paused, though, when I got to the box of my mother's journals.

I had vague romantic notions of sharing them with Sloane someday, but I knew no one was ready for that. Still, I couldn't throw them out; I liked the idea of occasionally glancing at their neat spiral spines, recalling how the pureness of their honesty had helped both me and my mom, years apart.

My truth about Dave had settled with the finality of a pebble tossed into the stillest pond. He would not be the love of my life; he would be my ex, the guy who was decent during our divorce after that sliver of a marriage. The one who would wind up being shockingly easy to let go.

"I'm fine," I said. "I'm going to California in October."

"I heard about that plan."

"How are you?"

"Good. Just filing my toenails. Polishing my one table. Washing my jeans, you know."

I laughed. "The important stuff."

"Right. By the way, Selena really thinks you're helping them."

"I'm glad."

Sloane had asked me whether I could stomach being a marriage counselor in light of the demise of mine. "Of course," I'd automatically responded before reflecting that she did have a point. Fundamentally, though, I still believed in the institution—its beauty and its ability, in the right case, to tether people together through hardship. I still asked people what they wanted. It was a good question, I had concluded, as long as you knew not to impute too much permanence to the response.

A yellow leaf spiraled off a tree and landed in our path. "I'm happy it's fall," Percy said.

"Me too," I said. "The best transitions are ones where you know exactly what to expect. The same every year."

"Not necessarily," he said. "I bought a lamp. Spur-of-the-moment purchase. It's given me no end of joy."

"Wow. What's next?"

He shrugged. "I'm thinking a bar stool or two." Before I could respond, he stopped and stood directly in my path, right where the leaf had landed. "I've thought about you."

"Oh."

"I haven't wanted to intrude. I figured you were dealing with what you were dealing with."

This was the hard part: to recognize my pull toward Percy and will against it. If I hadn't known my husband, how could I trust myself with someone who was essentially a stranger? Without warning, he reached out his fingers and brushed my cheek. "Eyelash," he said, holding it out for me to make a wish. We both glanced at his finger, and I let myself feel the bolt of certainty.

We think that truths are immutable—we rely on them like bedrock—but they last for mere moments, shifting and changing and dragging with them our lives as we've known them and sometimes, those whom we love. In that moment, I wanted—I trusted myself enough—to risk it, whether I turned out to be right or wrong about Percy.

Percy's eyes focused on mine the way they had that night in the hammock. Just like that night, I felt a charge in the air as we stood in the public openness of the park road. I hesitated, because after the contracts and sworn statements that I'd signed in the past three months, with the newsprint still darkening my fingernail beds from a week of packing up my belongings, a kiss seemed rushed, too much.

He didn't lean forward, though. He stepped aside and one pace ahead and turned, holding out his hand. "Let's just walk," he said.

So I held out mine.

Photo by Anne Joyce

L. Alison Heller, a divorce lawyer and mediator, lives in Brooklyn with her husband and daughters. *The Never Never Sisters* is her second novel.

the

never never

sisters

◆

L. ALISON HELLER

A CONVERSATION WITH
L. ALISON HELLER

1. What was the original inspiration for the story?

It all started with Dave and his betrayal. If you think you know someone better than anyone and then you learn something that disrupts your narrative about that person—what do you do? Your choices are either to change your narrative or do backbends trying to smoothly incorporate the new fact so that it fits into what you've previously believed.

I think people probably do both—and maybe degrees of each every day, and I wanted to explore that. The story grew to encompass Paige's relationship with not only Dave but also Sloane and Vanessa and even Franklin. But Dave was the springboard for that more global examination of how trust is earned and of what we tell ourselves about the people in our lives whom we think we know.

2. There are a lot of communication problems in the book—occasions where characters either don't say what they're thinking or say too much or build walls in the face of someone else's admission: Paige and Vanessa, Paige and Dave, Sloane and . . . almost everyone. How do you see conversation (or lack thereof) fitting into the development or erosion of connection between characters?

Obviously conversation—and more specifically the exchange of crucial information—is a key to connection. The right information communicated between the right people is how intimacy is formed. Don't you feel closest to the people with whom you can be completely honest, and who you feel can be honest with you? Navigating this—what you share with those close to you and what you keep for yourself—is, I think, definitely more art than science for most people. We share because we're moved to by a moment or someone else's admission, but there are also times when we divulge—or don't—as a matter of strategy and, of course, those choices help relationships move along or stall.

At the beginning of the story, Paige would claim that she knows everything that matters about both her mom and her husband. She's willing to accept certain areas of silence between them because they're not critical to her *here and now*, but as she delves deeper into family secrets, she starts to see that those silences have had a great impact. And that she's troublingly capable of maintaining her own strategic silences too.

When you really start to think about it, there's a necessary leap of faith in all relationships. You can't know everything about a person, and even when you think you know someone's heart and soul, you can't know all of his or her thoughts.

3. And the corollary to that leap of faith seems to be the ability to forgive. At the end of the book, Paige has loosened the strings of some of those crucial relationships and reinforced others. Without giving too much away, do you agree with her choices on what can be forgiven?

I don't know that I would've made the same choices as Paige, but I definitely respect her process. She (finally!) went with her own gut decision, which was a big deal for her. Her upbringing was a real mix of being overly coddled and also exposed to some pretty heavy stuff—and she desperately needed to make this decision by and for herself.

I purposely didn't give Paige and Dave any shared burdens or distractions (dependents, financial stresses, bad health). I wanted the book to take place while they're still in a honeymoon period so that, on the surface, at least, they're two happy people with everything going for them.

There's this romantic ideal about two people going off into the sunset on a horse (or in a carriage or a flying convertible like in *Grease*). But you know once they've been on that horse for a while, someone will get thirsty while the other will want to keep going until they reach the destination. Someone will want to help that guy on the side of the road, and the other will think he's a serial killer. Everyone makes bargains in their relationships. Everyone lets their principles slide or evolve at some point to make things work—it's just a question of knowing where your lines are at any given moment.

4. It was so interesting how Paige, a marriage counselor, helped couples find their way back to each other as she grappled with issues in her own marriage. At one point she says to Percy, "I'm not like my clients." Did you make her a marriage counselor to provide that contrast?

This is an especially funny question because Paige did a lot of floundering in the early drafts, before she became a marriage counselor. She tutored a bit for standardized tests. She dabbled in grad school (medical, dental), and she spent a lot of time and effort beautifying and mixing up health shakes filled with things like flaxseed and kale protein powder. (I don't know if there is such as thing as kale protein powder, actually. But it does sound healthy, and it would have totally been up Paige's alley.)

None of that felt one hundred percent right, though. Paige had to be a woman of opinions, someone who thought she'd figured out all the answers for relating.

Paige's job change felt very natural. It made a lot in the story click and, really, she was much happier and stronger as soon as we gave her that job. (My editor and I both breathed a little sigh of relief.) Frankly, it was nice to anchor her a bit, because she gets a lot thrown at her, including that being a marriage counselor doesn't give you an automatic answer guide to your own relationships.

5. I really enjoyed Giovanni. Whenever he showed up in the book, I laughed. Was that a deliberate choice to make him light?

I'm so glad! Giovanni made me laugh too. He was probably the most fun to write. (Although Vanessa was a close second.)

I've known (and envied) people like Giovanni, who just don't seem to get in their own way. Initially Paige underestimates him because of the games and the jokes, but he's very good at distilling things to their core simplicity and talking about them.

And, yes, Giovanni provides some much-needed contrast to the Reinhardt women. He's reductive where Paige is alternatively oblivious and hyperaware. He's sunny where Sloane is moody, and he's an open book, in stark contrast to Vanessa. I think he and Sloane will be just fine.

6. What surprised you the most in writing the book?

I love this question because being surprised while writing a novel is unavoidable, as well as one of the best parts of the process.

Aside from how very many drafts it took, I'd say the biggest surprise was the evolution of certain characters. A lot shifts as I write, but one constant here on the journey from idea to completed manuscript was the substance of Dave's "lie" and how it impacts Paige and Dave's marriage. I was not expecting to become as fond of Dave as I did, or that there would be such genuine compatibility between him and Paige. I'm so glad I stuck it out with him, because it complicated Paige's choice and forced her to explore her personal belief system: what makes one transgression forgivable and another not? I'm very curious how readers felt about Dave throughout the book, so please— shoot me an e-mail. I'd love to hear!

Vanessa surprised me too. She's tricky: she builds massive walls but is also incredibly, piercingly honest, especially in her journals. I loved writing those entries. I think a lot of people tap into something different with respect to voice when they write, and that was a very liberating way to explore her thought processes.

Obviously this is primarily Paige's story, but Vanessa helped *The Never Never Sisters* come together. She mines a lot of the themes in the novel—how the struggle to find your own truth dovetails with the struggle of those closest to you, how one's own narrative and identity impact parenting style and experience and the role of familial expectation in all of it.

QUESTIONS
FOR DISCUSSION

1. Before Paige sees Sloane, she thinks of her as "apart," not a member of her family. By the end of the book, how do you think Paige would redefine her family unit?

2. How are Paige and Sloane similar and/or different? Whom did you relate to more at the beginning of the book? At the end?

3. At what point do you think Paige starts to trust Sloane? What are some of Paige's obstacles to forgiving her sister for the long absence, and ultimately how does she get over them?

4. At what point did your opinion of Dave change (if it did at all)? Was it because of something he did or Paige's growing awareness?

5. How do you think the dynamics of Paige and Vanessa's relationship affected Paige in the years before the month during which the book takes place?

6. What do you think of Vanessa's strengths and weaknesses as a parent? How much do you think her parenting style affected her daughters' personalities?

7. At the end of the book, what, if anything, did you think was left unsaid between any of the characters? What do you like to think will happen to each of them in the years ahead? Do you think the Reinhardt family is stronger as a whole at the book's end?

8. In several different instances throughout the book, the way two characters relate to each other is tied into the actions of a third character. What are some examples of this?

9. Of all the characters in the book, whom do you relate to the most and why?

10. In your opinion, who is the most honest character in the book? The least honest? Why?

11. Did you agree with Paige's conflicting feelings about Dave's betrayals (real and perceived) as she was experiencing them? What about Paige's betrayals of Dave?

12. Did you consider Paige's flirting with Percy harmless or meaningful? Did your feelings about it change at the end of the book?

13. Did you feel that Paige's professional training helped or hindered her ability to express her own emotions? Can you name examples of moments when her desire to understand other people gets in the way of self-comprehension?

14. Percy and Paige discuss the difference between facts and perception. What are some other moments in the book where the same facts mean different things to different people? What are the effects?

15. What is the role of "silence" in the book? Were there situations in which shared knowledge might have altered how things unfolded in the story? If you were Vanessa or Paige, what might you have done differently?

16. In your life, have you ever been in a situation where you've learned something surprising about someone close to you? What have you relied on in figuring out your next steps?

17. At one point, Paige notes that Dave's greatest strength (ambition) is also his greatest weakness. Are there examples of other instances in the book where a character's strength is also—in extremis—his or her greatest weakness? Have you seen any examples of this in your own life?